THE DAMAGED BILLIONAIRE

THE BALTIMORE BOYS

BOOK 3

SAMANTHA SKYE

ISBN 978-0-6457144-5-6 (ebook)

ISBN 978-0-6457144-6-3 (Paperback)

ISBN 978-0-6459897-79 (Alternative Paperback)

Cover Design: Angela Haddon

Editor: Nice Girl Naughty Edits

Proofreading: Kimberly Dawn

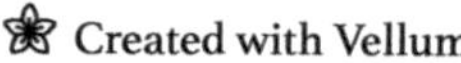 Created with Vellum

CONTENT WARNING

My stories contain spice and suspense and as such they can contain scenes and information that maybe triggering to some people.

This book contains scenes that include;

- Infertility/PCOS
- Kidnapping/Blackmail
- Assault/Violence

1

WILLOW VALENTINE

Our heels click on the dark wooden floor as we walk out of the elevator and into the elegant lobby of this five-star hotel in Soho.

"Okay, I am off," my sister, Saide, says with a big grin.

"Wait, what? Aren't we going for a drink?" I ask her, my steps toward the hotel bar faltering as I frown in confusion. I dressed up tonight. Heels, tight red dress, shiny hair, perfected makeup—the whole shebang.

"I have a date." Her smile dazzles with her admission.

"A date? What do you mean, a date?"

"You know, a *date*. Maybe it's hard for you to remember. It's one of those things that people do. They go for drinks or dinner, laugh and talk, then maybe end up having amazing sex throughout the night. A date." Her grin is still a mile wide, so I find it hard to take offense that my baby sister is ditching me so last minute.

"Saide, this is supposed to be a girls' night away. Just the two of us." I look at her almost pleadingly because I was really looking forward to tonight. I haven't had a night off work for months. My job is so demanding; I have trouble remembering what day it is most weeks.

"But Jacob just texted me... He is in town..." she purrs, trying to look innocent, whereas my teeth start grinding at the mention of his name.

"Saide..." I growl in warning.

"It is only one night. I haven't seen him in weeks," she moans like a petulant child.

"That's because he is *married* and has probably been home with his *wife*."

She has been having an affair with a married pilot, and I don't approve. Not one bit.

"Listen, don't wait up. I'm not sure what time I will be back." She completely disregards my comment, stepping away toward the door. Seeing the back of her is becoming a common occurrence now. Her high-flying life as an air stewardess keeps her from me more and more.

"What am I meant to do now?" I call after her.

"Go to the bar. Meet a man. Have slutty sex all night. God knows you need it!" she yells across the hotel foyer, and I don't miss the doorman as he looks my way.

I sigh and rub my head. She drives me crazy sometimes. If I knew my sister was going to bail on me tonight, I would have stayed in, got room service, relaxed in the big tub with a glass of wine, and had an early night. I need that kind of night. I *deserve* it.

Spinning on my heel, I walk two paces back to the elevator bank, when the bar sign catches my eye.

"One drink won't hurt," I mumble to myself and put all my frustrations with my sister into my step as I strut into the space. It's just how I predicted—dark and seductive, with soft music adding to the moody ambiance. I make a beeline for the warm lowlights that illuminate the back of the bar.

"A glass of white wine, please," I quip to the bartender as I grab the nearest seat and throw my handbag on the bartop.

"Wait, no, not wine. I think I need a cocktail. Can I get a margarita? On the rocks, with extra salt?" The cute bartender gives me a small smile as he nods and gets busy making my concoction. I blow out a breath, groaning to myself at how this night took a turn.

"Doesn't look like you need extra salt," a deep voice says from beside me, and I look across to meet the most soulful eyes I have ever seen. I'm only now realizing I have perched myself on a stool right next to a man who is currently eyeing me over the top of a glass of what looks to be whiskey.

"What is that supposed to mean?" I ask, my question sounding sharper than I intend. It's been a long day of Saide and I shopping and eating our way around New York. This girl time was much needed, even though we head home tomorrow.

"You seem salty enough. Have a bad day?" he asks in a softer tone, and I sigh. It isn't his fault that my baby sister acts like she is still seventeen rather than twenty-four.

"Family troubles," I murmur.

He huffs, nodding. "I know all about those." As he takes a sip of his drink, I take the opportunity to look at him further. I always find it so sexy when men drink that smooth amber liquor, especially over a beer or countless shots. It's the kind of drink you don't rush consuming, the tumbler you swirl as you sit and ponder instead of rage on. When his Adam's apple bobs with a swallow, I find myself swallowing too. He has a slight shadow of stubble on his jaw, his brown hair falling a little over his forehead. I watch his large hand grasp his glass, wondering what it would feel like on my body. He is by far the most handsome man I have ever laid eyes on.

"My little sister is having an affair with a married man," I blurt out, then wish I could take it back. I haven't even had a sip of alcohol yet. I suppose I needed to get it off my chest.

Seemingly interested in my story, he turns my way, looking at me like he's waiting for the rest of whatever's on my mind. Thankfully, before I can think to say anything more, the bartender drops my drink in front of me, and I grab my bag.

"On my tab," the man next to me says quickly, waving the bartender off, him leaving almost instantaneously.

"You don't have to do that."

"A woman should never have to buy her own drinks. Especially one like you," he says with a small smile playing on his lips, which I return easily. I take a sip of my cocktail, trying to settle my nerves, and enjoy feeling the alcohol as it burns down my throat.

"So what about you?" I ask, sitting back into my seat. I might as well get comfortable while I am here, even if it is only for one drink.

"What about me?"

"What ridiculous things has your family member done?" He looks too perfect and seems too smart to even put up with anyone's drama. What kind of troubles would follow a man like him around?

"How long have you got?" He raises his brow in question.

I watch him for a beat. His eyes twinkle in the mood lighting from the bar, making me smile a little more. Saide is right; I forget what it is like to date, having not been on one in a long, long time. The feeling of excitement at the initial flirt, the desire that swirls when getting to know one another. My stomach has butterflies already fluttering around in my belly, just being in his presence.

"I've got all night." I don't miss this way his lips curve up at the corners before he takes another slow slip of his drink.

"I have a crazy mother, a famous brother, two other extremely successful brothers, and a dead father." The words fly out from him quickly, and my lips purse as I hold back my wince.

"Okay. You win," I say, smiling sympathetically.

"Thank you." His shoulder lifts in a small shrug as he reciprocates my smile. Lifting my glass to his in a mock cheers for our problems, he clinks his glass with mine, and we both share a laugh.

"Parents?" he asks me in return. I am usually not one to open up to anyone, let alone a perfect stranger. But for some reason, I feel totally at ease with this man, and I don't even know his name. He drapes his arm on the back of my chair as he settles into his seat, getting more comfortable. Our new proximity has those butterflies traveling south as I get a whiff of his delicious cologne.

When our eyes meet, I can't help the shiver that moves through me.

I have all of his attention. And I really, really like it.

"Alive. Well. Old. In the Midwest," I offer, and I think I feel his fingers twitch a little on my back, but I can't be sure. My heart is thumping out of my chest as I try to keep my cool. Be the confident woman I am. Sure, I have been out before, met men in bars even, but it's been a long time. I have been married to my job for the better part of two years, so my time in the sheets has been somewhat lacking.

"Midwest? You're a long way from home then, aren't you?" Is he asking another question or making a statement? I'm not sure. What I am sure of is that if he keeps staring at me like he is, I am going to have to change my underwear. He looks like he wants to eat me whole.

"My sister and I left there years ago. DC is my home now. What about you?" I notice him still watching me intently as I take a sip, his pupils dilating. My mouth hits the salty rim of my glass, and I lick my lips, tasting the salt. I think the temperature in this room just went up a few degrees.

"Maryland is my home, always has been," he says simply. He's intriguing to me. One minute, he seems more playful, the next, almost stoic. I'll keep this conversation going all night if he lets me.

"So are you here on business or pleasure?" My head tilts up at him, my hair flowing down to his finger which I am now certain twitches against it.

"Was business..." he says, and I can hear the *dot-dot-*

dot. My body screams at my mind to take the opening and run with it.

"And now pleasure?" I ask, our eyes locked in what seems like an unspoken exchange.

"You tell me." He puts it out there, confirming my thoughts, and I suck in a breath. To have a man be this forward is giving me a sense of power I didn't know I wanted.

"Mmmm. You are too smooth for your own good," I murmur, smirking. I watch as his eyes travel down my body, taking in my face, the curve of my breasts, down to my bare legs, and I feel like I am going to melt right here on the spot. I am so glad I dressed up tonight.

He swallows roughly, his jaw clenching subtly, and I squeeze my thighs together in response. This is the hottest moment I have ever experienced—and we haven't even done anything. Yet...

"Is it working?" A cheeky grin pulls at his lips, lighting up his wicked gaze, causing me to laugh.

"Maybe," I say, my eyes never leaving his. And as the soothing bar music plays in the background, I realize I am without a doubt going to sleep with this man tonight.

2

———

TENNYSON LANGFORD

Her voice coats me in comfort from the inside out, and if I didn't know any better, I would say I am five whiskeys in. Given I am still on my first glass, and it is only two fingers, I know that is not the case.

I couldn't miss her as she strutted straight up to the bar and plonked herself next to me, huffing and puffing the entire time. My eyes have been glued to her ever since. Curves for days. Red pouty lips, a dress doing everything it is meant to for her incredible body, and I already want to strip it off her.

That is what I like about New York. It is a melting pot of people. It's why I stayed an extra night, because even though my face might be familiar in Baltimore, less people pay attention here. There are no paparazzi bothering me, especially when there are Hollywood celebrities down the street they can chase. New York gives me anonymity, time for me to just be myself. Not the Langford I was born to be.

"Married?" I ask her, already predicting that she isn't. If she was upset with her sister for being the other woman, I doubt she'd flirt with me if she was taken.

"To my job. You?" she fires back to me, then takes another sip of her cocktail. My eyes lower from her playful gaze to her lips as they glisten around the glass. As she pulls away, I notice a flake of salt sticking to her bottom lip, and I bite my own so I don't lean forward and lick it clean.

"Never. Don't plan to be," I state, because it's true. I never want to get married.

"Why not?" Her question is simple, but the way she's looking at me holds more curiosity. She sinks back into the chair again, her body almost molding into my arm. *Almost.*

"I haven't had a good experience with marriages in my family." Even though my two older brothers have found their happiness, it doesn't mean that is my life path. I'm still scared of what a lifelong commitment could be from witnessing my parents' diabolical shambles of a relationship.

"Not many people do. Let's take Jacob for instance," she says, turning her body toward me, her bare leg brushing against my trousers. The need I have to touch her tanned, glowing skin and run my hand up her long legs almost has a growl breaking from my chest.

"Jacob?" I ask, already hating another man's name on her lips. My mind is racing, feeling a little drunk on her already.

"The married pilot who is currently fucking my sister." As soon as the swear word leaves her mouth, my eyes drop to her lips again. Her tongue darts out and licks away the salt flake I wanted for myself, and I am now so fucking hard it is difficult to sit straight.

"What about him?" I press, rubbing my mouth with my hand and trying to keep it together. I want to keep her talking, but... *God, her legs would look fantastic around my head.*

"He earns a decent salary, lives in Connecticut behind a white picket fence, flies around the world and probably plays golf on the weekends," she says with a bite, sitting forward and taking another sip. But with her frustration, the sip turns into a long pull that almost has her finishing her drink. When she sets it back down, I notice her chest is rising and falling a little quicker, bringing my attention to her cleavage. My hands tingle to trail across her bare shoulder and slip the strap of her dress off her body to see more of her.

"Probably," I agree as I realize I've been in my own head for too many seconds when she looks at me with a quirked brow. Or have I just been caught checking her out? I clear my throat, and she continues.

"So, what about his wife? And with his seemingly perfect life, why is he leading my sister on? A smart, beautiful woman, who is at least a decade younger than him." She asks me this like I can speak for all men.

"Well, my father cheated on my mother, and while he died before we got any answers to that question, I can surmise one thing," I say, throwing back my whiskey, needing the burn.

"What's that?" she asks, swirling her drink.

"He isn't getting something at home so he seeks it

with your sister. That or he and his wife have an open relationship." My father may be a cheating asshole that left a trail of women in his wake. But my mother is a monster, so she is not innocent. Not by a long shot.

"Hmmm, maybe. What about you? Ever cheated on a girlfriend?" Her gaze sears into mine, her finger lightly tracing the rim of her glass. How is that action so damn sexy?

"Never," I answer with complete honesty.

"Never?" Her eyes narrow, like she might not believe me.

"Never had a girlfriend," I clarify because it is true. I play the field; I never commit.

"Not ever?" she says, her body turning closer to me, her expression one of shock. Eyes wide, lips parted. I'd like to make her look like that while she lies beneath me.

"Not ever," I say with a shake of my head. "What about you? Boyfriend?" I tease again, not really caring for the answer anymore, because I plan to have her squirming tonight, whether she is single or not.

"Married to my job, remember?" she replies, brushing her hair over her shoulder. It's a disregarding move in a way, like she thinks I wasn't listening to her before. That sass has me wanting to spank her.

"So that takes all your time, then?" I ask.

"Mostly. Sometimes it is twenty-four seven. It can ebb and flow." She rocks her head from side to side like she is stretching out the kinks in her neck, and as I take in the delicate column of her throat, I have never wanted to put my mouth on anything more in my entire life. This woman is killing me and doesn't even know it.

"So, when it ebbs, what do you do with yourself?" I ask her, but I can't hold myself back when she leans closer. Her hair falls forward over one shoulder, and I reach up and brush it off and down her back. A shiver scatters through her as I touch her soft skin, but she doesn't stop me or lean away. And when our eyes connect, a coy smile curls her pretty lips.

"The usual things. Spend time with my sister, exercise..." she says, giving me a look that tells me everything I want to know. That we're on the same page.

"What exercises do you do?" My voice is low, screaming with innuendo.

"Anything that can get my heart rate up." And there it is. Exactly what I needed. Our eyes haven't disconnected since I touched her, my hand still resting on her back, my thumb rubbing lightly. Electricity ripples between us, the tension so thick it's hard to breathe. I decide to go with it and hope that she is thinking the same things as me. That I'm not completely delusional with lust.

"Want to get out of here?" I ask, and immediately she tamps down a smile, biting her lip.

"What exactly did you have in mind?" Her tone taunts me with seduction, as she's going to make me spell it out for her. Finishing her drink, she slides her empty glass on the bar to meet mine.

"Oh, I have a lot of things on my mind," I almost growl, trailing my touch from her back to her shoulders, up to the nape of her neck. I press my thumb into the muscle she was stretching, massaging it lightly, but with enough pressure that she not only melts beneath my touch, but lets out the breathiest sound that zings down to my aching hard-on. I *have* to hear more of that.

"You do? Tell me one of them," she almost purrs, her eyes closing slightly as I continue my soothing rub. I take my time, drinking her in, and I don't miss the way her thighs clench and her pupils dilate under the heat of my gaze and the feeling of my hand.

"Well, the night is still young, and I have a room upstairs..." I put it out there more directly, sitting forward slightly, our faces now closer, and I see her smile at my suggestion.

"And what shall we do in this room of yours?" I feel her breath run across my lips, and it takes every ounce of will I have to not kiss her. God, she is something.

"We could grab dinner," I suggest with a cheeky smile. She lets out a light, airy laugh, but then straightens her expression. She likes playing this game just as much as I do.

"Hmmmm, what shall we order?" she asks, but it's merely a whisper. I run my hand around to the front of her neck and strum her throat with my thumb, feeling her racing pulse.

Turning my head, I position my lips near her ear. "For the appetizer, I want you to put those glorious legs around my head so I can lick your pussy."

She gasps, her hands moving to my knees as she moves another inch toward me. It's all the welcome I need to continue when she hums, "Mm-hmm."

"For the entrée, I want you on your knees so I can feed you my cock." Her fingers dig into my thighs at that, and she nods for me to keep going. "Then for the main, I am going to pull you onto my lap so you can bounce your perfect tits in my face." I pause as I swear I hear a moan rumbling in her chest, but I'm not done yet. "While I don't normally have a sweet tooth, I know tonight I'll need more of you to satisfy my craving. When you're all messy and sated, I plan to palm your perfect ass, lift you onto my body, and fuck you in the shower as I work to get you clean. Or even dirtier. I'll leave that up to you."

I pull back a little and look at her, her lips right in front of mine. She remains quiet now, her expression lax and unreadable, and I raise an eyebrow, wondering if I pushed her too far.

"Answer me one question," she whispers, and I don't miss the feeling of her hand as it travels higher up my thigh, resting so close to my rock-hard length that it makes my own breath catch this time. I clench my teeth, giving her a silent nod.

"Will there be seconds?"

3

WILLOW

We barely make it inside the room before we're on each other like it's our last day on earth. The elevator ride up was filled with so much tension, I'm not sure how we even made it down the hall. I thought I'd combust with just his hand holding mine.

As he pushes me against the wall, my back arches into him immediately, my body like a magnet that's already seeking out more of his touch. He kicks the door closed, then cups my face in his hands as his lips finally find mine. We openly devour each other—lips, tongue, pants, nips—as we share moans and groans like they're our next breaths. We are a tangle of tongues and limbs, frantic for each other, moving at a pace I've never known.

"God, you are so fucking beautiful," he growls, his hands now everywhere. They explore up and down my body, scorching me with need.

"Off, off. Get your clothes off," I almost demand, my hands pushing at the jacket he has on, trying to get it off his broad shoulders. He grips his lapels and rips his suit jacket from his body, then throws it across the room. But it's not just any room. It's the penthouse. The best room in this swanky hotel and bigger than my entire house back home. But I have little time to look around as I start to kick off my shoes.

"Keep them on," he tells me quickly, and I smile. Holy hell, he is so handsome. His face almost looks feral, his desire for me so strong that my knees nearly buckle from one look.

Stepping forward, he pushes his body against mine, his lips slamming into me again. I whimper into his mouth, my body turning liquid as he pushes his erection against my pelvis. God, he is big too. How is it possible? So far, he is a perfect ten. Good-looking, smart, masculine, and can hold a conversation. This is definitely my lucky night.

I reach forward with eager hands and start to unbutton his shirt. I'm desperate to discover what is underneath, and my fingers fumble with the speed. His hands leave my hips, and he grabs his collar, ripping his shirt from his body, causing buttons to go flying across the room.

That is by far the hottest thing I have ever seen.

"Shit," I whisper to myself as my eyes rest on his bare torso. I am reasonably confident that his body is either contoured by a professional makeup artist or fake in some other way. It's just too damn perfect. He smirks, letting me know he heard my admiration before he lowers down my body.

His mouth trails from my neck, down to my chest, his

hands gripping my breasts. Something about his touch is unlike anything I've experienced before. It's so strong and sure, but just gentle enough to keep me craving more. As my body heats, my heart races, and I can't actually believe any of this is happening. My hands run across his bare chest and up his neck, wanting to feel all of him, but then this gorgeous, half-naked man falls to his knees before me.

"I'm fucking starving," he mumbles as his hands slowly push my dress up my thighs, and I squirm a little already at the friction, my underwear soaking.

"Time for the appetizer?" I breathe out, playing this teasing game we have going all too well. I have never felt as sexy in my life as I do right now.

"You have great fucking legs," he says, running his palms up my legs to my hips and rolling my dress at my waist. His compliments keep coming, and I feel like I am having an out-of-body experience. It all feels too good, and we haven't even really gotten started yet.

"I am keeping these." He grabs my lace underwear, pulling them down my legs slowly, like I will break. And I might if he keeps this slowed pace from where we started.

"They are La Perla..." I am not sure why I tell him my underwear brand, maybe because they weren't cheap enough to be giving away, but he smirks as he pockets them. His hands are instantly back on my legs, caressing my skin like he can't not touch me.

"Goddamn perfect," he says huskily as his gaze zeroes in on the part of me he just unwrapped like a present. The way he's looking at me, the barest part of me, is so intimate, but I revel in it. Goosebumps of anticipation cover my skin as he grabs one of my legs, lifting it and placing it over his shoulder, and I find myself relaxing against the wall, ready for whatever he's about to do to me.

We haven't even made it two steps inside the room. We are still in the foyer of his penthouse, and I am opening myself to him, a complete stranger. This is so far out of my ordinary persona, I might as well be on Mars.

He presses kisses up my inner thigh and my breath quickens all over again. His large hand holds my upper thigh before slowly moving to my ass and gripping tightly, just as his mouth hits my center.

"Ohhhh," I moan at the contact, my hips jolting forward, but he holds me still. It has been so long since I have had a man's mouth on me, I almost forgot what it felt like. My fingers dig into his scalp, keeping him there, and he groans against me.

Like a reward for my greediness, his tongue swipes up my opening, his lips suctioning on my clit. He sucks with little pulses, tongue flicking and swirling, before repeating the action with another long swipe like he needs to taste more of me. He is slow one moment, taking his time, relishing me like I am the best meal he has ever had. But at the sound of my whimpers or moans, he returns my pleasure with a groan, doubling down his attention like he needs to devour me whole.

"You are so fucking delicious, so fucking wet and delicious." His voice vibrates into me, his mouth not leaving me for a moment as he goes right back for more.

"Oh God." I pant at his words. "Yessss, like that. Please don't stop." Biting my lip, my hips begin to rock against his face. My head pushes back against the wall harder, my eyes closing as I try to suck in the air I am lacking.

My hold in his hair tightens. Heat coats my skin as I start to sweat when he buries himself completely between my legs. Glancing down, I take in the fact that I'm still fully dressed besides my panties, and for some reason that makes me feel even hotter. How we couldn't even wait to finish stripping each other before this. Watching him work me over is the sexiest thing I've ever seen. He's so into it, his eyes closed, nose pressed against me, jaw flexing.

I whimper, but it's more like a sob without tears. At the sound, his eyes open and lock on mine, and when he sees the look on my face, he smiles. The only part of it I can see is the lift of his cheeks and spark in his eye, and it's so sinful. I can't believe I nearly went back to my room for a bath and a glass of wine instead of this.

With his eyes still on mine, his other hand glides up the inside of my thigh before I feel him insert a finger, and I almost combust on the spot.

I am moaning and panting like a porn star as he moves his finger in and out, massaging that magical little spot inside me with every pass. His mouth keeps up its unrelenting rhythm, and his grip on my ass grows almost bruising. And I can't get enough of all of it.

"Don't stop, don't stop, don't stop," I chant, feeling my muscles clench before I let go with a scream.

The orgasm that overtakes me is so intense, I clench every muscle in my body to the point of pain. He doesn't let up as each wave of euphoria rolls through me, my limbs shaking and my breaths quick. With one last shudder, I heave like I have run a marathon, trying to get a grip back on reality. He presses one last kiss to my clit when I whimper from sensitivity, but I can't even move or think for a beat.

"That was..." I breathe out, my eyes darting around the room, yet looking at nothing. Swallowing, I try to bring moisture to my lips and center myself again.

"Just the appetizer," he murmurs, his lips still on me, dragging up my body as he starts to come back to eye level, bringing my dress with him. "Time to get you naked. I want to see you and your beautiful body while I feed you." My dress slides up, popping over my breasts, and I raise my arms into the air as he scoops it off my body.

I stand there in front of this stranger, now totally naked except for my shoes. I don't do one-night stands. In fact, this is only my second one ever. So I shouldn't feel comfortable or safe in this situation, but I do. I also feel feminine, sexy, wanted, desired, worshipped. It has been a long time since I have felt any of those things.

"Look at you..." he says in awe, taking a small step away to look at me, but keeping hold of my hand. "You are breathtaking," he adds in almost silent wonder as his eyes run down the length of my body and back up again.

"Let me look at you," I say as I step toward him, full of confidence that I didn't even know I possessed, placing my hands on his belt. He doesn't move, and neither do his eyes that stay on me as I look back, unflinching. I open his belt buckle and button on his pants before slowly lowering his zipper. The heat in his gaze is intense, and I see him swallow roughly just before I push his pants down. My hands slide into the sides of his boxers to the top of his ass, and I slowly push them down too. They pool at his ankles before he kicks them away, and I just about lose every sense as I see him fully. I let my eyes wander, coming to the conclusion that he is, without a doubt, the sexiest man I have ever been with.

We stand in front of each other, entirely naked, not even knowing each other's name. But I feel no nerves, only excitement that I get to enjoy him.

"Are you ready for entrée? Because I'm ready to serve you," he grits out, and my eyes flick back down to his groin to see him red and throbbing.

"It appears that you are," I say, my mouth already watering, wondering if I can manage his size. I slowly lower to my knees in front of him, the only other movement his hand as it grips on to mine, ensuring I am steady. It's good to know this mystery of a man is also a gentleman.

"Bon appétit."

4

TENNYSON

My teeth are grinding as she lowers her naked body in front of me. I wasn't lying when I said she was breathtaking. Her voluptuous figure is fucking fantastic, with breasts and an ass that are round and full, the size you really want in your hands all the time. So much pretty flesh to grip and caress and spank. Her waist skirts in a little before flaring out again at her hips, making her the curviest hourglass I've ever seen. She is all woman, and I fucking love it.

"You look good down there on your knees." The urge I have to heap praise on this woman comes through me strongly. I like sex. I like a lot of sex. And while I usually have a good time with my partners, there has never really been anyone who's ignited this kind of visceral need within me.

"I look better on my back," she murmurs, her sparkling eyes gazing up at me with mischief as her hands teasingly trail up my thighs to feel my abs and back down again. My insides flare as my length twitches for attention, and I need to clench my other hand to ensure I am actually living this moment. It feels too good to be real.

I already want to have her on her back, on all fours, in the shower, in the bed, fucking everywhere and in every position. I re-clench my hand in hers, because if I don't, I think I will lose my self-control and end up taking her fully before I'm ready. I need to enjoy her in every way I can before the night is up.

"I want that pretty mouth of yours on my cock." I am hard to the point of pain, and I watch her as she looks up at me again with a coy smile, gives me a wink, and decides to use action instead of words as she leans in and trails her tongue up my length from base to tip. She moans as my precum lands on her tongue, going back again for another taste.

"Holy mother of God…" I murmur, my cock pulsing at the contact. My head falls back, and I look at the ceiling of this room and pray I don't come too soon.

I feel her other hand slide up the back of my thigh as her lips move, taking me into her mouth just a little. She sucks my tip softly before swirling her tongue around me again. She repeats this small action, effectively teasing me. But each time, she takes me a little farther into her mouth.

"That feels fucking fantastic." I keep my eyes on the ceiling, not wanting to look at her yet, because I am so close to coming it would be a crime. Even imagining her red lips wrapped around me is enough to drive me close to the brink.

Her free hand moves to my ass, and she grips on to

me as she slowly takes me all in, right to the back of her throat, and I almost fall to the floor. My head drops forward on instinct, my chin hitting my chest as I gasp for air at the feeling. I knew when I first saw her, those lips of hers would weave magic, and I wasn't wrong.

Looking down at her, I almost come on the spot. Her hair is dark and shiny, curling around her shoulders, playing peekaboo with her breasts as her head moves forward and back. One arm around my ass, wanting to keep us close, the other still encased in mine, our fingers woven together at my side, neither of us wanting to let go of the other. Her lips—pouty, red, and glossy—slide up and back on my cock, and I bite my own at the sight. This visual is spectacular.

"That's it. Oh, that's it. You are so fucking good at this, so fucking good." I groan, long and loud, watching every movement she makes. My dick's so hard, I feel like I am going to come for days. I have had a lot of blow jobs in my years, but I fail to recall one as good as this. I don't even need to tell her how I like it; instinctively, she seems to know.

I move my free hand then, needing to touch her, and place it at the back of her head. Her hair is soft, just like it looks, and I wrap it in my fingers tight, pulling it at her scalp, needing her to know how much I want this. Want *her*. Her gaze flicks up to me, and I bite my lip so hard this time that I will probably make it bleed, because her eyes are like molten fire, the desire swirling in them evident. As my attention drifts lower, I see her nipples from behind her silky strands, hard and showing her arousal. I can't wait to have my mouth on them.

"I'm going to come. Fuck, I am going to come so hard in your perfect fucking mouth," I grit out, feeling my balls tighten, my muscles clenching, trying to hold out a little longer. My hips are thrusting, she is moaning, our hands are clenching each other tighter.

"Are you going to take me? Are you going to swallow me down?" I ask, almost panting. If she is not, I need to pull out now.

"Mm-hmmm," she responds with a moan, her hand on my ass gripping me closer, leaving marks from her nails, no doubt, and she slides my dick so far down her throat, I almost see stars.

"Good girl. Such a good fucking girl. Jesus, I'm coming. I'm coming so fucking hard," I growl out almost unintelligibly as I slam into her mouth, holding her hair in my hand. I roar to the room as my release flies through me at a speed I haven't known before, and she takes it all, still sucking me down as I slow my pumps. Feeling my shoulders lower slightly, my eyes remain glued to her, and I watch her swallow as she pops off my length. Our hands are still gripped tight, her lips looking a little more red and pouty than before, some of her lipstick now coloring the base of my cock. My gaze doesn't waver when it locks back on hers, and when she sits back on her heels, she makes this moment even better.

She fucking smiles.

"I like you feeding me," she says playfully, and I see her perfect breasts rise and fall as she takes in some air.

"Good, because my appetite for you is growing," I growl as I pull her up by our joined hands before I grab her around her ass and lift her up onto me. She laughs then, a carefree, relaxing laugh that has me grinning like a fool. She wraps her legs around me, her warm, wet core now pressed against my stomach, and I walk us to the bathroom, feeling lighter than I have in years. "Let's have a shower because I want to get you filthy again. I want to spend the night making you come, and not only will I feed you seconds, but God, woman, we are going to have a midnight snack and a full buffet breakfast too."

"Hmmm... I like the sound of that," she says, burying her head into the crook of my neck, and I feel her tongue and lips nibble my skin, the feeling running down my body and making me warm all over. "Oh, but I have one request," she says as we reach the bathroom, and I turn on the hot water, steam encasing the room immediately.

"What's that?" I ask, knowing I would easily give her anything she asks for.

"No names. One night. My life is busy, and I don't need strings." She sounds almost shy as she says it, but she's still confident in her delivery, and the mix is somehow unbelievably attractive.

"I'm going to fuck you so hard, you won't even remember your own name, darling." I grin at her as she lifts her head to look me in the eye. She is the perfect woman, and for tonight, she is all mine. I'll take whatever she wants to give me.

Stepping into the shower, our hands and eyes stay on nothing but each other.

We spend the night with our bodies in sync, palpable heat and desire in every touch. The way I felt with her, it was life-altering, mind-blowing. It created a longing inside me for more before we were even finished.

And that only made the cold bed beside me harder to fathom when I woke up in the morning alone. She left without saying goodbye, and for the first time ever, I don't like it. Not one bit.

5

WILLOW - SIX MONTHS LATER

The black-and-white kitten stares at me with sad blue eyes through the glass window at my back door. It's small, has a cute little face and shaggy hair, looking a little worse for wear. It knows what it's doing. It did the same thing last night. We both know how this will end.

"Willow. You are the best at what you do, and with Harrison looking at moving into a bigger role in the future, then we really need to ensure everyone surrounding him has a great presence, strong leadership, and dependability," my longtime friend, Beth, says over the phone. We met years ago through work and kept in touch on and off throughout the years, although, I haven't seen her in a long time, as her life is so busy now that she is Maryland's First Lady.

"So are you concerned for Tennyson Langford or concerned for your governor's reputation?" I ask Beth point-blank as I look through my kitchen cupboard to see if I still have that dry cat food I bought last month. If Beth wants my help, then I really need to know what exactly is prompting this situation.

"I love my brother. But I am going to be honest and say we are a little worried for him," Harrison replies instead, and even though it is late, I get an image of him and Beth still sitting in his office with me on speakerphone.

"Well, if you want to be president one day, then your whole family really needs to be supportive and aware of the scrutiny that comes with such a position. In my experience, a lot of the time, votes are won or lost not only on the candidates' behavior but also that of their families. Tell me more about your brother."

My hand lands on the packet of cat food at the back of the cupboard. I pour a small amount into a plastic bowl I have for just this occasion. This is not the first stray cat to sit on my back porch. In fact, I'm starting to wonder if all the neighborhood strays have little cat meetings at the local park to discuss which house has the best food, knowing I will serve them each and every time.

Harrison clears his throat. "Tennyson is smart, successful, and the third eldest in our family. He is the CEO of Langford Construction, our construction firm. He and the team are responsible for many of the commercial buildings around Baltimore, and he also manages our international projects, currently working on some builds in Asia and other regions." Harrison offers me the brief rundown of the man whom I know absolutely nothing about.

"So, what's the problem?" I take everyone at face value, and so far, Tennyson sounds like a catch. But everyone has skeletons in their closet. Some are just better at hiding them than others.

"He is... somewhat..." Harrison struggles to find the words, and my body stills at the kitchen counter, mid-pour, waiting with anticipation.

"He is a party boy; the paparazzi follow him everywhere because they know he will give them a good story. And they're unfortunately not always positive. He loves women, spends too much money, and we just need him and his reputation to be a little more... conservative." Beth takes over, giving me more of a glimpse into the enigma that is Tennyson Langford.

"Black sheep?" I ask them as I grab the small bowl and walk over to my back door. The kitten sits in the same spot, its little tail flicking slightly, awaiting the feast it is about to get. I open the door slowly, trying not to startle it, then slide the bowl in front of it before I slowly close the door again. I think I will call this one Betty.

"Black what?" Harrison asks, sounding almost offended.

"Is he the black sheep of the family? You know, perfect family, perfect brothers, yet he is the one who always seems to find trouble, not as put together as the rest?" I have worked with that type a lot. My career in communications and brand management has varied over the years, but I have now fallen into the very niche area of reputational management. I am not even sure how that happened. One minute, I was doing publicity for the not-for-profit sector, being underpaid and undervalued. Not that I minded, since helping people is what I strive to do. The next minute, I was knee-deep in trying to dig a charity boss out of a whole lot of hot water he found himself in and he came out of it all relatively unharmed. My new skill set was then born, and I haven't stopped since. Unsurprisingly, reputational management is an area of great need in the political capital of DC and my client list is long.

"Yes, I guess... but not always. I mean, he has always been on the edgier side, maybe a little tough and mysterious, but for the last six months or so, he has gotten worse," Beth murmurs as I take a seat at my kitchen table and tap on my laptop, deciding to do a quick search on this Tennyson Langford. The Langford name is well known, although mainly in Baltimore. Here in DC, there are so many political personalities that I haven't really ever had to focus on helping people in other cities too much.

"When he was younger, we cast a blind eye. All boys play a little when they are in their early twenties. But now that he is older, many in the community look up to him, and my brothers and I are trying to work with him as a family to help him out of the worsening routine he is in. We just need someone with your expertise to help manage his external persona," Harrison explains, and I can hear his concern and frustration through the phone. It is a hard predicament to be in. He obviously has eyes on a presidential campaign in the future and knows to have a good run at something like that, he needs a clean house.

An image of Tennyson Langford flashes up on my screen, and I almost fall off my chair. Staring back at me are the eyes I have never forgotten. He is just as handsome as I remember. My hands are suddenly shaking, and although Beth is talking, I am not listening to a word she is saying. It has been months since that one night in New York, when I had the best sexual experience of my entire life. No names were exchanged, no personal details, but we gave each other everything. That night is burned so deep into my soul, I dream about it, and any touch I have had since then is never up to par. My body heats even now, just thinking about it.

Do I tell Beth I know him intimately? Do I refuse to take the job? I don't want to let her down, and she is right; I am excellent at what I do. But I am not sure I would be able to work with him, not without picturing him naked and with my leg draped around his shoulders.

"Does he know you are talking to me?" I ask, because if he is aware, then he may already know who I am. My mind is in overdrive, not yet understanding if I should or shouldn't take the job. Working with the family of a potential president would be great for business. But can I be professional while working so closely with the man who fulfilled every promise he made me that night, including giving me seconds?

"No," Harrison sighs.

Looking at the caption on this image of Tennyson Langford, the picture was taken at a charity gala a few months ago. I click to the next image and the next, all paparazzi shots of him with his head down, walking either out of a club late at night with a model-esque woman following closely behind, or him again wearing the same clothes, walking out of the Four Seasons hotel the next morning and jumping into a flashy red sports car. Not a good look, and my stomach turns a little.

"So he is out with different women a lot?" I ask, not liking the vulnerability in my voice all of a sudden.

"Every weekend," Harrison says, almost like he is exhausted from the fact. My stomach curls onto itself at that. We weren't special. It wasn't anything to him. The one night that had flames licking at my skin was probably a mere blip in his existence. I take a breath and steady myself. I can do this. I am a professional. I have worked with politicians, athletes, international celebrities. All I need to do is push the memories aside and do my job. It will be easy. I can put up my armor. It is not like we declared our undying love for each other. It was one night. One hot, scorching night of tongues and sweat and tangled limbs. But I can ignore it. I can do my job and do it well.

"We were hoping you were free this weekend. We have a children's fun day on Sunday at Harrison's brother's estate, just outside of Baltimore. We wanted to introduce you there. You know, with kids around, we were hoping he would be more open to the idea of his brothers getting involved in his affairs," Beth offers. It is clear they have thought a lot about this.

I click through photo after photo, all of him with different women over the past few months. It cements my thoughts. I have no doubt that Tennyson would not even remember my face. I was just another notch on his post, another mark for his black book. He will have no idea who I even am. But I need to tell Beth. I expect full disclosure from my clients, and I need to give it to them in return.

"Let me pull all this together to ensure I have it correct. You are concerned for Tennyson, both for him personally but also for the public perception about him. You want me to work with him to clean up his act so that it is more favorable for your run into a presidency opportunity, if and when that arises in the future. At this stage, he doesn't know anything about this, will most likely not be receptive to it, and you want me there on the weekend to meet him and answer any questions he might have about the process? Does that sum it up?" It is not my first rodeo, but family interventions don't usually go well, and while Harrison is a great guy, I have no idea about his brothers. The research I now need to do in the next few days in preparation for the weekend is already building in my mind.

"Yes, that pretty much sums it up." Harrison seems pleased with my brief overview. I take a deep breath, readying for the hard part.

"Full disclosure, I have met him before," I say, and even though I try to be subtle, my tone gives me away.

"Shit," I hear Harrison curse.

"It was over six months ago, and I'm sure with the way he's been living, he won't even remember, but I wanted to be upfront with you both. I am happy to take on this project, and I will ensure it is all handled professionally."

"We wanted the best and, Willow, you are excellent at this kind of thing. We know you are the right person for this, and I hope you have room on your books to take this on?" Beth asks, not digging into the history. I smile a little, feeling a warm sense of pride from her words. Beth knows me well enough to know I will get the job done for her and get Tennyson in golden boy territory, right where he needs to be.

"Beth, of course I will be there this weekend. Send me the time and address. And don't worry, we will get this all sorted and have Tennyson turned into a poster child in no time," I say, smiling as Tennyson Langford's dark, brooding eyes look back at me from my laptop screen. They are deep, his face swirling with emotions I can't yet decipher. I have a feeling this is going to be my hardest project yet.

But I do love a challenge, and by the looks of these photos I have found, that is exactly what Tennyson will be.

6

TENNYSON

Am I dead?

This is the first thought I have as I feel the thumping pain in my head that vibrates down my neck, before it settles in the familiar spot on my shoulders. I peel open my eyes, taking a look around the room. It is trashed, empty champagne bottles and clothes strewn everywhere, and remnants of a late-night pizza I have no recollection of ordering or eating.

I try swallowing, but my mouth feels like sandpaper, my tongue sticking to the roof. I need water.

Ding.

My cell phone pings at me, the sound like a knife hitting my brain. Groaning, I roll over, ignoring it. The bedsheets are rumpled, and I spot a red lace bra draped over the armchair in the corner of the room.

Ding.

I press my palms to my eyes, hoping whoever is trying to contact me gives up and leaves me alone. The thumps in my head increase as I start to move my body, the slug-gishness making my limbs feel heavy.

Ding.

"All right, motherfucker," I say out loud to no one. To nothing. My body aches and not in a good way. I am tired. Bone-tired. I haven't slept well in months; the only thing getting me through is whiskey and women, and even then I am lucky if I even get a few hours of shut-eye.

As I sit up, I hear a shower running and see a small amount of light peeking through the ajar bathroom door. Not for the first time in my life, I have no idea who the hell is in there. Squinting at the sun streaming through the gap in the closed curtains on the opposite wall, the thumping gets worse. I scrub my face with my hand as my eyes flick to the bedside table to see the logo of the Four Seasons staring at me from the notepad. At least now I know where I am. Grabbing my phone from the nightstand, the bright lights of the time flash into my face. Eleven a.m.

"Shit," I mumble as I rub my eyes again, trying to get some type of life into my body. I have message after message from my brothers, all asking me where I am, and as I start to type a reply, Ben calls.

"Hey," I groan into the phone as I drop my head into my hands, wishing I was still asleep.

"Where are you?" he demands, and I can tell by his tone that he is pissed.

"In bed. Why?" I ask innocently, trying to remember what day it is.

"Why?! You are meant to be here with the kids. Get

your ass up and to my place *now*," he says gruffly before ending the call.

"Love you too, Benny Boy," I murmur to myself, feeling like shit for an entirely different reason now. Letting down my brothers is the one thing I hate doing. And I seem to be doing it more and more lately. That and hangovers. I can't remember the last time I woke up without one.

That is a lie. I do. It has been six months, two weeks, one day, and about twenty-three hours. That mystery one-night stand still haunts my soul. I rub my eyes again. Those memories are not worth reliving, especially since I woke up that morning alone. A first for me. I crack my neck and think about the day ahead. The fucking kids. The schoolkids that Ben and his girl Em look after. The school that all us boys now support in one way or another. They are cool kids too. Time at the estate with them is always fun. But right now, I feel like I could sleep for days.

I stand up, grabbing my head in the process. Cool air hits my skin, and I look down at my naked body, wondering what the hell I got up to last night. Although it doesn't take long to remember, as I notice two ripped condom packets on the carpet. At least I wrapped myself, something I always ensure I do. The shower stops as I reach for my pants, putting them on quickly, ignoring the spinning that starts, and just as I pull on my shirt, the bathroom door opens.

"Oohh, you're awake?" the feminine voice purrs. It should make me want to strip again and crawl back into bed with her, burying myself deep, but it doesn't. It has the opposite effect.

"Morning," is all I say, cringing a little at the abruptness that falls from my croaky morning voice. She is not familiar, even though I am sure I had this woman screaming in pleasure last night. I look up and see Kim or Kerry... maybe Kaylee, as her eyes roam my body. *I think she is from out of town.*

"I didn't want to wake you. In fact, no, that is a lie, I did want to wake you, but I thought I might do that with my mouth." She saunters her naked body toward me in what I am sure is her way of being seductive. She is a pretty girl, just not the woman I want. Every woman since that night has been a placeholder to make me forget... not that it's working.

"No morning glory for me, sweetheart. I need to go." I try to soften my tone. I don't want to be a total asshole, even if I can't remember her name.

"So soon? But we had so much fun together..." My skin crawls, making me want to scratch it at her tone.

"Thanks for a great night. Let me get your phone," I say as I walk over to where I think the safe is. It is my standard behavior. As soon as I am alone with a woman, I ask for their phone, and I lock it away in the safe. That way, they can't take photos of me naked while blackout drunk to sell to the nearest gossip site. I may be a bed-hopping asshole, but I have learned how to play the game a little smarter than I once did. My brothers, I am sure, are all relieved.

"You didn't really think I would take any photos, did

you?" she says as I pass her cell phone over and pocket my own.

"Thanks for the night," I offer, giving her a peck on the cheek, completely ignoring her statement before I retreat to the door.

"I'm in town until Wednesday. Call me if you want to catch up again!" This time when she speaks, I pick up her slight accent. I think she was from Kentucky. I give her a smile and a nod that hurt my face without making any commitment, before I walk through the door, shutting it firmly behind me.

Because even though I fuck a lot, I never fuck the same girl twice.

7

WILLOW

The sound of kids squealing in laughter fills the air, and the sun shines down, illuminating them all as they run and play. My nerves are at an all-time high, and my heart thuds in my chest from uncertainty. I have no idea what is going to happen today when I see Tennyson; I just hope I can put on my professional face and get on with the job and not imagine the night we had... even though that is all I have thought about these past few days. I gaze around this estate. While I have been to many beautiful homes in and around DC, I am at what could only be described as perhaps the biggest and most luxurious estate in all of the East Coast.

"Seriously, did you see their bathrooms? I could swim in their tub," Josh says from next to me. My best friend, even though he is only twelve.

"I didn't bring you here to swim, so stay clear of the bathrooms," I murmur as I look around at everyone and everything from behind my sunglasses.

"Why am I here?" he asks, and I look at him as though he is crazy. Just like Betty the kitten, Josh turned up at my back doorstep a few years ago and has been hanging around ever since. He is my neighbor and his mother works a lot of shifts at the local hospital, so I normally watch him whenever I can to help her. Given I work from home and have no personal life to speak of, that is often.

"Someone has to watch you. Besides, I thought you would love it here." I wave my hand around at the extravagance. There is a petting zoo, face painting, balloon animals, even those ridiculous Segways that kids are driving all over the place.

"At least they have a soccer pitch," Josh says as he bounces his soccer ball between his feet, onto his knee and back again. While not exactly a soccer pitch, it is the greenest, largest lawn I have ever seen.

"Just be careful with that ball. I don't want you to break anything or hurt anyone," I warn him, because he has been playing soccer for most of his life. The ball is something he takes everywhere and his right kick is powerful.

"So, are we on a job?" he whispers like we are doing something sneaky.

"Just visiting a friend." I offer him nothing, but he is a smart kid. He knows. Mostly because he knows what work I do, ever since I caught him peeking at a file I had in my house when he was over one day about a year ago. The work I do is not for little eyes or ears, but he is much older than his years.

"Yeah, like you hang out with these kinds of people," he mutters with a roll of his eyes.

"What is that meant to mean?" I ask him, slightly offended.

"You're cool, Saide is cool. These people are..." he comments about my sister and me as he looks at the adults situated around the gardens.

"Hoity-toity," he says, firm in his assessment.

"Hoity-toity?" I ask, trying hard not to laugh. "What does hoity-toity mean?"

"Stuck-up snobs." I don't need to ask where he learned that phrase from. His mother is Australian; it runs in his blood.

"Not all of them look snobby. What about her over there?" I point to a woman who is talking to the kids. Dressed casually in jeans and a shirt, her hair is tied back, and she has a wide smile on her face. I recognize her from my research. She is Emily Carr, a schoolteacher who's engaged to Benjamin Langford, owner of this estate I find myself in today.

"She's okay. But look over there." He points, and I see our governor. The man who invited me here today. Dressed in a shirt and suit pants, I assume he has come from a meeting or something, because he is not really dressed for a family fun day. He is watching me from afar. In fact, the other two men standing with him are as well. Obviously, all three Langford men are discussing how today will go. I give them a small, reassuring smile and wave. We have already said our quick hellos, but I am sure there will be lots more to talk about later. Surprisingly, all three of them have their faces painted like the

Ninja Turtles, looking equal parts ridiculous and kind of endearing.

"What, you don't like the ninja turtles?" I tease, because he grew out of cartoons years ago. Josh is more likely to watch the BBC global world news with me now than kid shows.

"Pfft. They don't even realize that there are four turtles, so their attempt at being cool with painted faces is severely underwhelming," he says with a bored sigh before he continues kicking the soccer ball and we walk farther into the crowd of kids.

"What about him? He looks okay." I nod toward an older man helping the kids. Beth introduced me to him earlier as George, who's friends with the Langfords via Emily Carr, and he also happens to be the principal of the school that's here today, enjoying the life that being wealthy brings.

"He looks cool," Josh concedes with a shrug, having already lost interest in dissecting the adults, his eyes now firmly on his soccer ball. I watch him bounce and bounce the ball, changing it from his knee to his feet and back again. He is far enough away from people that it isn't harming anyone, but I know he is itching to kick it.

"Hey, Willow," a man's voice says from beside me, and I turn and look up. These Langford men are so tall and broad compared to me, my neck is already cramped from my chin rising so far.

"Governor, or should I say, Donatello?" I try not to laugh, but my smile is wide. The face painter actually did a really good job.

"Yes, well, it is a good cause. We try our best to help

where we can. Tennyson should be here soon. Do you have any questions?" he asks, looking a little nervous, and that only reignites my own nerves. I have no idea what to expect, but if I had to guess, I think there will be yelling and probably some hostility between the brothers. I again wonder if he will have any recognition when he sees me. But as soon as the thought comes, I lock it away. I am a professional on a job, and that is how I need to remain.

"About babysitting your brother, you mean?" I quip. After a few days of research, I have come to the conclusion that Harrison and Beth's breakdown was spot-on. Tennyson Langford is a self-indulgent party boy who beds a different woman every weekend, maybe two. Parties too much, loves to flash his wealth, and he's currently in the bullseye of every media outlet because he gives them exactly what they need to feed more gossip. "Don't worry, Harrison. I will do my best to tidy up your black sheep. Your reputation will stay clean." This is my bread and butter. I do this type of reputational management all the time. Usually after one of our esteemed politicians gets caught doing something that is unbecoming. I now have a small team, all of us working remotely across the country. I love having my own business, but I am confident that it won't stay small for long. There are many people who need my skill set and it is growing by the day.

"Believe me when I tell you we have tried everything. But Tennyson is his own man, who does things his way. Which is good. But his spending, womanizing, and party boy ways need to stop." I nod, pushing my lips together in a tight smile. It's getting harder not to show my nerves as the minutes pass. He could show up at any time now.

"Well, I am sure he is going to be thrilled by the surprise intervention that you have planned today," I say sarcastically, raising my eyebrows.

"Hmmm," Harrison says, looking at me before his eyes flick up again. "All right, well, he is finally here. I will let you know when we need you." My head whips around to where he was looking so quickly, I almost trip over my own feet.

"We will stick around here," I murmur in agreement as he stalks off to the side of the house, where Tennyson has just walked out, carrying a tray of food. My eyes remain glued to the man I will be managing. He looks the same. Handsome, strong, tall, in control, and I push my nails into my palm to wake me up from my dreaming, restoring order in my limbs. He puts the tray down before one of the kids grabs his hand and pulls him to the face painter. I huff a small laugh as I watch the interaction. Tennyson, with his dark sunglasses on and his hair ruffled, looking possibly hungover and like he got ready in a hurry. He has a scowl on his face, but he goes with the kid willingly.

I watch as he sits in front of the female face painter and removes his sunglasses, and I think I see her swoon from here. I scoff to myself. Clearly, he has a way with the ladies, and like an idiot all those months ago, I fell for his charms. I wonder how many other women he has picked up in bars. She gets busy on his face while he watches the kids as they all talk over each other while trying to tell him things.

His dark hair falls a little over his face, and as my gaze drifts down, I take in how he fills out his shirt all too well. He looks casual, with a don't-mess-with-me air about him. The kind of look that I am sure attracts women in droves. The face painter is quick, probably because he looks like he would rather be anywhere else. Once she's done, he stands, rolling his shoulders back before slowly walking toward his brothers, the four ninja turtles now complete.

"Hey, Willow, check this out," Josh says from beside me, and I look at him just in time to see him take a big kick. He has been itching to do it since he arrived and saw the massive green space. Normally, I encourage his physical activity, as kids playing sports is important. But as I watch the soccer ball fly through the air, it moves in slow motion, soaring across the green lawn, and my eyes widen as I see where it is going to land.

"Watch out!" I yell, but I am too late. This is not going to be good.

8

TENNYSON

The kids are too loud, this face paint is itchy, and if I don't eat something in the next ten minutes, I feel like I am going to turn into the Hulk.

"Glad you could make it," Harrison says, his purple painted eyes staring at me, the sarcasm dripping in his tone not something I miss.

"I slept in." I shrug, wondering if Ben has any whiskey around here.

"You're late." Eddie punches his words, and the headache I had before starts to come back again.

"I made it, though, like I said I would. What time did you all get here?" I ask, taking a swig of the bottle of water I grabbed on the way through. My eyes flick between them all, knowing it is midday and surely, they only just arrived themselves.

"Nine. We had a big breakfast for the kids before playtime. Their day is almost over," Ben says accusingly, and I cringe a little.

"Sorry, I thought it was lunch," I murmur, feeling like a sack of shit for letting him down.

"What the hell is going on with you?" Harrison asks as his eyes pin me. It is a question he has asked before. I huff out a laugh as I straighten my shoulders, trying to stand up to his pointed question. He looks concerned.

"Nothing. Why?" I ask, sounding nonchalant, hating the emphasis on me. I have always been able to fly under the radar with my family. Harrison was always in the spotlight; his sights set on the governorship is what drove him and our family for years. Then he met Beth and achieved his dream, so we all looked to our second older brother, Ben, as he took the reins of our family law firm. He fired one of our most profitable clients and got an instant family in Em and Rosie, hence the reason we are all here today.

"You're never on time, you are always out late, you look like shit," Eddie says, and I look at my younger brother for a beat. I always see him as the baby, but he has grown up a lot these past few years, despite being the only one of us boys who still actively speaks to our mother. The mere thought of her sends a shiver down my spine. She has been too quiet lately.

"Not here..." Ben growls, eyeing my brothers, and I look at him sharply. He is Raphael, the red eye bandana face paint doing wonders at hiding his grimace.

"What do you mean, not here?" I look between them, confused, as they all look at each other, and for the first time in my life, I feel like I am not privy to all the information my brothers are.

"Let's go inside and talk," Harrison says, taking a step toward the house.

"Wait, what *fuck* is going on?" I ask. Now I really need that glass of whiskey as my shoulders stiffen.

"Fruit!" Ben hisses at me, and I roll my eyes but nod, acknowledging the kids within earshot.

"We want to talk with you about your lifestyle choices," Harrison says in a voice that drips with uncertainty, and I look at him with narrowed eyes. For the first time, my brother, the governor, of all people, seems nervous, and that makes me feel on edge.

"Lifestyle choices?" I tilt my head in question, my voice rising slightly.

"Tenn, you're out every weekend, sleeping your way through half the city; you're not looking after yourself; you're flashing your cash too much..." Ben adds, and I can see the empathy in his eyes behind the stupid face paint, but my skin starts to crawl.

"So you have all been talking about me? Discussing my behavior behind my back? Planning to what? Confront me all together? Reprimand me?" I press, bewildered, wondering how long they have been in discussion for.

"Hey, you all look great," Beth says, smiling as she walks up to us. But as she really takes us all in, her smile starts to fade. "You did it here?" she hisses at Harrison accusingly, and my eyebrows shoot up.

"You're in on this too?" I ask her, shocked.

"Tennyson, we are all worried about you. You're out late, you're partying a lot..." she offers as her lips press into a thin line, eyes wide with pity—pity that isn't warranted.

"I am not partying too much. So I like women and whiskey, who doesn't?" I shrug, waving off their concerns, but I already know it's not going to shut them up.

"You need support," Eddie says, the look on his face making me feel sick to my stomach.

"I don't need fucking rehab." I spit out the words under my breath, anger starting to swirl. I might enjoy a drink or two, but I do not have a problem.

"*Fruiting!*" Ben hisses at me again, while looking around at all the kids who laugh and play nearby.

"No. Not rehab. Willow," Beth says, her smile small and warm. A woman offering me genuine affection is a novelty to me, and my anger subsides a little.

"What?" Is Beth talking in code because of the kids or am I still drunk? I am pretty sure I finished off the best portion of a bottle of fine Japanese whiskey that I ordered from room service last night when I was with Katie. Or Karen... or whatever her name was.

"What the fu... *fruit* is Willow?" I ask, drilling my eyes into each of my family members, wondering what the hell is going on.

"Who," Beth corrects, looking clearly pleased with herself, and I know now that she has organized something.

"Who what?" I seem to be the only one who's confused, since nobody else is asking questions.

"Willow. Willow is who is going to help you," Beth says, and I sigh and run my hands through my hair, wishing I didn't look like a fucking turtle.

"Again, *who* is Willow?" I ask, trying to keep my voice down, but I can't help but be frustrated. I wish they would all just get to the point and stop talking in riddles.

"Watch out!" I hear a woman yell from behind me, but my reflexes are slow this morning, and it takes a beat to register.

"*Strawberries!*" Ben shouts, and I see him move just as I turn and get hit from behind. The thwack of a ball slamming into my head is loud enough for the entire country to hear, my head jerking forward on impact, almost knocking it clear off my shoulders.

"*What the fu—!*" I groan as my brain rattles in my head, deep throbbing vibrating across my skull, annoyance now crawling up my spine. A soccer ball bounces straight off my forehead and into Eddie's waiting hands.

"*Fruit!*" Ben yells, giving me a death stare. "No swearing in front of the kids," he grits out.

"I just got hit in the head by a *fruiting* soccer ball. I think my *fruiting* head almost fell of my *fruiting* neck!" I yell back at him, all three of my brothers now almost choking on their laughter while my dehydration, pain, and frustration all start to swirl into growing anger.

"I'm so sorry, he has a mean right kick," a woman's voice says from behind, and I spin around, ready to give her a piece of my mind, but the words get stuck on my lips.

It's *her*.

Am I dreaming? I turn quickly and look at my brothers and Beth to ensure I am not imagining this, before my eyes land back on her. She is just how I remember. I never thought I'd see her again. But now she is here. In front of me. In the flesh.

"Tennyson, this is Willow Valentine. CEO of Valentine Management and your new babysitter," Beth tells me tentatively from beside us as my brothers look on.

"Willow..." I say her name, liking the feel of it on my lips.

"Tennyson," she says quietly, and I see recognition in her eyes. I step toward her, my eyes glued to hers, and am about to grab her elbow and pull her close, but she retreats. I still, watching her swallow, her jaw set. She doesn't want me to touch her.

She doesn't want me...?

I look back around at my brothers; all eyes are on me, and I feel like a deer caught in headlights.

I need to get out of here. I need a fruiting whiskey.

9

―――――

WILLOW

"Willow is who we have hired to help you get on track with things. She is a good friend of mine and will be great for you. She can help you with everything from media and interviews, positive press, and reputational management in terms of how to elevate your personal brand," Beth says by way of explanation as she and Tennyson's brothers walk swiftly behind Tennyson as he stalks into Ben's house.

I follow behind them all, observing him to get to know his mannerisms and traits. I feel like a total bitch. He came to me, and I stepped away. I didn't want to. I wanted to do the opposite. But I knew if I touched him, I would feel something I shouldn't, and even though I will be working closely with him over the next few months, I also need to keep my distance emotionally.

I never get involved with clients. It is my number one rule.

My nerves dance in my stomach, keeping me on edge.

I don't normally feel like this with a new client, so I need to get my head in the game. I need to remain professional. The first meeting is always when I must cement my dominance. They need to see me as their boss, which is hard, because most of my clients never have to answer to anyone. They are the ones at the top of the pecking order. That all changes, though, when they work with me.

"You have hired me a fucking babysitter?" Tennyson seethes as we all gather behind him, and I watch as he heads straight to the bar. So predictable. Most people in stressful situations consume alcohol. They use it as a crutch, and it appears Tennyson is no different.

"Willow works with politicians down in DC. She is excellent at her job," Harrison says, and his comment fills me with pride. It is nice to have the governor acknowledge my skills. Tennyson huffs out a laugh as he pours three fingers before turning to look at us all standing behind him, the glass firm in his grip.

His eyes fall to me, and I meet his gaze before my eyes drop to the glass in his hand and back to his face again. I can see the moment when he realizes that he is now proving their point. I watch his jaw clench and almost feel his frustration from where I stand near the doorway. I know his brothers have judgment in their faces, but I try to remain impartial.

As his gaze washes over me, it's like he is seeing me for the first time. There is still heat in his eyes, accompanied by some hurt. He is very confused, both by the intervention that his brothers have sprung on him, but also from seeing me. I force myself not to melt under his attention. My heart lurches for him, my empathy radar almost pinging out of my chest for how he must be feeling. This is why I am good at what I do. I can tell when my clients need me, but I am an expert, and in many cases, I have to be tough on them, the media, and the people around them. I haven't made it this far in my career by falling into my naturally soft and compassionate personality. I bring the heat, I put on my tough exterior, and I show them who is boss when necessary. I have to; otherwise, my clients would walk all over me. Instead, I mix the two; it is what has made me and my business so successful. My body remains stiff as I push all my feelings for this man to the back of my brain, locking them up tight.

"You have got to be fucking kidding me!" he seethes, slamming the full glass back on the bar and stalking toward the window, now wanting to get as far away from it as possible.

"And you two are in on this as well?" he asks his other brothers, both who have been quieter than Beth and Harrison. They both nod solemnly.

"Firstly, I don't have a problem with my reputation. My reputation is excellent," he says as he rubs his head, the lump already starting to form from the soccer ball. His statement causes me to roll my lips before I laugh out loud. His reputation is so close to being in tatters and he doesn't even realize it.

"Secondly, I don't party every weekend," he continues, but no one in the room is believing a word he is saying.

"Thirdly, I am not sleeping my way through the city," he finishes, glancing at me before he looks down. I now understand why law was not what he went into. He is terrible at proving his points. He doesn't buy what he is selling and neither does his audience.

All his brothers look at me, defeat clear on their turtle faces. Interventions never go well. It is always hard for my clients to see that they could make improvements. It is often not until they make a massive mistake that tarnishes their reputation for years that they finally admit they have a problem. Lucky for Tennyson, his brothers got onto this early, and we have time to turn it all around without a big issue arising.

It is my turn to step in.

"Tennyson," I say, his name falling from my lips too easily, and he looks at me. I can tell in his eyes he needs a professional like me; I just wish his gaze didn't hold so much desire. It would make it a lot easier. "Partying every weekend, hooking up with a variety of women, drinking, spending like you do, none of these things are necessarily bad. In fact, most men are active in all these areas. It is pretty normal for a wealthy single man in the city these days." I shrug because it is true. I slowly walk farther into the room, acting as if it is no big deal, and all his brothers look at me as though I am crazy.

"See!" Tennyson gestures to me like I am proving his point, giving me a small smile, accompanied by a look of hope.

"But..." I continue, and his head swivels back to me. "You are not a normal man, you are a Langford. You are brother to the governor. A governor who would like to make a run for presidency of this country in the coming years and will have no hope of winning if his family is not the clean-cut, all-American family he needs to portray.

He will have enough trouble with your mother, so he doesn't need to manage your activities as well."

"You want to run for president?" he asks, his eyebrows rising as he looks to Harrison.

"It is something Beth and I have been talking about. Something I would like to do." Harrison nods, and I see Tennyson smile. I feel my nails dig into the skin of my palm again as I try not to be affected by his obvious affection for his brother. I swallow, tuning back into my business exterior. My work personality. The tough side.

"And you also have an excellent lawyer in Ben, who is currently trying to spend as much time with his new daughter as possible, maybe even thinking about extending his family. But he's finding it hard to put them first when he spends all of his weekends calling every social publication and media influencer in the city, trying to take down photos and videos that people take of you doing things you shouldn't be." Tennyson's eyes widen before landing on Ben.

"It isn't every weekend," Tennyson quips, tilting his head in question.

"Every Sunday, without fail. I usually have to miss Rosie's swimming lessons," Ben admits, sadness in his tone, and Tennyson's brow crumples.

"I can go on if you need me to. There is the obvious issue of your mother and her antics that the media also love to dig up," I offer, and the look on his face would cause a wildfire, there is so much anger in it. I straighten my spine, because my good cop act is now done. I need to bring bad cop out to drive my point home.

"I don't need a babysitter," his grits out and he steps

toward me slightly, almost in challenge. I can't back down. He needs to know I am his boss, and for the next few months, he has to listen to me, do as I say. He may have been able to control our night together months ago, had me in every way imaginable, but he won't be able to go anywhere or do anything moving forward without clearing it with me.

"If the shoe fits," I sass, and his eyes flame.

"Your kid gave me a migraine," he says as he steps closer to me, his eyes squinting, appearing to accuse me of something I am not yet sure of. We are now almost chest to chest. There is an undercurrent of electricity humming, my body more on edge than usual. I am stepping way out of my comfort zone here, my skin prickling as his eyes look deep into mine.

"Maybe he should have kicked harder and knocked some sense into you." I see his lips quirk, and I know I have won this round. Our banter is natural, just like that night in New York. His eyes lower down my body, taking me in as he looks from my eyes down to my feet and back again. I see appreciation in his gaze, and warmth spreads through me before I tamp down any wayward thoughts.

"So you're going to follow me around, then?" he asks, his face now softening into a cheeky smile, giving me a new insight into the infamous Tennyson Langford.

"You have enough women doing that. You don't need another," I offer, and disappointment flickers in his eyes.

"But you do have to do everything I say for the next few months, including laying off the whiskey, lightening your spending, and keeping your bed empty." His nostrils flare, not liking his options.

"Do we have a deal?" I ask, tone stern and ready for pushback.

He looks around the room at his brothers before looking back at me, his expression now dancing with delight that should concern me.

"We have a deal, Willow Valentine. I just hope you can keep up," he says before he walks back to the bar, grabs the glass of whiskey, and swallows it in one gulp, giving me a wink in the process.

10

TENNYSON

My assistant, Melody, puts a steamy cup of coffee on my desk and gives me a look I haven't seen before.

"What is that look for?" I question her, taking a sip of the warm liquid and peering at her over the edge of the cup. It has been exactly twenty-four hours since the intervention at Ben's house and exactly twenty-four hours since my last drink. I didn't even have my regular nightcap because my thoughts were consumed by her. Willow Valentine. At least I now know who she is. I was shocked to see her at my brother's house, and I wanted to do so many things with her, but one look at her, and I knew she meant business. So I will toe the line. For now.

"I'm looking forward to meeting her," Melody says with a wide grin, and I keep my face blank, even though I have thought of nothing else but the beautiful pocket rocket since our night together. Her teasing smile and sassy personality heighten my senses. Her long dark hair and her lustful eyes—I fell asleep thinking about that vision last night, and for the first time in a long time, I slept for more than a few hours.

"I did some research, and she is supposed to be *the* person to go to for personal branding. She has even worked with the White House!" Melody offers, obviously excited about Willow's experience, and my eyebrows shoot to my hairline. I am intrigued, if not a little pissed off that Harrison has arranged her for me. The last thing I need is a woman telling me what to do, regardless of her good looks or the way her body curves in all the right places.

"Hmmm, let's see what she says when she gets here," I murmur, keeping my cards close to my chest, not giving anything away, and Melody purses her lips.

"Well, I will send her in when she arrives. She already called this morning, and we have synced diaries, so she now has a full visual of all your activities and whereabouts," Melody says as she stands and rushes out the door, closing it behind her before I can respond. Beth mentioned Willow needed all my contact details and social media access, but diary oversight is something new.

My eyes lower to the screen in front of me as I look over *The Society News*, our local Baltimore social paper, where my brothers and I often grace the pages. Today is no different. There are shots of us all from an event we went to on Friday night and from a ladies' lunch that was held on Sunday, where my mother's face makes an appearance. Just the look of her makes my shoulders stiffen.

I click to the next page and see an image of me, my

shirt ruffled and untucked from yesterday when I was making my way out of the Four Seasons before I went to Ben's. I had no idea the cameras were there; my mind so preoccupied with racing to my brothers, I paid little attention.

My brows furrow. I look like shit.

"Tennyson, Miss Valentine is here to see you," Melody's voice interrupts my thoughts through the speaker.

"Send her in," I mumble as I flatten my tie and clear my throat, trying to rein in my insane desire for this woman.

There is a knock at my office door before it opens, and I look up to see the woman who has been on my mind for months. I grit my back molars so I don't open my mouth in awe.

She is stunning. Breathtakingly so. Her long hair is down and wavy, and she's wearing a simple yet elegant pair of black tailored trousers with a black satin shirt that ties at the neck with a bow. The contrast between the black clothing and her complexion is striking.

"Good morning, Tennyson!" she singsongs, her smile contagious. After the intervention yesterday, I thought she was on my side. But the compassion in her eyes disappeared quickly as she stepped into the tough businesswoman she is obviously known for.

"Morning," I say slowly, drinking her in, my eyes wasting no time going back over her body.

"Here, I brought you a cupcake." Placing a brown paper bag on my desk, she sits uninvited in the armchair facing me.

"A cupcake?" I question, not moving to grab it, my shoulders stiff. Nobody brings me anything. Aside from my brothers, I don't even get birthday presents. I know this is her being sweet, trying to soften me up before she stabs me with a pen or something. I have to say, though, I like both sides of her. She is like a lioness, friendly until she pounces. She keeps me guessing.

"Yes, a cupcake. You know, the small little cakes with cute icing. Not only do they taste amazing, but they look adorable. This one is death by chocolate," she says with a teasing smile. Isn't she just a ray of fucking sunshine this Monday morning.

"Do you often provide baked goods to people?" I ask, trying to get more of a sense of who she is. She is firm, strong, and professional, but also soft, delicate, and feminine. A deadly combination.

"Sometimes. I like to bake," she says with a shrug like it is no big deal.

"Is this what we are doing? Pretending we don't really know each other, giving each other morning tea?" I ask, interested to see where her head is at. I let her get away with it yesterday because we had an audience, but now it is just the two of us, and I would prefer to use my lips to eat her rather than a cupcake.

"Yes. This is exactly what we are doing. Your brothers have hired me to do my job. That job is looking after the reputation of a man who has probably slept through the entire female population of Baltimore City," she says matter-of-factly and in a tone that I am sure many others never question. But I see the hurt in her eyes before she regains her composure. It was fleeting; if I had blinked, I would've missed it. I feel like shit again. A common occurrence for me these days.

"Our night was different," I murmur, taking a breath. I hate talking about my feelings. I hate reliving past events, but she has been on my mind every day without fail. She is not my past; she is very much my present. I don't want her thinking she's just like every other woman.

"Let's just get on with it, shall we?" she says, a fake smile now plastered on her face, and I want to remove it. It doesn't feel the same as the one she walked in with.

"You were the one who left me there. I woke to an empty bed, remember? And you didn't mention you had a kid." My tone is harsher than I mean it to be. We didn't exchange too many personal details that night, so I shouldn't be upset that she is a mother.

"We agreed no names, no strings, remember? Besides, he is not my child; he is my neighbor. But let's get back to the job at hand, shall we?" She obviously doesn't want to relive our night.

"Fine," I say, almost in a challenge, because I know what she is doing. She is trying to erase me from her memory, but I struggle not to smile, knowing that I am as much burned into her as she is to me.

I have spent months trying to find her, but meeting and not exchanging names or details about work or friends, I had very little to go on. But now she is right in front of me and will be managing me for months, so it is game on. I will have her in my bed again, a plan already forming in my brain.

"Grouchy already, this should be fun," she says sarcastically.

"There is only one way to get me to smile, and since you have banished all women from my bed, then it is unlikely to happen. Unless you are offering your services?" I lean forward on my desk, quirking a brow. Because right now, I know that is what we both want. A repeat. A repeat of New York, preferably every night for the foreseeable future.

"I am a professional and have been hired to manage you. I don't mix business with pleasure, Tennyson, and neither should you." Any other woman would already be on their knees, or at least blushing, but not Willow. I admire her.

"Married to your job, I remember," I say, my grin widening as I see recognition in her face again. But she collects herself quickly and launches straight into work mode.

"Okay... So, the way we will work together is pretty simple. I will meet with you regularly throughout the week. And I will arrange with your assistant, Melody, to approve or cancel any social outings—outside of business meetings—that I deem not appropriate. My team will manage your social media channels, and I will be managing your press and any endorsements that arise including charity events and the like. Your part in all this is to not drink, no women, and to do everything I ask of you, with cleaning up your image in mind," she says without taking a breath.

"How often is regularly?" I ask, wanting to know exactly how much time we will spend together.

"Oh, well, I will pop in every Monday morning to see you and also every Thursday or Friday. You can call me at any time, though, if you need me. Melody has all my details and she has put them into your contacts."

I smile. Twice a week and direct access to her is all I need. I will have her underneath me in no time.

"Great! Now, I have been over your diary this morning, and I have a few adjustments that we need to make this week." She pulls out a small tablet from her large black handbag and taps it to turn it on.

"What kind of adjustments?" I bark back as the reality of what needs to happen sinks in all too suddenly. My weeks are busy, work is stressful, and I have a million other things I need to be doing this morning.

"Monday through Thursday is all fine. Friday evening, you have a scheduled dinner at the Latin Rose Club that we need to cancel. Golf on the weekend with your brothers is all well and good. I have also added in a business dinner coming up in a few weeks' time that Beth mentioned to me that you will be encouraged to attend, but no after-party and definitely no drinking," she says before she peers at me, waiting for my confirmation.

"Why no Latin Rose?" I ask because I love that club. I usually meet some business contacts there every Friday night to blow off steam.

"Because it is owned by an overseas conglomerate that has ties to slavery and child labor—none of which would look favorably to anyone associated with a potential presidential campaign," she fires back quickly, but does so with a genuine concern in her eyes. I had no idea that was the case, but I guess it makes sense. I can tell she is passionate about that point, another puzzle piece about this woman now sliding into place in my brain.

"And what about the dinner? What am I meant to do, drink water all night? Turn up without a date?" I quip because that sounds like hell.

"Exactly!" she says with a bit too much pep, and I look at her like she is crazy.

"I can't do that." I shake my head, making my thoughts clear.

"Why not?" she presses. I am not used to a woman pushing me; they usually give in to everything I want. For some reason with her, it's as irritating as it is arousing.

"Because my mother will be there. That alone warrants whiskey," I huff out.

"Yes, I have learned a little about your mother over the weekend. Do you have a good relationship with her?" she asks, sitting forward slightly.

"Hell no. I fucking hate her," I admit a little too quickly and see her eyebrows rise.

"Well, still no drinking, because we don't need any images or gossip featuring you anymore. We need you to be boring, home in bed at ten p.m., sensible, straitlaced, while doing it all with a wide smile on your face." She looks at me with her beautiful big blue eyes, and I almost crumble.

Go alone. No alcohol. How the hell will I deal with my mother if I can't drink?

"Fine. Will you be there?" I really hope she will be. That might get me through.

"Yes, actually, I will be. Beth has asked me to come along, to get to know the Baltimore scene a bit better," she says with a smile, and the tension in my shoulders eases a little.

"Fine. I will not drink. I'll leave before the after-party, and I'll leave with no women," I say, already not wanting to even go, but knowing I have to. This event is something that Harrison and Beth have arranged. But I can't remember the last time I was sober and in the same room as my mother. I need the alcohol to drown out the memories that seeing her continue to raise.

"Great, I am sure yo—" she starts to say before an alarm sounds on her phone. She grabs her cell and taps the screen, her brow furrowed slightly.

"Everything all right?" I ask as she looks slightly panicked.

"Oh, yes, it's just Betty," she says, sounding relieved.

"Betty?" I ask, raising my eyebrows in question.

"Yes, the neighborhood cat that loves my food." She's smiling to herself as she puts her phone back into her bag and looks at me in a way that makes the world feel a little off-kilter.

"So that's what you do, huh?" I ask.

"What do you mean?" she asks me, confusion written on her face.

"You take in broken things and fix them? Me, the stray cat, your sister who is having an affair with a married man?" I offer her more of my memory of that night, putting the pieces together on how she might like to operate.

"I like helping people, helping animals. I enjoy looking after things. It is probably why I fell into personal brand management and now enjoy my job. What about you? Did you always want to work in construction? It seems at odds with your behavior." I forgot how quick and easy our banter was.

"My behavior?" I question as I sit forward a little more, interested in her assessment of me.

"Well, yes. Construction is about building, developing, creating something that, for the most part, is bigger and better than what was there before. But that is in contrast to your personal life, it seems, from what your brothers and the media tell me, which is all about drama and social gossip that your behavior feeds. It keeps expectations of you low, when you are so much more. Your work alone speaks volumes about your talents, Tennyson. You build massive shopping centers and apartment buildings that have not only provided your family immeasurable income for years, but also won awards in design, and you have even received environmental accolades. But all of that is totally overshadowed by stories and gossip of your personal life, resulting in the myriad of social media messages that are now burned into my eyes from a night of trying to clean up your overflowing inbox."

Not for the first time, this woman makes me stop and think. She is not cold or opinionated about any of it; she just holds up a mirror to my behavior. I don't usually consider my achievements. I'm too busy trying to build the business, ignore my mother, and just enjoy life. But the way Willow highlights it all, I feel accomplished. I feel proud and even happier that she notices.

"I think we both know that I was unaware of the impact my behavior was having. I always thought I was flying under the radar, although not anymore, it appears," I murmur, still digesting what she just said.

"We need to let everyone else see what I can already see," she says, making me want to grab her and put her firmly on my lap and not let her go.

"What's that?" I ask, and I hold my breath for her response.

"That underneath this devastatingly handsome, charismatic man, there is a very smart businessman who has single-handedly tripled his family's bank balance and brought in more money than both the governor and lawyer combined over the past three years." Her blue eyes are now twinkling just for me.

"You think I'm handsome?" I ask with a broad grin, and she rolls her eyes at my teasing. Although I don't miss that her cheeks tint, and she doesn't refute the comment.

"I will leave you to it for the week, and I will come back on Thursday to go through the social media plan and discuss some key media opportunities for the next few weeks." She shuts down our friendly banter, her tone now back to being professional as she stands and grabs her handbag.

I lean back in my chair and watch her. Every inch of her is elegant perfection. Her black patent leather heels are high, the kind that I really want wrapped around my neck again.

"See you then," she says, her cheeks now flaming brighter at my open ogle before I watch her swallow roughly, then turn and walk out the door.

I sit in the quiet of my office for a beat, eyes on the

door, thinking about our interaction. She is everything I remember and more. My parents showed me exactly why not to get involved with anyone. But she is tempting me. I close my eyes, the vision of her naked dancing in my mind. My hands on her body, my lips on hers, her moans, her pants, the feeling of her in my arms... I shake my head of the thoughts and gulp down the remainder of my now cold coffee and get to work. The fire in my belly that I didn't think existed is now burning brighter today than it has in a very long time.

11

———

WILLOW

"Have you seen my pink top?" Saide yells at me from down the hallway, where she is packing for another trip.

"I ironed it and put it on the laundry countertop," I yell back as I sit at the kitchen table with a hot water bottle on my stomach, wishing I could curl up in bed and get through the pain. But I need to finish off the social media strategy for my new client—Tennyson Langford.

I only saw him this morning, yet just the thought of him has my pulse racing. I tried to be professional, when all I really wanted to do was crash into his arms. The thought alone unsettles me. I have never been like this. I have a borderline crush on my client, and I need to get my head in the game. I roll my neck, the stress of the situation building. I forcefully had to remove the thought of how good it would be to have him peel the clothes from my body and put me on his desk. Just watching his big hands wrap around his coffee cup had me forcing myself back into the chair, because I know what they feel like on my skin and I really wanted to feel that again.

"Thank you. You are such a lifesaver," my younger sister says as she waltzes past me and into the kitchen. The two of us have lived together ever since we moved out to the East Coast from small-town Wyoming as soon as we finished college.

"Oh, period pain again?" she asks me, looking concerned.

"Just the usual," I moan, because I have PCOS and my hormones are all over the place. As are my periods. Sometimes they come, sometimes they don't. I get pain, I don't get pain. It is exhausting, not to mention almost debilitating sometimes. But I am somewhat used to it, as I have had these issues my whole life.

"What are you working on?" she asks, grabbing a glass from the cupboard and getting herself a juice.

"Just finishing the strategy for his digital presence." My eyes stay glued to the screen in concentration.

"I can't believe Josh kicked the ball into his head," she snorts. I told her all about the weekend and my new client. She also knows all about the night I left Tennyson asleep in that penthouse at four a.m. after our night of sexual escapades, having to quickly grab my things and take a car straight to DC for work. I didn't lie when I said I was married to my job. That early morning escape was evidence of that fact.

I rub my hand to my temple as I relive that morning. To say that day was one of the longest in my life would be an understatement. The regret of sneaking out without so much as a goodbye still stings to this day.

Saide gathers her things and moves around the house like a tornado. We have lived here for years, in a small cottage with a yard, a mile away from the business of the city. It is my sanctuary, and when I found it for sale a few years ago, I didn't hesitate. My sister, however, prefers a busier life. Younger than me by a few years, she's used to the rich and powerful. An international air hostess who manages the first-class cabins, Saide has seen the best and the worst of them.

"Where are you flying this week?" Every week she is in a different country. Last week was Brazil, the week before France.

"Australia," she states, leaving her dirty glass near the sink and the open bottle of juice on the counter. "I am staying there for a while because I need a break. I won't be back until later next week, at the earliest." My eyes narrow at her, because I know why she is staying longer, and it has everything to do with aligning with Jacob's schedule and very little to do with a break in one spot for a while.

"Ohhh, is that him? He is gorgeous. Is he single?" she asks as she looks at the photo of Tennyson I have up on my laptop. Her question makes me bristle. My sister is beautiful and has men falling at her feet on the regular. At last count, she has had over five marriage proposals, and that number doesn't include the one from Eastern Europe, where I was offered two camels as a dowry a few years ago.

"Yes. If you don't count the endless models who fall into his bed every weekend," I offer, feeling sick at the thought, before I close my screen and look at her.

"Well, given how good you said he was, he had to learn it all somewhere. I wish he was on one of my flights. He is serious eye candy. You should ask him out!" She flicks her hair, and I see her blemish-free skin shine in the late morning sun. Jealousy coils in my stomach as I look over my own appearance. Messy topknot, college sweatshirt that really needs to be thrown out, my pen sticking in my hair and my glasses on, contact lenses not needed today.

"I can't ask him out; he is my client. Besides, our history is exactly that. History," I state, drawing a firm line in the sand.

"Willow. I can't even remember the last boyfriend you had. You have been married to your job for years. You said you had a fantastic night with him in New York, so why don't you go back for round two?" My little sister starts lecturing me, and I sigh.

As I think about what I know of Tennyson, from my research and his brothers, I know he would be perfect for someone like my sister. But all kinds of wrong for a girl like me. I like the simple life at home. Saide is a jetsetter. I prefer a good book on the couch over a night out on the town. I like my work, and Saide likes to party. I've seen too many lives upended due to that type of lifestyle, and I am more of a white picket fence girl. That is why I am more like a mother to Saide. I wash her clothes, clean up after her, and pay for this entire house, even though she lives here too. I hold the responsibility, and Saide throws it all out the window, but I love her. She is my best friend.

"I don't need to date. I need to work," I say, pretending

to tap a few keys and get back to it, even though my mind is now somewhere else.

"You need to start dating again, Willow. In fact, you just need to start dating period," Saide harps on the point, and I know she won't let it go.

"Fine. I will go on a date." I offer her the only words she wants to hear. I don't particularly want to date right now. I don't have the time for one. But also, every man I meet is never a good fit. Some don't even turn up to the dates. Others just want to get in my pants. It is exhausting. But it may help to get my mind off Tennyson. It will also help cement that personal boundary. *I wonder what his reaction would be if I told him I had a date?*

"I want photographic evidence," she demands, making my eyes flick to hers, and I see that she is serious.

"Fine. I will go on a date and provide you with photographic evidence." She smiles, seemingly appeased. It sounds too easy. Find a date, have a nice meal, please my sister... and get Tennyson off my mind, potentially showing him I am unavailable, thereby he'll lose interest in me, allowing me to reinstate professional boundaries and focus on the job I am hired to do.

"So what have you found out about tall, dark, and dreamy?" she asks, looking over my shoulder at my screen again.

"Well, now that I have access to his socials, I can see messages every day from women, all offering him something, none of it good," I say, getting a sore hand from blocking them constantly, their blatant sexual advances more than I have ever come across before.

"Believe me, a guy like that would be getting offers

multiple times a day, I am sure. So what are you up to this weekend?" Thankfully she changes the subject, folding some clothes nearby as she finishes packing.

"This weekend is work and spending time with Betty," I say with a smile as the stray cat I have unofficially adopted walks tentatively around my kitchen, sniffing our feet.

"You're not going to turn into a cat lady, are you?" she teases me, but it is highly likely.

"There are worse things in the world."

"There are also better ones. Like your client. I bet he would be better to snuggle with than some stray cat," Saide says with a sly grin.

"Never mix business with pleasure, Saide. Don't you know that?" I ask her with a pointed look. She really is in deep with Jacob, and I hope she finds her way out of it soon. Hearts are going to be shattered, and I already feel anxious about it.

Beep, beep!

"Saved by the bell. My Uber is here. I have to go." She runs past me, kissing me on the cheek before throwing the folded clothes in her bag, zipping it, and heading out the door.

"See you next week!" she yells before the front door slams, and I get busy cleaning up her mess, while trying to sort through the mess in my head.

THE HOUSE IS CLEAN. I have showered, shaved, and fake tanned, and now as I'm about to curl up in bed, when my cell phone rings. Grabbing it, Tennyson's name flashes on the screen. It is almost eleven. It's late. Not an hour that a call would be classed as conversational. I wonder if something has happened.

"Tennyson?" I answer, concerned.

"Hey," he says simply, his voice sounding normal.

"Everything all right?" I ask as I climb into bed, my body weary, the soft duvet calling my name.

"Fine." Only one word again, and this time I sense stress.

"What's going on?" My phone is always open to clients. I offer them my services whenever they need it. Most of the time, late-night calls are due to them being caught doing something they shouldn't be, and I wonder if that is the case with Tennyson now.

"I had a conference call with my team in Hong Kong tonight and now I can't sleep," he murmurs.

"Okay. Was there something in particular that is an issue?"

"Everything," he huffs, still not giving me much.

"Are you building a new high-rise over there or something?" I ask, changing my questions to be specific to see if he'll give me more to get to the bottom of his call.

"A new shopping center, right on the water. Biggest in the Southern Hemisphere," he says, his voice starting to relax.

"Wow, sounds like a big project. Must be stressful?" I can't imagine managing a project of that size.

"It is delayed. We can't find good workers, and the building suppliers are having trouble getting us the materials. I also found out today that the company we secured to fit out the internal furnishings is not signed up to the Modern Slavery Code," he says with a sigh, and I get to the crutch of the issue. I must say, it is a first for me, having a client call me over something like this so late at night, but I am starting to understand that Tennyson is anything but normal.

"Okay, is that a contract you can break? Can you choose someone else who is?" I ask, sinking into my bed. I spent a lot of money on this bed. On the sheets, on the pillows and blankets. I need something every day that feels luxurious, safe, and calming. Somewhere I can turn off from the day, the myriad of bad press, negativity, and pressure. "It is things like this that the media will take and run a story on if Harrison ever runs for presidency. In fact, they could run it now since he is governor, as it will still get clicks." I know Tennyson understands this now; otherwise, he wouldn't be calling me.

"I've got Ben and my legal team on it. This is why I need my regular whiskey nightcap. I can't sleep, and whiskey normally helps, but since you took that away, I am now lying awake, my mind racing." Even though I feel for him, I roll my eyes. He's being a bit dramatic with the rules.

"You can have a nightcap, Tennyson. It is more about limiting your drinking when you are out. So you can make smarter decisions in that external environment," I clarify.

"My decision-making is fine," he mumbles.

"I beg to differ." I shake my head to myself. If I wasn't in control of his life right now, I already know the decisions he'd be making. Most of them blond.

"What are you doing?" he asks, and I imagine him lying awake, staring at the ceiling. The question is innocent enough, but it takes my mind out of work mode and into personal. The flutters in my belly warm me and make me feel slightly giddy. I shouldn't entertain this, but it is nice of him to ask.

"I just crawled into bed. It's been a long day."

"Hmmmm. What are you wearing?" he asks smoothly, and my body stiffens.

"Tennyson! Cut it out," I admonish, but my warning is soft at best. I am already looking down at my sloppy t-shirt and my unflattering bed socks, immediately knowing this is not how men imagine women sleeping. Yet here I am. No wonder I'm single.

"Relax, I'm teasing." He chuckles, the sound new to my ears, but I feel good for making it happen. "So are you married yet?" he asks jokingly, and I relax a bit more.

"No, Prince Charming hasn't entered my life in the six months since I saw you last." Bantering with him is one of my favorite things to do. We bounce well off each other.

"Well, you could have met someone the morning you left me. He'd be an idiot not to put a ring on your finger." I stop breathing. My heart thuds, literally feeling like it is going to burst out from my chest cavity. I swallow, deciding to skirt over his comment.

"No. Still married to my job," I offer, because I want to be honest, even if my dull life makes him fall asleep. I am okay with that.

"Boyfriend?" he continues, and again, I sigh.

"No. No boyfriend."

"Girlfriend?" he asks, his tone changing slightly.

"No, Tennyson, I am single. Why all the questions?"

"You now know everything about me, so I think it is only fair I get to know you too," he says, and his argument is sound. We know each other intimately, yet know nothing about each other at all. And he is right; while I have done my research, he wouldn't know much about me.

"*Why* are you single?" he asks, and I scoff.

"Probably because I sleep in an old t-shirt and fluffy bed socks," I say too quickly before I balk and scrunch my face. This bed has me too relaxed; it is like it inserts truth serum into my body.

"Bed socks? How old are you, like sixty?" he teases.

"Bed socks help me sleep. I hate my feet being cold." I defend my choice of sleepwear, when really, I should just hang up the phone.

"I bet you look good in fluffy socks." He laughs lightly.

"Tennyson…" I moan his name in frustration as I roll over and bury my beet-red face into the pillow. *What am I doing?* I should have ended this conversation already. But it feels good to chat. It has been a long time since I talked like this with a man. But he is my client, and I need to put a stop to it before it gets out of hand.

"What color are they? Pink? Purple?" he asks, teasing me some more.

"Oh God, stop it," I say again, now with a smile on my face.

"Blue? Green?" he continues, and I need to stifle my giggle. *What the hell is wrong with me?* I am a professional. This is so outside the work limits I set, yet I can't seem to cut him off.

"Yellow, okay. They are yellow. It's my favorite color," I say, again not sure why I am sharing so much.

"Hmmmm... yellow is a sexy color..."

"Oh my God, go to sleep, Tennyson, it's late," I scold him lightheartedly.

"Maybe I need some bed socks too," he murmurs.

"Good night, Tennyson." I hate how hard it is for me to say.

"Tenn," he says quickly.

"What?" Where is he going with this?

"All my friends call me Tenn. Call me Tenn," he says seriously. But we are not friends. We can't be friends. Or shouldn't be. He is my client. I need to reinstate the professional boundaries before they disintegrate completely, regardless of if he warms me from the inside out.

"Okay. Now go to sleep," I say softly, vowing to erect a stronger barrier tomorrow.

"Night, Willow."

I end the call and lie staring at the ceiling, where I remain for the rest of the night, my mind racing, my heart thumping, feeling things I haven't for a very long time.

For the one person I shouldn't be feeling them for.

12

TENNYSON

I stare at the ceiling, willing my eyes to close, but just like last night, I am wide awake. Grabbing my phone, I see it is just past eleven. I know I shouldn't, but with no whiskey and no women, she is all I have. Our banter is natural, the visions I continue to have of her so colorful and vibrant in my mind, I am struggling not being able to touch her. I shouldn't call her. I know she wants to remain professional. Our relationship is nothing more than manager and client, but I can't stop wanting to talk with her. It is too much fun, and I haven't spoken like this to anyone in such a long time.

I hit her number and wait.

"Tennyson?" She says my name in question, just like she did last night.

"Willow?" I do the same to her, a small smile coming to my mouth at the mere sound of her voice.

"Everything all right?" she asks, probably assuming the worst. Who knows what other jackasses she has had to deal with down in DC before. It is nice to be asked, though. My mother never gave a shit about me; my brothers are the only lifelines I have.

"Yeah." I sigh, already feeling the tension from my workday leave my shoulders. "Just can't sleep." I offer her my excuse for calling, waiting for her to hang up, but she doesn't.

"Me neither. Betty is extremely hyperactive for some reason," she murmurs, and I imagine her running around, chasing her stray cat.

"I can't believe you are a cat lady." I may love pussy, but I dislike cats. It is like they can look into my soul, understand how black it is, then want to scratch my eyes out. Happens every time I get near one, and I don't imagine Betty to be any different.

"Well, I never thought I would be either, but here I am, taking in cats and feeding their friends."

"Friends? So there is more than one now?" I ask, holding back a laugh.

"Another guy showed up yesterday. A big tom cat who must have caught on that Betty is being fed."

"Oh, so tomorrow you will have all the neighborhood cats then," I say, my laughter sneaking through, to which she huffs.

"No! I hope not. I don't mind feeding and looking after one, but I don't have time for any more," she says, almost panicked.

"I just don't get the appeal," I say honestly.

"What is wrong with cats? They are smart, good companions, clean." I hear a meow in the background, like Betty's agreeing with her.

"I'm more of a dog person myself." I couldn't think of anything worse than a cat in my apartment.

"Oh, you should get a dog! Yes, it will be perfect. It will give you responsibility, and it would be great for your reputation," she offers, her voice rising an octave at her idea. I laugh at hearing her immediate excitement. Even when she is about to sleep, her mind still is in work mode, thinking of strategies and tactics for her clients.

"I'm not sure…" I start to say before she cuts me off.

"You could rescue one. You will have to look after it, train it, walk it, feed it. It is a great addition to keep you busy, but also you get to save a pet that someone else abandoned," she continues, and the fact that she appears so happy with the thought is almost enough reason for me to agree on the spot.

"I don't have time for a dog." Work is kicking my ass at the moment. It's a good excuse.

"Of course you do. I have seen your diary. You can walk the dog every morning, take it to work with you, and play with it at night." Her mind's already made up. I rub my face, thinking about how Willow knows almost every move I make and how I spend my time. I don't know how our conversation turned into me getting a dog, but there is no way I could ever say no to this woman, especially not now that I've heard how happy this makes her.

"I have no idea where to even look for a dog." I have never had an animal before. My mother never liked having them around after Harrison had a dog and it dug up all her roses. She was always about appearances rather than happiness, even back then. The mere thought of getting a dog now just to piss her off even more sounds rather appealing.

"I will do some research and schedule something in your diary." I imagine her tapping on her tablet, getting it all sorted. "How is the work situation going?" she asks, and my mind moves to the other issue I am battling.

"My lawyers have found a loophole in the contract, and I released the interiors firm today, much to their displeasure," I tell her. The decision is still weighing heavy on my shoulders. This change will push the project back a few months at best. This simple decision will cost us money. A lot of money. I don't like losing money. I don't like losing. Period.

"Have you found anyone else who is up to standard to take the job on?" Willow asks, and I can hear the rustle of her bedsheets and know she is tucking in for the night. I wonder briefly if she is in her bed socks again, the thought making me smile and relaxing into my own sheets.

"We have a few companies that we had on file from the tender initially, so my team is going back to them to see if this is something they are willing to jump on. I also have my brother and his legal experts reviewing all the contracts for all our suppliers to see if we are using anyone else who isn't signed up to the anti-slavery laws, and if so, we will need to switch them out too." Even though it is a lot of work, and a loss of money, I am proud to be making this change. It is overdue, something that me and my brothers should have done with all our businesses and it's something I will bring to their attention.

"Sounds like you have it all under control. You are

good at your job, Tennyson. Anyone can see that." That small compliment from her, in the peacefulness of the night, flutters over my skin, almost encasing me in a warm hug. Genuine compliments are not something I receive a lot of. It feels nice.

"Unless it all goes to shit, and I bankrupt the firm with the changes," I say with a huff of sarcasm.

"You could always go into dog training..." she says, and I laugh. After a quiet moment, I hear her yawn, and I know she is battling sleep.

"I will let you go. You need your sleep," I say quietly, imagining that she would talk to me all night, probably putting my needs in front of her own.

"Good night, Tennyson," she says quietly, and I can hear the sleepiness in her tone.

"Good night, Willow."

I end the call and toss my phone on the side table, feeling lighter and happier than before. It's been three days since I first saw her again, and I have been horny for her ever since. I have never thought about a woman like this before. I sleep with them, get them out of my system, and move on. But Willow, she is constantly on my mind. I want to talk to her. And I ache to touch her, though I know I shouldn't. She is changing everything I thought I wanted and making me see things clearly for the first time.

I think back to that night we had, not only how hot her body is, but how great our banter is. Her long hair as it fell down her back, the way she rocked on my body and gripped onto my neck when she saddled me. Her perfect breasts as they bounced in my face. I want her. I want her badly.

Putting my hands under the covers, I grab myself. I am fucking hard as a rock, and I close my eyes tighter as I think more about the night we had. Her laughs, her smart comments, her quick wit. My grip is firm, my cock throbbing, and I stroke myself to the memory. Her moans, her whimpers, her pants, her lips as they wrapped around me. Fucking her in the armchair, tasting her against the wall, her on her knees in front of me. I start to get breathless, my skin feeling hot as I jerk myself firmer and quicker. I remember our time in the shower, when I pulled her up on my waist, pushed her against the wall, and fucked her so hard and fast neither of us could get enough.

"Fucking mine," I grit out, just as my cock releases in my hand, my orgasm coating my stomach. I lay my head back, breathless for a beat, as the stress of the day leaves my body. As I slow my breathing, my body feels relaxed, and I walk to the bathroom and clean myself up before climbing back into bed. And just like last night, I am asleep within five minutes, the second deepest sleep I have had in years.

13

TENNYSON

It is Thursday, and Willow is supposed to be here any minute. I feel antsy, and energy hums through my body as I pace around my office, not able to sit still. My sleep this week has been better than ever, thanks in most part to my nightly telephone calls, followed by chasing my release with images of her. My motivation's high, my eyes clearer, my brain firing on all cylinders, and I haven't felt this good in months.

On Monday night, her admission of wearing yellow bed socks was enough to lighten my mood. I have imagined her naked in nothing but yellow bed socks since. I called her on Tuesday night, because I still couldn't sleep, and I learned all about Betty, the stray cat she had taken in, and somehow, I agreed to rescue a dog. Wednesday's call we talked about her cupcakes, revealing that baking is something she does when she is stressed or angry. I had vivid memories of devouring that cupcake once she left earlier in the week. It was the best thing I have eaten in a long time. In at least six months...

"What are you doing?" Willow's voice breaks through my thoughts as she stands in the doorway, looking at me. She is in a black dress this time, the type that is extremely professional, but shows off her curves. Her hair is again down, glossy and over one shoulder. I stare at her as I swallow around the lump in my throat, my mouth suddenly dry. This is the third time I am seeing her beauty this week and each time is better than the last.

"What do you mean?" I ask as my mind slowly comes back into the present.

"Why are you pacing your office? What happened?" she asks, now slowly walking in and putting her coat and bag on the armchair, but not making any move to sit down as she watches me.

"Sometimes I pace when I need to think," I offer with a shrug.

"Did something good happen?" A small smile plays on her lips as she tentatively walks toward me. Fuck me, she is stunning.

"No. Why?" The urge I have to put my hands on her is growing by the day, even more so as she comes closer.

"Because you are smiling," she says, her smile now wide on her face, making mine grow wider. "Whatever you were thinking about obviously makes you happy, so continue to focus on that. It can be what you pull on whenever you are stressed or angry." If only she knew I was thinking about her.

"Oh, I brought you something." Turning away from me too quickly, she steps back to her purse, where she rummages around and pulls out two brown paper bags.

I know what one is immediately, as the smell of

freshly baked goods hits my nostrils. Moving back to my seat, I keep the desk between us, so I don't do something stupid, like smash my lips against hers.

"Here. Red Velvet this time," she says, putting the two bags in front of me, and I peek inside, seeing the cupcake with thick white icing and a sprinkle of red glitter. My eyes flick back to her.

"Why were you stressed?" I ask her, concerned, knowing now that she bakes when she is upset.

"Oh, no reason." She waves me off, her smile not as bright as it was before. I know she isn't being completely honest, but I let it go as I open the second bag and see a small pile of green fluff before I upend the bag and a pair of socks falls onto my desk.

I bark out a laugh as I pick them up. They are soft, bright lime green, and look like they will reach my knees.

"Bed socks. So now you can look as ridiculous as me every night," she says, her voice too sweet for her own good.

"You think these will help me sleep?" I ask, feeling their softness. They are utterly absurd, but I already can't wait to put them on.

"Well, you should try everything. Never underestimate a good night's sleep," she says simply, but to me, it's not simple at all. She went out of her way to get these for me.

"But talking to you helps me sleep. I will just call you," I say, taking the tags off the socks and pulling one onto my hand to get the feel of it.

"Yes, but our calls need to stay about work." My smile leaves my face, but I check myself quickly.

"But they are about work. By talking to you every night, I am staying out of trouble," I say to her before I give her a wink, my smile turning into a smirk. She knows I am playing with her. Her lips thin, and she sighs, trying to ensure she does the right thing while all I want to do is the wrong thing. The very wrong thing. With her. Over and over and over again.

"But I won't be there every night. In fact, I won't be able to chat with you tonight." My head whips up to look at her.

"Where will you be?" I ask before I sit back a little, knowing that it is probably none of my business, but I am intrigued to know what Willow does in her spare time.

"I have a date," she states, looking a little uncomfortable as I feel my morning coffee spinning in my stomach.

"A date?" I repeat, my eyebrows hitting my hairline, not liking that piece of information one bit. I move in my seat, unsure how to take this news. It's not like I can forbid it, tell her not to go. My chest feels tight as I try to process, wondering how on earth I can get her not to go on that date. She is a catch, one who no one else can find.

"Yes, a date," she confirms with a bit of sass I'm not expecting, and I feel my teeth grinding before I try to relax.

"With whom?" I press, my eyes thinning, trying to sound like I don't care. I want to find out who it is and break his legs so he can't go and needs to cancel.

"Oh, a guy I met on an app." Grabbing her tablet, she taps it to life to start our meeting like she didn't just drop this bombshell on me.

"An app?" I ask a little too loudly, making her eyes snap up to me.

"Yes, an app," is all she says, and I'm about ready to pull my hair out.

"Do you know what kind of men are on those apps?" I seethe. Does she have any idea what she is doing? Those men are animals. I know, I am one of them.

She sighs. "Yes, I know. I have received more dick pics to my phone over the past few days than I care to admit."

"So, cancel it. Tell him you have to work," I say, almost demanding it.

"But I don't have to work," she says with a shrug, ignoring my tone. "Besides, my sister told me I need to get out more and meet people, so that is what I am doing. Now, let's review your social strategy. I want to ensure you are across it all before we put it in place starting tonight." Putting her tablet on the desk between us, she effectively signifies an end to our conversation.

She talks me through the new plan, and while I crack my knuckles under the desk, my face remains impartial. She is good. The entire strategy is like something I would expect from a large corporation or one of those really trendy media companies. She has thought of everything from content, imagery, timings, collaborations, and sequences.

"So you are happy with it all?" she asks, packing her things, about to leave.

"It looks good, and I trust you," I say, standing and walking around the front of my desk, just to be a little closer to where she stands.

"Good. My digital manager will roll it out starting

tonight." She gives me a small smile, her face soft and free of judgment, her eyes sparkling in my office lights.

"Speaking of tonight, where is this Romeo taking you?" I can't help myself, I need to know. I can't stop thinking about it. Who he is. What they will do. *Will she let him touch her?* Fuck, now I want to hit something.

"Oh, just a small restaurant in DC, nothing too fancy." I swallow so I don't say what I really want to say, which is, "*Don't go*. Come out with me instead." I will take her to the best restaurant, fuck, I will fly her to Paris for a meal in the Eiffel Tower if that will impress her.

"Well, have a great time," I grit out, still not liking this situation, but not sure how to stop it. I can't say anything. I can't push her.

"Thanks. Oh, before I forget, I updated your diary. We are going to find you a dog this weekend," she says, her smile wide.

"This weekend? So soon?" How can I get out of this harebrained scheme she has hooked me into? I am not sure I am ready for such a commitment, but then I look into her eyes, see her beaming up at me in delight, and I crumble.

"Yep. Be ready!" she singsongs as I nod and watch her turn and walk out of my office. I remain standing, gripping my desk to ensure I don't follow.

I need to tread carefully. Balance the professional expectations she has with the very unprofessional thoughts that I have and hope that the date bombs.

14

WILLOW

I feel like a moron sitting here. Candlelight creates a dim glow on the small and very intimate tables. The decor and music are on point for a romantic evening. It is all way too much for a first date. Already, the expectations of tonight are sky-high, and I am slightly nervous.

I had to swipe a lot to find this man, and even though he was reasonably good-looking and his profile said he worked in finance and loved animals, there was something about the few text exchanges we had that didn't leave me filled with confidence that this evening would be a success. Maybe because I would prefer a different man to be sitting opposite me tonight. I could tell that Tennyson was jealous when I told him about my date. Part of me wanted him to say something. Tell me to cancel it and go out with him instead. But I know this is for the best. I need to push him, and any thoughts I have of him, to the side.

Besides, my sister was right. It has been months since

I have been on a date. That one night in New York was the last time I was intimate with anyone, and I need to get out in order to find a yin to my yang.

But as I look around the room at all the other couples who look lovingly into each other's eyes, hands grasped together on the table, my own hands start to shake slightly, and I take a tentative sip of my water. My date is late. And if there is anything worse than taking that first step of agreeing to a date, it is being stood up.

I try to act busy, looking over the menu, staring at it for so long that I already know I would like to have the farm roasted chicken with baby carrots. I then take out my cell and check my emails. I see my social manager has started with Tennyson's newly curated feed and I look over image after image of him. He's so hot my cell phone nearly melts in my hand.

"Willow?" a man's voice says from beside me, and I jump a little in surprise.

"Yes. Roger?" I ask, subtly putting away Tennyson's sexy smirk and slipping my phone back into my purse as I give him a warm smile.

"Sorry, I'm late. I got caught up at the office," he says, taking a seat opposite me, and I look him over. He is different from his online photos. *Very* different.

"Wow, you look just like your photos. You're beautiful," he says, smiling as the waiter fills his water glass.

"Oh, thank you. You look... a little like your photos as well," I say with a forced smile.

"Well, I will admit those photos are a little old. I have aged somewhat." That's quite the understatement.

The man in the photos looked to be in his midthirties,

maybe late thirties, showing him mountain climbing, then in a suit, then swimming. The man sitting in front of me, I would guess is pushing fifty, has filled out a lot, and his hair has receded and thinned to the point of being almost nonexistent. Not that I mind bald men, but he is nothing like he portrayed, and already I wonder what else he would lie to me about.

As Roger looks through the menu in front of him, we fall into an uncomfortable silence. I think again of Tennyson. His presence just lights up a room. His personality acts like a magnet, his conversation just as attractive as his looks. Obviously knowing what he will order, Roger places the menu down and looks at me.

"So your profile mentioned that you work in finance. What kind of work do you do?" One of us has to talk, even though this night is already not going to go the way I had hoped.

"I work in mergers and acquisitions at the top end of town," he says, his eyes going from me to around the room and back again. I hear my cell vibrate in my purse, and I grab it to ensure there is no emergency. I don't care if I seem rude for it either.

Tennyson: How is the date?

Of course it's him. I swiftly type a reply.

Willow: Great. Lovely restaurant.

I drop my cell back in my purse and pick up my menu, burying my head in the words. I feel frustrated.

Frustrated because this is a waste of my time. I have a hundred other things I could be doing, speaking with Tennyson on our late-night calls being one of them. My chest lurches a little, knowing that I would be having a much better time tonight if he was with me instead.

"That sounds like it would be high pressure? Do you enjoy it?" I ask another question since he's yet to ask me one. But I hear the vibration in my purse yet again as I do. I ignore it this time.

"I do. I have always worked in finance. But being here in DC, I will say that I am getting some political aspirations."

"It is that kind of town," I say with a smile. I know better than to talk about politics. It is a topic that I like to stay clear of, because in this town, people are very opinionated on the matter. My purse vibrates once again, and I smile to myself and ignore it. I will talk to Tennyson later. I just need to get this date over with.

"Are you ready to order?" the waiter asks, stepping up to us.

"I will have the steak. Medium rare with a side of steamed greens. She will have the same," Roger orders for me and I am a little taken aback. The waiter leaves almost instantly, effectively dismissed by my date's flick of a hand, the menu whisked from my grasp so quickly I sit and wonder what the hell just happened.

"So are you a Democrat or a Republican?" he asks just as I take a sip of water to steady my nerves, and I almost choke. *That* is the first thing he's asking me. *Really?*

"Oh, I'm so sorry, it went down the wrong way." Grabbing my napkin, I dab my mouth. My purse vibrates again, but Roger doesn't notice. "Please excuse me. I just need to freshen up," I say as I stand, grabbing my purse and heading for the ladies' room. I weave between the tables, making my way in the low light of the restaurant to a small bathroom toward the back. As I push open the bathroom door, relief floods my body, and I hold on to the vanity and take a breath. *What am I doing? Why can't I find a nice man?*

My purse vibrates again, and I open my bag and grab my cell.

> Tennyson: Who is he?
>
> Tennyson: Where did he take you?
>
> Tennyson: Has he even asked about your bed socks yet? Because if not, he is not worth wasting your time on.

I laugh at his last message, my mood lightening instantly. I am acutely aware that our conversation is not on work at all, though, which is dangerous territory. His keen interest in my date is a problem, and I debate on whether to lie and tell him the date is amazing or go with the truth.

The truth wins.

> Willow: No bed socks. It's been ten minutes, and I already want to escape. The bathroom window looks very inviting.

I tap my reply quickly before grabbing my lip gloss and touching up my makeup. I didn't ruin it, but I am not ready to go back out, so I take a selfie in the bathroom mirror. Evidence for my sister that I am, in fact, out and on a date. While it may not end how either of us had hoped, at least I tried. That should win me enough time to not try another dating app again for at least another six months. They are seriously depressing. I post the image to my social media, tagging her in it, knowing she will see it on the other side of the world, with her constantly being glued to her social pages.

Throwing everything back into my purse, I take a deep breath and head back out to my date. While I really wanted to order the chicken, I might as well enjoy my steak. Because after tonight, I plan to stay in work mode for as long as possible.

AFTER ENJOYING a bottle of red and a tender steak, I have discovered that Roger is one of the most arrogant and self-centered men I have ever met.

"So, you see, that is why I would be a good president. The financial acumen, business presence, and family ties all point me in that direction." I hate to burst his bubble, but he is most certainly not president material.

"Sounds like you have it all planned out," I offer, looking around for a waiter, wanting to get the hell out of here already. We have been here for almost two hours, and I think that is long enough.

"For you, madame," the waiter says, coming up to me from the side. As he puts a plate in front of me, a lone cupcake stares back. Vanilla with a sunny yellow frosting.

"I didn't order that," Roger spits out. His behavior

toward the waitstaff here tonight has been less than stellar.

"No, but I did," a familiar deep voice says, and I look up to see Tennyson Langford standing to my left, his hand now resting on the back of my chair. I am glad I am sitting down, because even though I have seen him in a suit before, this vision of him now would most certainly sweep me off my feet. Black suit, well fitted across his broad shoulders. White crisp shirt underneath, open at the neck. He is relaxed yet professional and looking like every woman's dream man.

"Who the hell are you?" Roger questions, looking less than impressed.

"Tennyson Langford," Tennyson says, holding out his hand in introduction.

"Roger Court." Roger stands, shaking his hand. It's clear he knows who Tennyson is, the Langford name more common now that Harrison is governor. Roger is the poster child for Pleasantville as he smiles and stares at Tennyson, probably thinking that he would be good to have in his political corner.

"I have paid your bill. Roger, you are free to go. I will ensure your date is looked after," Tennyson says, and I look around the room, seeing most of the people have left.

Roger looks at me then, like he is deciding whether to stay or go. I can't even speak. I'm shocked that Tennyson is here, and more than a little pissed that my date is considering leaving me with another man without consulting me. My mind is a whirl of thoughts before I feel it—Tennyson's hand on my shoulder. He rubs his thumb across my skin, and I instantly relax. I look up at Tennyson and see his eyes staring right at Roger, ensuring he knows exactly who is with me, and it isn't him. And then, I feel relief. Relief that, although my date is a total douchebag, I dodged a bullet. Relief that Tennyson is here. The touch of his thumb on my shoulder is barely anything, but the hum through my body has my skin pulsating and butterflies swirling. We are electric together. This touch only cements it.

"Fine," Roger mumbles, throwing his napkin on the table, then grabbing his coat and walking straight out the door, his free steak keeping his belly full. And the handshake with Tennyson will keep his story bank full for his next few dates, no doubt.

"What are you doing here?" I ask Tennyson as he takes a seat opposite me, the waiter scurrying to clean the table and leaving another cupcake, placing it in front of him.

"Well, I couldn't let my girl suffer all night," he says with a cheeky smile before he pierces the cupcake with a fork, taking a big bite. *My girl.* Those two words have my chest warming despite myself. I shouldn't be entertaining this, never mind enjoying it.

"How did you know where I was?" I ask again, not sure whether to be relieved to be saved from my disaster of a date or annoyed that Tennyson showed up at all. Especially when he will be out late and not adhering to my schedule.

"Your social media photo," he offers, taking another bite.

"Are you stalking me now?" I ask in jest, and he smiles.

"I am. You know where I am every minute of the day, so I think it is only fair. Are you going to eat that?" His fork points to the cupcake in front of me. It looks delicious, and my mouth waters, so I don't hesitate to grab my fork and dig in.

"Were you in DC? I didn't see that on your schedule." I went through his diary this week three times, and a visit to DC would have been something I noticed. I take a bite of the cupcake and moan. It is fresh, lemon, and so soft, I immediately want more.

"Fuck," Tennyson murmurs, barely loud enough for me to hear, and my eyes flick to him. He looks at me with heat in his gaze, and I raise my eyebrows in question.

"You all right?" I ask with a mouth full of cake.

"Your moan is just like I remember," he grits out, and I swallow, feeling myself getting hot all over. We are both dancing way too close to the flame. My feelings for him are hardly contained. The fact that he is here is all the evidence I need that he feels the same. I clear my throat and try to get us back on track. I can't think of him like that. He is a client. I can't go there.

"So how did you get here so fast? I took that photo only an hour or so ago." Squeezing my thighs together, I try to slow my racing heart. His eyes on me are everything. I feel wanted again, and it feels too good.

"I grabbed the chopper," he says, shrugging, like he is describing a trip to the grocery store.

"Are you serious?" I pull back, not believing my ears. *Did he say chopper?*

"What?" he asks, the last bite of his cupcake now in his mouth as he looks at me like a trip in a helicopter to DC is a regular occurrence. Maybe for him, it is. This is the spending that Harrison was talking about.

"You flew down here just to interrupt my date?" I ask, bewildered.

"No. I flew here to *save you* from your date," he reinstates with a satisfied smile on his face.

"In a helicopter?" This is crazy. I have never had someone even drive anywhere to pick me up. *A helicopter? For me?*

"No, in *my* helicopter." He sits back, a smirk growing on his face that I really want to put my lips on. I am shocked and sit unmoving for a beat, digesting the information. When I look around the restaurant this time, I see it's empty. Only Tennyson and I are left, and two staff polishing glasses over near the bar.

"Tennyson, you can't... I mean, we can't..." I try to think of the right words to say. As much as I want to jump across this table and feel his arms on my body, I can't go there. His reputation needs rebuilding. And if I am romantically connected with a client, my reputation may take a hit too. There are so many unknowns.

"I know, Willow. It's all right. Eat your cupcake, and then I will take you home," he says softly, looking serious, and I nod, taking another bite as he watches me in deep thought.

It is obvious that we both want the same thing. The electricity that runs between us is high voltage.

"I know we can't..." he starts to say, and I look up at him. I remain silent, waiting for him, my heart thudding so hard I feel the vibration across my chest. "But, Willow, I want to. I *really* fucking want to." It's so sincere the way he says it, like it's so much more than sex he's got on his mind, and I melt. He is laying his cards out. He flew here to me *in a helicopter* to rescue me from the date, because he wants me.

"We can't. My business means so much to me. I have worked hard over these past few years, and if I fraternize with a client, that could impact everything I have worked so hard for." My voice is merely a whisper. This is so hard. The battle between my head and my heart is fierce. But I need to pull it together. I am a professional, goddammit. I clear my throat and straighten my spine. Rolling my shoulders back, I take a deep breath.

"You're still coming to the business dinner, aren't you?" he asks me, and I appreciate him getting back to work talk. That dinner has been on my mind lately. Harrison and Beth are putting it together. It will be a great opportunity to meet potential new clients, spread my name further afield and away from DC to help diversify my business. I have since learned that the who is who of business will be there, so I also need to be focused on making sure that Tennyson is positioned in a good light.

"I will be there to support you and make sure everything goes smoothly. I just need to organize something to wear." My nerves dance because it will be the first time we will be together in a formal setting.

"You could wear a potato sack and look beautiful," he says the words low, but his statement hits me square in the chest.

"We should go. I have a town car here to pick me up.

He can take you wherever it is you need to go," I say, my feelings about everything almost overwhelming. But it must be this way. *Doesn't it?* His smile is small, but it is there. He knows. He knows it is merely a matter of time before I bend.

"Lead the way." He watches me stand before he does as well, grabbing my jacket off the waiter and draping it around my shoulders himself. He stays close as we start walking, his hand on my lower back as he guides me out of the restaurant and out onto the street, and he doesn't lift it until I am safely in the back of the car. His protective touch isn't making this any easier. I see him take a moment outside before he rounds the trunk and jumps in the back seat with me.

The two of us are ending the night not at all how we would like to.

"So this is where you live?" Tennyson asks as the town car pulls up to my house. I am itching to get out of this car. The tension between us has me on edge. Sitting close to each other, yet careful not to touch. Talking about business yet trying not to get too personal. I am usually excellent at keeping things professional, but it is already harder than I ever thought it would be. The way he sits with confidence next to me, the perfect conversation flowing naturally, and the way I constantly feel his eyes skirt over my body... it all has my body zinging. If I don't climb out of the car, I'll be climbing all over him.

"This is it." I admire my bungalow as it sits small and proud in my street.

"Suits you," he says before he quickly gets out of the car. I grab my purse and open the door, just as he stands there to help me out. His hand encases mine so easily it is almost my undoing. But I don't remove it. It is like my body, mind, and heart are all pushing me to him, and I can't seem to fully control anything anymore. My body hums for him, his hand feels nice in mine, and for once, I just want to be the girl the guy wants to hold on to. I blow out my breath slowly as the car door closes.

"What do you mean by that?" I ask him as he walks me up the path to my door. My legs shake a little as my hand still sits in his. It should feel all types of wrong, but it doesn't. It feels too right.

"It's small, elegant, welcoming, just like you."

"Well... there will be no welcoming tonight." I don't know why I say it. Maybe to remind myself. He only smiles, but it's the knowing kind. "Thank you for the drive home. Please get home safely." I am not sure how safe helicopters are at nighttime, but he's got to leave, no matter what. As we reach my porch, I make no move to pull my hand from his. The two are glued together so tight, neither of us wanting to be the first to let go.

"The car will take me home. It will only be forty minutes from here. You are closer to Baltimore on this side of town," he says with a grin. "You sure you don't want to show me your bed socks?" His thumb leaves my hand momentarily, stroking my upper thigh.

I laugh, smacking his hand playfully. "Good night, Tennyson," I say, smiling as he takes a step back toward the car, his handsome grin on full display, our arms still connected and stretching between us.

"Some other time then," he says, giving me a wink, and our hands release as I wait and watch him get to the car before I open my front door and slip inside. As I close the door, I lean back against it, my legs giving way, my body sliding until my butt hits the floor.

I have no idea how I am meant to get through this next month or so. Work comes first, it always has. It is my anchor, it is what drives me, gives me purpose. I can't jeopardize that.

All I have is my reputation. That is all I need to get the next job. People refer me. People learn about me and my services. If I were to start sleeping with a client, that could all go away in an instant. It would also attract the wrong type of clients in the future as well. I trust Beth, but I don't really know the Langford men at all. If Tennyson and I were to take that step, who knows what the governor would do.

15

TENNYSON

I t stinks, there are barking dogs everywhere, and my girl stops and makes a cutesy voice at every cage we pass, doing something to my insides that makes me feel like butter. *My girl.* I am not sure when it happened, but that is how I think of her. She is mine. I knew it the moment we met in New York. I knew it when I turned up on her date in DC. And I know it now.

"Ohhhh, look at this one! Hello, beautiful boy!" she says in a voice that makes me jealous for no other reason than she is calling something else beautiful and giving it all her attention.

"No. Too slobbery," I mumble, looking at the massive Doberman that is currently sitting on guard, looking like he is about to bite Willow the minute the gate opens to his pen.

"Hello, little man!!" she says again as we pass by a cage that has one of the smallest dogs I have ever seen.

"It looks like a rat!" I say, scrunching up my face, not loving any of these options. Willow has talked me into getting a dog, and after serious consideration, I tend to agree with her that it is a good idea. Although no doubt an adjustment, I think it will be a positive step. A companion, a running partner, someone around the house. Something just for me.

"Well, what about this one? He is so squishy!" Her voice pitches a little, her hands making a squeezing motion as we pass a pug, the round animal snorting and scurrying. I bet he snores.

"No, too fat. He won't run with me." I want a man's dog. One with stamina, strength, grace.

"Which one do you like then?" she asks, looking at me, her eyes shimmering, a smile on her face. I would buy the whole damn center just to keep her smiling like that at me.

My eyes flick to the street outside, and I see a paparazzo arrive on a motorbike, followed by another. Clearly, it is a slow news week. Before they have their cameras ready, I reach out my fingers and brush Willow's hand, the one I want to hold but can't. I just want to feel her skin on mine.

"None. Let's go," I say, looking for the nearest exit.

"No, you need to choose one. You can't leave them all here," she says, looking up at me, jutting out her lower lip, my eyes flicking to it quickly before I look back into her eyes. I want to lean down and bite it. I want to throw her over my shoulder, take her to my apartment, and spank her perfect ass. God, the things I want to do to this woman. She smiles at me then, her finger slightly curving around my own. We are not holding hands, merely touching, but the heat in our touch is everything. The two of us are so close to combusting, I can feel it. Her little touches scorch my skin, and I smile back, knowing that we are meant to be professional today, yet she can't help but reach for me. I fucking love it.

"You stick that lip out at me again, and you need to be prepared for the consequences, Cupcake," I growl, meaning every word.

"Cupcake?" she asks me with her brow raised.

"Sweet, individual, and delicious. Sums you up." It also helps that she smells as sweet as a cupcake most of the time, her baking skills obviously getting a regular workout. She looks at me with a smile that could light up the entire universe, her eyes sparkling. Happy Willow is fucking illuminating, and I want to have her glowing every damn day.

"Paps have arrived," I say to her, not wanting to break the moment, but I am already protective of her.

"Hmmm…" she hums, looking out the window as she snatches her hand back, and I scowl.

"Okay, back to these dogs. You can't leave without one." Her tone turns professional now, her eyes running over the cages.

"I can. They were here when we got here." One thing I have learned from our time together is she is focused on work, and right now, I am her work, so getting me a dog is something she is taking very seriously. "What about when I travel? Who will look after it then?"

"A kennel or your brothers or depending on which one you get, I can dog sit." All of a sudden, I want every damn dog in this place.

"They look happy enough here, no?" It is clean, the staff seem friendly, and the dogs are well kept.

"Yes, but they need a forever home, Tennyson." I see the sadness in her eyes, knowing if she could rescue all of them, she would. This woman may be sassy and smart, but her heart is huge.

"Let me guess, you want to rescue all of them, am I right?"

"They should all have homes..." she grumbles, looking around at all the dogs as they bark and run around in their designated areas.

"Maybe I should just buy you this entire facility as their home for good," I tease her, kind of liking the idea actually.

"Don't you dare. We have to rein in your spending, not do more of it," she sasses, thinking about me and my reputation again.

"Fine, what about him?" She could ask me for anything right now, and I would agree. I flick my head to one I have been eyeing since we came in, which I am sure is a mix of breeds, but looks like he has a bit of life to him.

"Ohhhh, too cute! His name is Bob!" she says, walking up to the cage and reading over his information.

"Bob? Who the fuck names a dog 'Bob'?" It needs to be something more manly. Like Buster or Beast.

"I named a cat Betty," she says, coming chest to chest with me.

"Yeah, but that's you," I say with a shrug.

"What's that supposed to mean?" Her hand finds her hip. It's supposed to be feisty, but it's adorable.

"You know. You're…" I look her up and down, my favorite sight, and I wave my hands over her appearance.

"I'm what?" Her eyes thin, her brow quirked.

"You know, cute and stuff." I'm not able to hide the small grin appearing at ruffling her feathers.

"Cute? You think I'm cute?" she asks, her stance softening a little.

"Among other things, but cute is the most G-rated option I can think of." Her body relaxes, and she rolls her eyes.

"Are you rolling your eyes at me?" I don't think anyone else has ever rolled their eyes at me before, not like she does.

"So what if I am?" she asks, her stance strong again, and I chuckle. I am going to have so much fun fucking the sass right out of her. I am about to come back to her with a smart quip of my own, but I see a flash of cameras, and I straighten my spine. Willow does the same, putting distance between us that I don't like.

"How about it, Bob? You want to come home with me?" I ask, squatting down to look at my new family member, and he lets out a bark and runs in a circle, chasing his tail. He is light brown in color, his eyes blue, his tail wagging happily.

"That sounds like a yes to me." Willow says from beside me with a bright smile. This day is already feeling much better than any other morning I have had in recent months, and it's all from seeing that curve of her lips directed right at me.

16

WILLOW

I push through my front door, the groceries hanging from my hands, leaving marks on my skin. Why I struggle to bring everything inside and not make two trips, I'll never know.

"You're home!" I hear Josh yell from next door. I look up and watch as he jumps the low hedge and runs up the front path to me, flashing me his big smile, yet eyeing the bags, knowing that they contain snacks for him. I hold the door open with my foot as he follows me inside.

"Yep. Are you hanging out with me today?" I ask. I can't remember if I said I would watch him today, or if his mom is home and he is just after my candy jar.

"Nah, Mom's home. But she is sleeping," he says, flopping on my sofa and turning on the TV like he owns the place. Josh slept over here because she worked the night shift last night, so she must still be sleeping it off. "Did you get Cheerios?" he asks. They are his favorite, and he knows I am a sucker and buy them for him.

"Yes, in the bag. Help yourself." He jumps up and

joins me in the kitchen, the two of us moving around each other, him making a mess, and me cleaning it up. My cell rings and Tennyson's name flashes on my screen.

"Tennyson?" I ask in question, tucking the phone between my shoulder and ear. I thought he would be too busy with his new sidekick to call me. I would like to say Bob has settled in well, but it's been a week, and they are still having teething issues.

"He is eating my furniture, my new shoes are ruined, and he pissed on the kitchen floor!" he yells, his words coming so fast they run into each other.

"He is probably just excited to be in his new home. It is all still new." I roll my lips to stifle my laugh.

"I need a new fucking sofa!" I can't stop the giggle as it leaves my lips.

"Are you laughing? Go ahead and laugh. You are the one who now needs to come furniture shopping with me," he says, still upset, although a little less stressed.

"Have you walked him?" I ask. "Maybe he just needs to stretch his legs?" I wonder if Tennyson has actually read the fact sheets on dog ownership I sent him.

"Yes." Tennyson is short with his answer.

"When?" I don't believe him. I should get his assistant to put it in his diary and make it a priority. I write a note down for myself to do exactly that.

"Last week," he offers.

"Last week? You need to walk him every day." I shake my head, my eyes rolling. "And take a photo so we can put it up on Instagram this week." I might as well get some good content to push out the old.

"I know, I know. I had plans to run with him every

morning, but work is kicking my ass at the moment with early morning conference calls and late meetings." He moans, but I can hear the clink of the lead so I know he is getting ready to do just that.

"Bob," I say again, trying not to laugh.

"What?" he bites out.

"Bob, his name is Bob," I repeat, knowing he hates the name.

"I am not calling him Bob." I can't wipe the smile from my face.

"Well, what are you calling him, then?" I ask, juggling the milk and juice as I put them in the refrigerator.

"You have a yard, don't you?" he asks me, changing the subject so fast I get whiplash.

"What?" I ask mid milk placement, the fridge door banging against my arm.

"A house with a lawn? I'll bring him over. We can go through the week, and he can run at your place. Easy." I can hear his elevator closing, knowing he is already on his way.

"Wait. What?" My bed socks and a movie with Josh isn't how my afternoon is going to play out now, I guess.

"See you in thirty minutes."

"Tennyson?" I say, but the phone is already dead. He's gone, and now I need to change and clean the house before he gets here.

As promised, thirty minutes later, there is a knock at my door, and I open it to see Tennyson standing before me, looking tired with Bob in tow. The two make a very good-looking sight, Tennyson is in his jeans and white top that is stretched over his well-formed chest. His broad shoulders and thick arms are nearly my undoing and my grip on the door tightens a little so I don't do something stupid like jump him.

"Hello, boy, look at you so cute and cuddly," I coo as I squat down and give Bob my full attention so I don't swoon over his owner. I scratch behind his ears, which earns me a slobbery kiss in response.

"Hey, I'm up here. Do I get a greeting like that?" Tennyson quips, but his eyes are soft as he takes me in. His shoulders are relaxing now that he is in my home.

"Hello to you too," I say in a mock coo and scratch behind his ear, but his hand shoots out and grabs my hips and he pulls me close, giving me a peck to the forehead. The move looks innocent enough, but there is so much electricity running between us all the damn time that we could power all of New York City.

"You drive me crazy, woman," he mumbles. This new familiarity between us is nice, even if the urge I have to strip him naked runs wild in my mind.

"Come in," I say, opening the door wider and letting them both in before walking to the back door and opening it for Bob who shoots out and immediately starts running and exploring my small yard. I peer out, ensuring Betty is not in the way, but the coast is clear.

Turning back around, I see Tennyson sitting slumped at the kitchen counter, looking at me. He seems even bigger in my small cottage, taking up the counter space, and his presence almost takes over the room.

"You look exhausted," I say with a small smile, although I am concerned. I wonder if he is sleeping.

"The mutt keeps me up all night. Crying every time

I turn out the light. I have to sleep with the hallway light on. Then last night, I finally got to sleep, only to wake up and he was on my bed. Do you have any idea how much those Egyptian cotton sheets cost? Now there is dog hair all over them," he says, rubbing his tired eyes.

"He will settle down. Coffee?" I ask, moving around the kitchen.

"In an IV would be great," he murmurs, sighing.

"What are *you* doing here, Ninja?" Josh asks with bite, not offering a warm welcome to Tennyson as he walks into the kitchen, dumping his dirty cereal bowl in the sink. He eyes Tennyson warily, and I can only assume it is because this is the first man who has been in my home— ever. It's cute that my twelve-year-old best friend is so protective. He will make some girl very happy one day, I am sure of it.

Tennyson's brow crumples, and he looks at him with confusion on his face before his eyes flick to me for information.

"Michelangelo, wasn't it?" Josh asks, opening the fridge and peering inside, before grabbing an apple.

"Soccer ball kid?" Tennyson guesses, and I watch the interaction with interest.

"Surprised you remember. Thought an old guy like you would have suffered memory loss," Josh quips before he takes a bite out of the apple, and I cough to stifle my laugh.

"I'm not old!" Tennyson almost yells at Josh as he struts out of the room, back to the living room where he is holding my TV hostage.

"I'm not old," Tennyson murmurs to me as I slide across his coffee. "Although today I feel fucking ancient."

"Early night tonight, then," I offer, standing next to where he is sitting at my small kitchen counter.

"Yes. You coming?" he asks, then takes a sip, his eyes staying on mine as he watches me over the rim of the mug. His constant teasing about wanting me continues. If only it was that easy. My body quivers at the thought. I want to. Jumping into Tennyson's bed is an inviting prospect, one I think about often.

"Tennyson." I catch myself and growl his name in warning, my eyes flicking to him over the top of my own coffee cup. My body betrays me more times than not when I see him. But my work and my business are important to me. I wonder for a moment if I could have both. Would it be possible? Logistically, yes, but is it smart, for either of us right now? I really don't know. Maybe I should just throw caution to the wind. Be more like Saide and live a little.

"I know. I know. Professional boundaries, I get it. So, the photo shoot is booked?" he asks, and we dissect his diary for the coming weeks. Something I usually do on Mondays in his office, but he has now saved me a trip.

"So we have a shoot with Natasha Libermans. She is a photographer for the *Manhattan Men's Magazine*, does lots of editorial and fashion shoots. I have arranged for a stylist to have a rack of men's designer clothing collections from fashion week, and I want both suit and corporate shots, and maybe something a little more relaxed," I say, already picturing how handsome he will look in everything.

"You will be there with me, right?"

"Yes, Tennyson, I will be there," I confirm with a nod, his eyes on mine. "I will even meet you at your office and we can go together."

"Good. What else do we have going on?" he asks, almost finished with his coffee, and my eyes raise in question.

"IV, remember," he says, and I get busy making him another one.

"We have the business dinner with Harrison and Beth coming up," I mention.

"Shit, I forgot about that. You're going to be there?" he asks me again, clearly not happy to go without me by his side.

"Someone has to keep you in line. Besides, it is good for business to start mingling and networking with some of Baltimore's finest." I am happy to attend his event, but it is much bigger than I first thought. The stress I have to look after Tennyson and hope he does a good job in front of the governor is building. I need to show them how far he has come, because so far, he is doing a great job.

"Good. Anything else?" he asks, sipping his coffee and taking in all the information.

"You have a quiet weekend next weekend. Nothing is planned so far, so I thought you might like to spend next weekend with Bob." While I could parade him out and about at a charity function, sometimes keeping my clients out of the spotlight makes room for someone else to step in it and take the focus away. We don't want Tennyson out of the media completely, but a little space to make him more elusive will provide us some time to build up the positive press in the background.

"That will be nice if nothing else comes up. I have another conference call tomorrow with the Hong Kong team. The project is slowing, but not yet stopped." I see his shoulders get heavy as the words leave him.

"Good, well, progress is progress, no matter how slow and steady." I try to be encouraging, but from the look on his face, it's not helping.

"It would be faster if Newcomb got out of my way. He is looking at cannibalizing the market over there and has people in his pocket. It is getting tougher to get traction." Tennyson is so deep in thought, I don't think he realizes I have no idea who he's talking about.

"Who is Newcomb again?"

"Geoffrey Newcomb owns a large construction firm that produces a lot of buildings here in Maryland. And he is a giant pain in my ass." From his tone alone, I can tell that they aren't friends.

"Why don't you go somewhere he isn't? Why not start a new foothold? I mean, I know Hong Kong is great, lots of progress and advancement, but you could look at Singapore? That is a really great country, with lots of investment in advancements and infrastructure that pushes the boundaries. Smart buildings that are tech enabled are a new frontier that you should look into," I suggest, having read something about it in the news just recently.

"You are just a wealth of information, aren't you? Smart as well as sexy," he murmurs, running a hand through his hair.

"I'm pretty sure I read about it in the Wall Street Journal or something, but think about a new plan of action. Change things up a bit," I say with a shrug. I have no real understanding of what he does, but I am happy to provide thought starters if they are helpful.

"A new plan of action? Changing things up? Sounds like my current life at the moment."

"You know what they say, a change is as good as a holiday." I smile at him, but when he looks up at me, there's something in his eyes that has my breath catching.

"Why did you leave me in the middle of the night in New York?" I blink, then blink again. I was not even close to being ready for this conversation.

"Tennyson..." I warn again, not wanting to delve into us whatsoever. I am hanging by a thread as it is. The urge I have to be with him is growing stronger by the day.

"I thought we were both having a good time. Your moans were certainly telling me you were." He looks at me in a way that makes me want to melt, desperate for answers that I shouldn't give him.

"We really shouldn't be talking about that weekend," I say quietly, my eyes flicking to the living room, conscious that Josh doesn't hear over the TV.

"Not talk about it? Willow, it is all I think about, and I know you do too. I am not going to lie, when I woke to an empty bed that morning, I was disappointed." His features soften, and I know he is genuinely telling me his feelings. I don't know how I know, but I think this is new for him to be this open. Something about our connection has us comfortable in other's presence without even trying. I could tell him anything and he wouldn't judge me, wouldn't throw it in my face, and would always have my back.

But I can't do this. *You love your job, Willow.*

"Do you ask all your one-night stands that question? Surely, I am not the only one to skip out during the night?" I push back on him and see his body stiffen.

"You were different," he murmurs, sipping his coffee, his jaw set hard. "We were different. We *are* different." I am not an idiot, I know he is a playboy and our night together was just that. One night. But hearing him now, along with his constant flirtations, it makes me feel a little better about the situation. Like, even though it was one night, it meant as much to him as it did to me.

"David Taylor Smith," I state his name, and Tennyson's back goes ramrod straight.

"You left me for fucking David Taylor Smith? The asshole baseball player who is serving time?" he asks, with shock and confusion on his face.

"I did," I say casually, nodding and sipping my coffee.

"Didn't he get locked away for drug possession and prostitution?" His brow crumples, like he's imagining us together.

"He did. He was picked up at a club in DC about seven months ago at three a.m. A massive bag of white powder and a questionable associate next to him. He got one phone call from the police cell. Who do you think he called?" I ask him, watching him closely to see when the penny drops.

"You," he states, sitting up.

"Yes, me. He was my client, Tennyson. I had just taken him on a few weeks earlier. I knew he was trouble as soon as I met him. There wasn't an honest bone in his body. But I took the job anyway, me and my optimistic notions that I can save everyone. He is the only client I haven't succeeded with. My only failure," I say remorsefully. David really pushed my professional boundaries in a totally different way. He was a challenge, one I didn't win.

"Married to your job..." Tennyson says in awe, relief evident in his face that I left because of a work emergency, not because I wanted to.

"Married to my job," I confirm, giving him a small smile, and I see his face brighten.

"So are you going to show me your bed socks?" he quips, his humor breaking any tension, and I laugh.

"You have your own to look at." I am not taking Tennyson to my bedroom. I already know that if we go there, we are not coming out. For days.

"At least the dog hasn't eaten them," he mumbles, and as if on cue, Bob barks. We jump up to look outside to see what trouble he has found, and I stand stunned. Bob and Betty have found each other and are currently in a standoff in the backyard.

"Betty! Come here! Here puss, puss, puss," I yell as I open the door, trying to get her away, but I see her back arched and her hair standing on end.

"Bob! Come here, boy," Tennyson yells, stepping outside with me as Bob jumps around like it is playtime, not at all aware that he is about to get his eyes scratched out.

"Shit," we both say in unison as we make a mad dash out the door, the two of us sprinting in opposite directions just as Betty pounces.

"I've got him!" Tennyson yells, jumping on Bob and grabbing him, pulling him up to his body and tucking him under his arm.

"Betty!" I say, trying to get her, but she is still not trusting of me, so she hisses some more and I watch as she flies through the air, her claws grabbing on to Tennyson's arm as she tries to get to his dog.

"Son of a bitch!" he shouts, turning swiftly, the cat dropping and sprinting to the fence, then scrambling away from the yard.

Tennyson lets go of Bob, who bounces around like he is having the time of his life, then marking his territory on a nearby bush.

"Let me get the first aid kit," I say, grimacing at Tennyson's bloody arms.

"Can you put a nurse's uniform on? I think that would help with the pain."

Rolling my eyes, I reach out and pull his arm toward me to look at the damage. It isn't deep and has only just broken the skin, but I know what cat scratches are like. They sting for a bit before they get better.

"How did you know I have a nurse's uniform?" I tease once I've looked him over.

"Jesus. You're serious? Now you really need to go in and put it on. I think I would like you to play dress-up for me," he says, smirking, my hands still holding his.

"Maybe I can be a naughty nurse for Halloween this year?" I act nonchalant, shrugging my shoulders, and he growls in response.

"There is no fucking way anyone but me will be

seeing you in a naughty nurse's uniform," he grumbles, shaking his head, and I huff out a small laugh.

"David fucking Taylor Smith. I hate him even more now."

"You and me both, Tennyson," I say, pulling him inside so I can clean him up, his fingers intertwined with mine.

And even if it's just for a moment, I revel in that simple touch.

17

TENNYSON

The morning dew steams from the manicured grass, and for the first time in a long time, I feel good. I'm sleeping better. My body isn't as stiff, my mind feels clear. I got up with ease this morning instead of with a raging headache. My mind is sharper and energy hums through me and I know it is all because of Willow. The changes we are implementing to my routine and lifestyle, along with her just being around, seem to be making a difference.

"What are you smiling about?" Harrison asks me as he walks past where I am standing to take his shot.

"I'm smiling because I am going to beat all you fuckers this morning," I say, feeling confident that I will win these eighteen holes, even though we are only up to the third hole. My brother takes his shot, and the ball flies through the air, landing near the tee.

"By the look of his shot, he is in fine form today," Ben murmurs as he and Eddie sit in the golf cart, waiting for Harrison and me.

"Seriously, what's with the stupid grin?" Harrison asks again as he throws his club in his golf bag and looks at me.

"What grin?" I ask, trying to ignore his statement, even though I do feel pretty good this morning.

"That grin." He points to my face, and I try to keep my lips down, but I know they quirk up at the sides.

"What? I have had a good few weeks is all," I say, shrugging as we jump into the cart, and Ben drives us down the fairway.

"How're things with Willow?" Harrison asks, and I don't miss as Ben's eyes flick to me in the small rearview mirror. I haven't spoken to my brothers in depth since the intervention, so there's no doubt in my mind that all of them thought I would be hard to handle.

"Fine. She's good," I reply simply, not really wanting to get into details.

"Have you spoken with her much? What is she like to work with?" Eddie asks, keen to get the lowdown on our arrangement.

I don't want to tell them the truth that Willow and I speak almost every day. Nor do I want to admit to wearing those bright-green bed socks to bed every night since she gave them to me. My bed never felt so cozy before. After crashing her date and hanging out at her place, I am still trying to get my head on straight with where we stand. I want round two, and I know she does too, but she is hesitant because of her work. I get that. I just need to find a way around it.

"Yeah, we have built a new social media strategy. Her team is now managing it all," I offer, and they seem pleased at that point. I was impressed by her strategy, albeit a little embarrassed by all the messages from women that I receive and all the photos I'm tagged in. I am so used to it, I ignore them all for the most part, but Willow has cleaned it all up and her digital manager is already implementing the new strategy, positioning me as a friendly, likable billionaire, who gives to charity and does it all with a wide smile. As the cart stops, I pull out my cell and take a selfie while on the course. The bright-blue sky behind me, the luscious green of the fairway in view. I send it to Willow.

"Sounds like it is going well so far, then?" Ben asks as we all walk to find our balls.

"So far. She has booked a photo shoot soon for some new images that we can use. Apparently, my Zoolander is not up to par." I find my ball and fall into silent concentration, hitting it just right for it to land on the green. The shot is so good, I'm smiling again.

"Sounds like I will get to go to swimming lessons again tomorrow, then?" Ben asks, and I look at him with a wince.

"Yes. You will, and I am sorry I didn't see what I was doing before it had such an effect on you. Willow will be at the business dinner tonight, and I am under strict instructions to drink water and be home by eleven p.m." He nods, and I feel like a weight has been lifted. Willow has no problem in telling me the cold hard truth. But I needed to hear it. I was oblivious to so much before, and the last thing I want is to negatively affect my brothers in any way.

"I already like Willow. She sounds like a great woman!

Who else could get you home by eleven?!" Eddie jests, and my eyes home in on him with a scowl. I don't like him liking her. Not one bit.

"What's that?" Ben asks, looking sharply at me.

"What?" I ask, my furrowed brow not relaxing.

"That look. What is that look?" Ben pushes, and I growl, not able to let go of the jealousy that coils after Eddie's comment. Harrison raises his eyebrows, and Ben looks at me with his mouth agape. Eddie stops mid stride in shock.

"What?" I look between them, wondering what the hell is going on.

"Do you like her?" Eddie asks, his eyes wide.

"What do you mean?" I ask, hoping they buy my stupid act.

"Do not get involved with her. You are her client. Don't fuck it up," Harrison warns, dead serious as he points his finger toward me. Something our dad used to do.

"Relax. I think she is the only woman I've met not to fall for my charm," I say, trying to keep the peace. It is not a total lie. I thought if we ever saw each other again, it would be so hot that we would run straight to the bedroom. Her halting that for us has me second-guessing myself.

"Smartest woman in the country, then," Ben teases.

"Yeah, she is smart. Like super smart." I rub my chin, thinking about the woman whose business acumen rivals that of the many business contacts I have.

"Just be careful, Tenn," Harrison says, still looking at me intently, and I meet his eyes and nod. "I know you have a history; Willow mentioned it to Beth and me on our initial call. But she promised she would remain professional," he adds, and my shoulders stiffen.

"She is excellent at her job. She is professional. But what she does outside of that, and who she does that with, is not up for us to discuss," I state, letting them know my intentions, because I am not about to let him put any of this on her. There is no way I can stay away from this woman, and if something happens between us, it doesn't mean she's failed at her job.

"Fuck," Harrison murmurs, rubbing his head. "Well... you have been a different man since she has come into your life. No more fucking everything with legs every weekend."

"That's true. We haven't seen any early morning pap shots of you escaping from a woman's bed in a while," Eddie says.

"Yeah, well, I know the last six months or so I haven't been great. But things are changing," I say to them, feeling the change in myself. All because of Willow.

"I hope that they are." Harrison looks at me questioningly, still not fully accepting it.

"How good have I been? I have been on the straight and narrow, done everything asked of me, and I don't plan to fuck anything up. But Willow is someone I have been looking for, for a long fucking time. Now she just shows up again, and I am meant to keep things professional?" My voice rises. I can't help it. This is starting to piss me off.

"What do you mean?" Ben asks, looking between Harrison and me.

"Willow was the woman I met in New York," I tell them, letting them all know the truth. I don't tell them much about my life, but after that night in New York, I did spend a few weeks trying to find her, and my brothers know all about that.

"Willow is your New York woman?" Eddie asks, shock evident on his face.

"Jesus, what are the chances?" Ben says, rubbing his head.

Harrison just looks at me in shock as he puts the pieces together.

"I will be careful. I am not stupid. I will keep things professional. But Willow is not like anyone I've met before," I say adamantly, and as I look at my brothers, steel determination settles in my bones.

I will have Willow again. It might not be as soon as I hope, but it will happen.

18

WILLOW

I have seen extravagance before, but as I walk around this room, it is next level. I am not sure what is in the water here in Baltimore, but even in DC, the elegance at events is more understated. Here, it is on full display.

This is one of the key business events for Harrison and Beth. The governor's office has brought together important stakeholders across a variety of industries for a formal dinner to build networks, enhance partnerships, and to amplify the Maryland business offering.

My shoulders are stiff due to the pressure I feel about ensuring Tennyson behaves himself tonight. It's his first big event since I have come on board, and I need to show him and his brothers that there is a tangible difference.

"Willow, you're here!" Beth says, grabbing me in for a hug. She was obviously waiting for me, but I only just arrived.

"Hey, you look amazing," I say, because she does. Her hair all pinned, a burgundy floor-length gown complementing her gorgeous figure, she looks a million dollars. Just like a first lady should.

I don't go out a lot, but at least in DC, I know everyone. Here, I know only a few, but that doesn't stop people from looking at me with interest, the gazes I am getting so intense I am continually checking my attire, wondering if I have a stain on my dress or something.

"So do you, and I am not the only one to think that," she says with a knowing smile.

"What do you mean?" I ask, confused.

"Every man in this room has his eye on you. Not only because you are new to the Baltimore scene and they all love fresh blood, but because you look stunning, and I must say, that soft blue dress does amazing things for your eyes."

"Oh stop. This old thing," I tease, and we laugh. We are both smart women; there is more to us than just the fashion we wear.

I haven't worn this dress in a while. I work so much that I am usually in yoga pants in front of the computer or in corporate attire for my meetings. Formal wear is something I don't pull out of my wardrobe very often. I forgot the leg slit was so high, but with little time to choose an alternative because Betty was being needy and wanting to be fed, I decided the chiffon flows enough to hide it, my leg only peeking out when I walk or if I step out on purpose.

"Ladies, you both look beautiful tonight," Harrison says as he kisses Beth on her temple. The two of them are so obviously in love it is almost nauseating. "Willow, how is it all going with Tennyson?" He gets straight to the point.

"The past few weeks have been great. Very productive," I say with a nod as I offer him a beaming smile. I don't want to go into specifics. One, because this is not the time or place, but two, my loyalty now lies with Tennyson. Regardless of the fact that Harrison reached out to me first. It is one of the reasons I am so good at what I do. I compartmentalize the noise and chatter and remain laser focused on my client. When they need me, I am there. Always in their corner.

"So he is behaving himself, then?" Harrison presses.

"So far, so good." I placate his concerns before looking around the room for the man in question. I still can't spot him.

"Excellent. He was a new man at golf this morning, so I hope that continues. Beth, we need to go over to the bar. I see someone we should have a chat with," Harrison says, already pulling her away.

"See you at the table later." I smile and watch as the two of them move as one across the room, like they own the entire country. I can actually picture them being the first family, and I am almost positive that Harrison should make a run for it in the next few years.

"Stunning couple, aren't they?" a man says, coming to stand next to me. I look at him, and like all men in this room, he looks dapper in his suit. His hair dusted with silver, his shoulders are broad, and he is very, very handsome.

"They sure are. Wonderful leaders of Maryland," I say with a smile.

"Geoffrey Newcomb," he says, extending his hand.

"Willow Valentine." I accept it, shaking firmly. His grip is solid, his hand large and encasing my own.

"I haven't seen you at one of these things before?" he prods subtly with a slight rise to his eyebrows.

"First time," I say, matching his grin. He is flirting with me, and while the woman in me is extremely flattered, I know exactly what he is. Trouble.

"Well, now I am glad I came," he says, taking a sip of his drink, his eyes sparkling in the lights as they run down my body and back up again. I can tell he is a man who always gets what he wants. I bet no one has ever said no to him.

"I'm fucking not." Tennyson's voice sounds from my other side, his hand warm as it runs around my lower back. His fingers curve around my waist and he pulls me slightly toward him.

"Tennyson," I growl at him as my brow crumples. This is not the professionalism I was expecting from him tonight. But his eyes continue to focus on Geoffrey.

"Thought you kept your distance from these things, Geoffrey." I look between the two men, their gazes locked on each other. Tennyson appears sober, but a little rattled.

"Tennyson," Geoffrey says, his shoulders now stiff, his lips pressed tight. He gives me a silent nod before he retreats and I spin around to face the problem.

"What the hell is wrong with you? You cannot go around this room greeting people like that," I hiss quietly.

"He is an asshole," Tennyson mutters, looking down at me. His hand remains, almost like he is staking his claim here in front of everyone. I should move, but I don't.

"It doesn't matter if he is or not, you still can't greet people like that," I tell him, my heart stammering in my chest.

Tennyson looks at me with thinned eyes. I match his stare, our silent disagreement oblivious to anyone else but us.

"Fine. Sorry," he mutters, offering me a half-assed apology. "Have you been here long?" His hand around my waist grips me a little tighter, tucking me in to him a little more.

"Not long. I arrived maybe ten minutes ago." I can't help but notice my voice is breathier.

"Hmmm, it didn't take him long then," Tennyson murmurs with a shake of his head as he looks over me. "You look..." His eyes dip, taking in my dress and the slight appearance of my leg as it juts out of the chiffon that runs like water down my body. "Like I need to take you out the back and trail my lips up your leg and bury myself in you for the rest of the night instead."

Any response gets stuck in my throat for a moment, my mouth parched, his words zinging straight through me. I am starting to see more and more that Tennyson is struggling not being able to get the one thing he wants. *Me.*

"You are very dapper yourself, Mr. Langford. But we are here to work. Remember?" I whisper, my eyes glued to his before we both seem to come to our senses and he slowly relaxes his arm. His grip is no longer possessive but gentlemanly.

"I have been here five minutes, and I already need a drink." I knew this would be tough.

"Oh, I brought you something," I say, remembering the small token I have in my bag. I pull it out and pass it to him, the keychain dangling in the light.

"A cupcake?" he asks, his brow furrowed.

"Yes. A cupcake. Put it in your pocket, and when you have the urge to do something you shouldn't, you grip on to this instead. Kind of like a stress ball."

"It is hard and glittery," he murmurs, taking the keychain and putting it into his hand, and I see little shimmers of glitter now coating his palm.

"It is. Something that you can feel in your hand, get your mind off whatever bad idea pops into your head at the time," I say, smiling as I see him pocket the little keychain.

"Ohh, I have lots of bad ideas. And dirty ones too," he whispers to me, his eyes searing into mine.

"Tennyson, hi!" a young blond woman almost squeals as she comes up to us, looking stunning with a bright-red smile and sparkling blue eyes. Full of energy and acting like she is a teenager, she lets out a little giggle as she approaches. I look at her and immediately know she is someone who knows Tennyson intimately. I stiffen, but Tennyson's hand grips around my waist again, keeping me close.

"Hi," Tennyson says with a nod, not saying her name and not introducing us, so I figure he can't remember who she is. I am not sure if that makes it better or worse.

"Hello, I am Willow Valentine," I offer her, and her gaze moves to me, her smile dropping as soon as it leaves Tennyson's face as she takes in how close we're standing.

"Hi, Katerina Newcomb." She introduces herself with words, yet her body language tells me she doesn't care who I am at all. I would like to say that I am not familiar with the type of woman Katerina is, but that would be a lie. Unfortunately, she isn't uncommon. Women like her are often surrounding rich businessmen, men who travel and cheat on their wives and usually do something they shouldn't before they end up calling me. I have come across her type before.

"Newcomb?" Tennyson asks, his eyes looking confused. "Any relation to Geoffrey?"

"He's my dad, silly. You know that," she says as she playfully claps her hand onto Tennyson's chest in a move that confirms they are very familiar with each other. She is too flirty, and I need to leave this conversation before I slap him. Jealousy coils on my insides, and I pinch my palm with my nails and take a breath.

"Oh, how wonderful," I say with a fake smile, turning to look at Tennyson, who now won't look me in the eye. Getting into bed with a range of women is one thing. Getting into bed with the daughter of your main business rival is entirely different.

"I need to freshen up. I will leave you both to chat," I say, gritting my teeth behind my smile.

"Willow..." Tennyson says, grabbing my elbow, his touch burning into my skin.

"I will speak to you later." I clutch my bag in my hand so tight I'm probably breaking the stitching. Pulling my elbow from his grip, I walk to the bar, following the same trail Beth made earlier. It isn't until I am ordering a glass of champagne that I feel someone come up beside me.

"Another cute couple. My daughter took a liking to Tennyson the minute they met. Even though she is in Kentucky at our ranch, her trips out here to see me are more frequent now. I thought perhaps she just missed being with her dad, but I soon realized that she comes to see someone else," Geoffrey says from beside me. The thought of Tennyson with anyone but me makes me feel sick. But I have no claim. I can't go there, no matter if I want to or not.

"Kids have a way of being sneaky like that," I offer, trying to shake off my anger at the situation and plaster on a fake smile that I have well practiced. I have no idea what kids are like, really, but if my little sister and Josh have taught me anything, it is that they only tell me the truth when they really need to.

"You have kids?" he asks, and I start to feel the familiar ache in my chest at the question. Since I have been single for a while, it isn't a question I get asked a lot. I want children. Desperately. My maternal instincts are strong, but who knows if I'll ever get to put them to use. While chatting to one of Tennyson's business competitors is not my idea of a good time, I don't see anyone else I know, so I perch myself against the bar and try not to look Tennyson's way.

"No. But enough experience with them to know that you give them an inch and they will take a mile," I say, and he laughs, making me smile. I take a sip of my champagne, needing the quench, and maybe even the buzz.

"Isn't that the truth. When Katerina was younger, she

snuck out of the house. I knew, of course, and had her followed and waited for her to get home. She tried to sell me some excuse that she was shopping for a Father's Day present. But I couldn't understand what shops would be open at eleven p.m. on a Friday night and why she needed the young boy down the road to help her." He chuckles at the memory.

"So she was a handful as a kid, then?" I ask, keeping the conversation going, my eyes looking from him to around the room and back again.

"Always has been. She has taken a shine to Tennyson. Not my ideal candidate for the job of being with my daughter, but I am afraid she has me wrapped around her little finger. I would do anything for her and to see her happy."

"My father is the same. Nothing is too much for his girls," I say, thinking of my dad whom I don't see enough of these days.

"I'm sorry if we got off on the wrong foot. Tennyson and I are business associates who don't always see eye to eye on things, so I apologize if I overstepped earlier." His apology takes me by surprise. I have read up a little on Tennyson's business and his competitors. From memory, Geoffery Newcomb is the main one vying against Tennyson in every aspect. The two of them obviously don't get along, yet maybe he isn't as much of an asshole as I assumed he was from the information that was given to me.

"Let's start over, then. Hi, I am Willow Valentine. I am here as a guest of Beth and Harrison." I offer my hand to shake.

"The pleasure is all mine, Willow, and I am glad I got to talking to you tonight." As his hand encases mine, we both smile. There is some activity across the room, and I see Tennyson's mother has arrived. Now that is a woman I have heard a lot about and one I already know is going to be a handful. I slip into work mode, and my protectiveness of my client and his welfare kicks in as I watch her saunter around the room like she owns it. I quickly look around for Tennyson, and I spot him over in the corner, chatting to his brother, Eddie, his eyes piercing mine. I don't miss the way his shoulders stiffen when his mother approaches.

"I'm sorry, Geoffery, if you will excuse me," I say with a small smile, and I leave my glass on the bar to walk over to the corner of the room.

It is time for me to play bodyguard.

19

TENNYSON

The night has barely started, and I already want to fucking kill someone.

"What's got your knickers in a twist?" Eddie asks from over his whiskey, one that smells amazing right about now.

"Nothing," I growl, not looking at him, not taking my eyes off Willow, who is laughing and smiling with Geoffery *fucking* Newcomb over near the bar. She looks amazing. That dress is almost painted on her, the slit up her leg doing nothing but teasing me and every other man in this room, and she doesn't even know it. Her eyes twinkle in the overhead lights, but I saw them cloud over when Kerry or Katrina or whatever her name is came over. It was a surprise to me that one of my bed fellows was the daughter of my archenemy—yet another fuckup I made. That list gets longer by the day.

I watch them both now with deep distaste on my tongue. It didn't take Geoffery long; the old bastard saw fresh meat when Willow walked in and is no doubt trying to get her into his bed. Which is not happening, because there is only one bed she belongs in, and it is mine.

"Ahhh, Geoffery Newcomb is here. Harrison and Beth's way of leveling the playing field in front of the Baltimore business personalities," Eddie says. "Or is it the fact that he is currently flirting with your publicity manager?" Eddie pushes me, and a growl vibrates from deep in my chest that startles us both. Eddie's eyes widen in surprise as he looks at me before his eyes flick over my shoulder and his face clouds over.

"Shit, don't look now," Eddie hisses, but it is too late. I see my mother walking toward us, and I want to run. It is my usual way of dealing with her, simply walking in the other direction. But given my back is against the wall and Eddie and I are holed up here in the corner, I have no escape route.

"Good evening, my youngest two." My mother's greeting is cold, distant, just like our relationship.

"Hi, Mom," Eddie offers, and she smiles at him. Her eyes then flick to me, and I remain silent, ramrod straight. I fucking hate her with everything in my being.

"Hello, Tennyson," she remarks, her lips pursing in displeasure.

"Mother," I grit out, my hands clenched in fists inside my pockets. I feel like I am about to explode. With a room full of guests, and Willow telling me to be professional, I greet her even though I don't want to. My hand grips on to the fucking cupcake that Willow gave me moments ago, and I feel it pinch into my palm.

"Oh, Tennyson, really." She scoffs at my lack of enthusiasm for her, and I am about to lose it. To hell with burning Harrison and Beth's business dinner with a public outburst.

"Really what, Mother?" I spit, and I feel Eddie tense beside me. This is the most my mother and I have spoken in years. The damage she caused to our relationship hit me young but has never dissipated. And usually when I see her, I am either drunk or I remove myself from her presence entirely. I want to scream. I want to yell. Without the whiskey or women to dull it, I found my voice, and I want to fucking use it.

"Tennyson, glad to see you can actually use that voice of yours, As your mother, I haven't heard it in what...? Since you were twelve?" my mother hisses and brings up memories that need to remain hidden.

I see Eddie out of the corner of my eye watching us both with interest, but I am burning hot. Anger, frustration, and every other negative emotion simmer to the surface of my skin. The need I have to rip this tie from my neck almost chokes me.

"You want to go there? Because I am fucking ready," I seethe, and I don't miss her eyes widen. Skeletons don't stay in closets forever and this one is ready to come out.

"Tennyson, don't be ridiculous." She waves her hand at me like I am being absurd smiling at some people walking nearby. God forbid, we are not the perfect family in everyone's eyes, even though our recent history is often splashed on every local newspaper in the state.

"Really? What—" I spit out before I stop. Warmth encases my arm, her body against my side in an instant, and I take a breath, smelling her scent. *Willow.*

"Good evening, Mrs. Langford. I am Willow Valentine, and I apologize for interrupting, but I am going to steal your son for a moment," Willow says, already pulling me away. My eyes are now on her, and my heart rate slows a little, my shoulders lowering slightly. I slip my hand into hers easily as we edge around the room, maneuvering between people. She is a woman on a mission, and I don't stop her, because right now I need air, I need space, and I know she will get me both of those. She leads me swiftly out into the corridor, into a nearby meeting room, and locks the door.

"God, I hate her. I fucking hate her," I tell Willow as I pace the room, running my hands through my hair before I yank at my tie, trying to get some air into my lungs.

"Breathe, Tennyson. Just try to relax." She comes to stand near me, and she is a brave girl to get this close to me when I am this angry. I would never harm her, but I feel on edge. I am brimming with hate and need to get it out.

"Relax? *Relax*? God, Willow, if you knew, if you knew what she really was," I say, undoing my top two buttons as she stands to the side, watching me.

"It's okay. You don't have to speak with her. You don't have to go anywhere near her," she assures me, her hands up in front of her chest like she is trying to tame a wild beast. Concern is laced in her features as she tries to help me calm down.

"That is very fucking hard to do when she is my mother. She is always there, always in my face, always digging into our lives. No doubt she is already trying to figure out exactly who you are and why you were holding my hand," I pant, trying to get air. The last thing I need is my mother coming near Willow. Hell will freeze over before that happens.

"Good. Let her see. I am not scared of her," Willow sasses, her hands landing on her hips, and I stop pacing to look at her.

"You are the first woman I have ever met who doesn't give a fuck that I am a Langford."

"Nope, your surname means nothing to me," she admits, and if I liked her before, then I idolize her now.

"She is so fucking deranged. Deluded. Horrible, conniving. I hate her. I just hate her." I am almost yelling, my hands clenching and unclenching.

"Okay, take some breaths," she says, her voice soothing, but I am so far gone, I can't rein it in.

"I can't," I admit, my voice almost panicked.

"Here, with me. Breathe in and then out." She steps forward and takes my hands. She watches me breathe a few times, but it isn't the breathing that is helping, it is her. And now my attention is only on one thing... what I want the most.

"Fuck," I yell out in frustration and step toward Willow, grabbing her around the waist and pushing her back against the wall. My forehead presses against hers, and I hold her hips tight. We are panting, her chest rising and falling in time with mine.

Her eyes widen as they look into mine.

"Tennyson," she whispers, her tone a mix of pleasure and warning, and it is nearly my undoing. I know I can't touch her. Not like I want to. But it is really fucking hard, especially because I know she wants me just as much as I want her.

"Fuck, I want you. I fucking want you, Willow. I have thought of nothing but you since that night months ago. I want you in my bed again. I want you screaming my name, moaning around my cock. I want to taste you, hold you, mold your skin to mine. I fucking *ache* for you," I grit out, barely hanging on, my fingers digging into her flesh as my pelvis presses into her. She makes me feel, for the very first time in a long time, and I don't want to run from it anymore. I want to run to it.

Her hands grab my upper arms, her body arching slightly into mine.

"Tennyson," she says again, her voice warning me, while her body is telling me something entirely different. I know she wants me, but the predicament we are in from a professional standpoint has clouded things. I don't let her finish.

"I know we can't. I know we shouldn't. I know you take your work seriously, and I would never jeopardize that. But God, Willow, what are you doing to me?" My voice is pained, like the feeling in my body.

Before she can say anything, there is a loud knock on the door.

"Tenn, everything all right?" Eddie yells. Obviously, he has gotten rid of our mother and is coming to check on me.

"Fuck," I groan, pulling back from Willow, frustrated that we got interrupted, but even more so at this entire night. I see her straighten her dress and hear her clear her throat. Our moment is lost.

"I want to go home," I say to her, defeated. Exhausted.

"Then let's go," she says, not asking questions. Not trying to get me to stay. It is then I realize she is on my side. My team. Here to help me. She has my back, and I will make sure she knows that I have hers too.

20

WILLOW

We both sit in comfortable silence as we relax in the back seat, each reflecting on the evening. By the time I got us out of the venue and into the car, Tennyson had calmed down. He was right on the brink tonight; I could see it. I could feel it. I am starting to learn that he is a passionate man with lots of layers. Telling me how much he wants me, though, that almost did me in. My heart hasn't raced like that for a very long time, and his declaration mixed with his proximity had my body almost jumping out of my skin.

I have no idea what it is about his mother that makes him so angry. I have done my research, and I know she isn't a nice woman. But to the extent that Tennyson gets upset, there must be more to it. It's very personal for him. Almost like it is raw and still carving into him. I'm not a psychologist but the deep-seated anger is probably what is pushing him and has created the reputation he now holds.

We lasted only forty-five minutes into the dinner

before we told Tennyson's brother, Eddie, to give our apologies, and we walked straight out the door to a waiting town car.

"Take a left here," I tell the driver, who looks from me to Tennyson, wanting his approval. Tennyson remains quiet, but nods. He glances at me quickly, then gazes back out the window. His shoulders are still stiff as his hand runs back and forth across his mouth, deep in thought.

"Just take the next left, and then pull over near the yellow building," I instruct the driver again, who nods this time, not looking at Tennyson for confirmation.

"Where are you taking me, Willow?" Tennyson asks with a sigh, his voice deflated. Any other client, I would have taken home straightaway. Probably called their manager or family member and told them where they went wrong. Tennyson is different. He is a client, but I care for him on another level. He is hurting, and I need to take his mind off things.

"You'll see," I say, not knowing if this will make him angry or not, but we need something to lighten the mood, and I didn't get dressed up for nothing. I give him a small smile, and his eyes soften.

He said a lot of things back in that room that are still swirling around in my head and between my legs. If Eddie hadn't interrupted, then who knows what would have happened. I think I was seconds away from shedding my dress and letting him bend me over.

The car pulls up right outside Softies, one of the oldest ice cream parlors in the world, taking me from my spiraling thoughts.

"Ice cream?" Tennyson asks, raising his eyebrows, his

lips curving upward. I know I made the right choice. Ice cream fixes everything.

"I heard that they have the best rocky road, and ice cream is really what we need right now," I say with a wide smile, glad to have him back to smiling too.

"You are what I need right now, Willow. If I need to eat ice cream to get you, then I'm okay with that. Let's go," he says quickly, not waiting for my reply, which is good because his words hit me in my chest. They are not the words of a playboy trying to get in my pants. He means what he says to me, I can feel it.

He steps out of the car, keeping the door open, and holds his hand out to me. The tension between us is still there. It is simmering, the raging inferno of earlier dimming a little, but not snuffed out. Taking my hand in his, I let him as he keeps me close, his body heat running up my arms. We walk inside, and I eat it up with my eyes. It is so fun and colorful. There is a small jukebox over in the corner, playing old-school tunes. A row of vinyl booths lines the long wall, the black-and-white-checkered floor and neon lights on the walls adding to the vibe of the place.

Luckily, it's quiet in here for a Saturday night. No need to be concerned about paparazzi or strangers snapping pics.

"Ahhh, hello, lovers, what can I get you?" an old man greets us from behind the ice cream selection as we walk up and take a look at all the flavors. But I already know what we're getting.

"Two rocky roads, please!" I say with a broad smile as I hold up two fingers, loving how even though he must be in his sixties, he is dressed up like an old-school ice cream server, with red and white stripes and a hat to match.

"My nanny brought me here as a kid," Tennyson says, not looking at me, but watching the old guy scoop the rocky road ice cream into cones.

"Really? You still remember?"

"I remember everything, Willow." He says it like it pains him. Like his memories are not good ones. "At the start of every summer. Mom didn't know. She wouldn't have approved. But my nanny was amazing like that," he adds with a smile.

"Here you go. On the house," the older guy says.

"Oh no, we can pay!" I say, not wanting to be in his debt.

"Don't be silly, you're all dressed up, so it must be a special night. Enjoy," he says before shuffling away as I call out a "Thank you." Tennyson and I take our cones and sit down in one of the empty booths along the wall, and I'm hoping he'll tell me a little more.

"So how long did you have a nanny for?" I ask, taking a lick of my ice cream and savoring the sweet taste on my tongue. Tennyson is quiet for a beat before he clears his throat.

"I had the same nanny from the moment I was born until I was about twelve. I then went away to boarding school," he says quietly, and it piques my interest.

"You must have been close. What was her name?" I ask again, not sure if I should push, because I feel like this is a sore spot for him.

"Helen. She was more like a mother to me than my

own, that is for sure." I notice his jaw's now tight, and so I move on to safer topics.

"So, how are those bed socks going for you? Is green your color?" I ask with a smile. I am sure he threw them out, but it was more of a joke gift anyway.

"Green was definitely my color tonight," he mumbles, admitting his jealousy. "How was your conversation with *Geoffery Newcomb* this evening?" he almost growls, and I hear him crunch on the rocky road pieces. Clearly, he's still not happy about me talking with Geoffrey. He is cute when he sulks.

"He was nice," I offer, trying to ensure I don't make it a bigger deal than it is. I know he is jealous, but he has no reason to be.

"Nice? He is my number one asshole. My main competitor. The continuous thorn in my side. You can't be flirty with him," he says, telling me how it is going to be.

"I was not *flirty*. I was being friendly. I can talk to whoever I want to talk to. It is important for business," I say, putting my stamp on things before taking a long lick of my ice cream. I need to keep the line of professionalism drawn. I can't step over, even though I really, really want to.

"Ahh, yes. Business. The sole reason we are here tonight, right?" he asks, calling me out on our little ice cream date. Would I do this with a normal client? No. But Tennyson is anything but normal.

"Tennyson. I can't be seen—" I start, trying to explain why we can't step over the lines, but he interrupts.

"You've got a little..." he says, pointing to his lip.

"Here?" I ask, wiping the side of my mouth with the napkin.

"Here," he says, sitting up and leaning over the table. Before I can even make sense of what he's doing, his hand grabs the back of my head and his lips smash into mine. My mouth opens on a gasp, and I fall into it for just a second, really feeling the softness of his lips, but then he pulls back just as quickly. I am left a little stunned, hot, and wanting more. My heart feels like it is going to thump right out of my chest as my knees shake. Nothing has ever felt so right as his lips on mine. Soft yet demanding. Cautious yet possessive. His hand on my head remains, our faces merely inches apart, and he looks deep into my eyes, searching them, looking for what, I don't know.

"I know you like control. I know you have full oversight of my life now and that is the way you work—by having full control of things. I know you are smart, successful, and as I have already established, beautiful. But let me tell you one thing, Willow Valentine. While you may control my life on the outside, I am calling the shots with us. In the bedroom, you are mine, and I can't wait for a repeat of New York. I will be patient, though. I will play this game of professionalism with you because I don't want to jeopardize your business, but be warned, whatever this is..." he says, his finger waving back and forth between us, "the flame hasn't flickered out after one night. If anything, it is burning hotter and brighter with each passing day, and you and I will combust, and I, for one, am absolutely looking forward to it."

I am left speechless as I watch him sit back in his seat,

smirking at me from across the table as he takes another big lick of his ice cream. He has always been open and honest about his feelings with me, and now he has literally told me exactly how he thinks things will go.

"We should finish up. We have the photo shoot this week and you need your rest," I say, clearing my throat, moving the conversation back onto safer topics. As we finish our ice cream and leave the restaurant, I am functioning on autopilot. His words roll over and over in my head, the kiss playing on repeat. My lips still tingle from the memory, and as I push through the door to my hotel, I flop on the bed, and it is then I realize that he is right. I will soon be putty in his hands.

Tennyson Langford is not the man everyone thinks he is. He is so much more.

21

TENNYSON

After I kissed her briefly in the privacy of our ice cream booth, I took her to her hotel and was a total gentleman when I said good night. Until I got home and took matters into my own hands, with her being on my mind ever since. It was good to have my lips on hers again, even if it was only briefly. She was quiet afterward, but I have come to learn that is how she processes. I know my words were correct. She wants me just as much as I want her. How she can act like the world didn't shift when we kissed, I don't know, but she hides it well. Better than me, because all I want to do is have my hands all over her.

Now, as our photographer, Natasha, gets into the groove, with tunes on in the background, me dressed in designer jeans and a tight white Henley top, I thought I would feel uncomfortable, posing in front of this small group of people, but I don't. Because Willow's eyes are firmly on me, and I can see her trying not to be affected.

But she is.

"That's it, Tennyson, just angle your head a bit to the left. You are a natural," Natasha says, before she lowers the camera and walks toward me. Placing her palm on my chest, she stands close, her eyes flicking up to mine as she runs her hand down my torso, smoothing the nonexistent wrinkles in my shirt before her hands rest on my belt buckle.

"How do you feel about a topless shot? I think it would be a great photo," she purrs. Her flirtations have been off the charts since I arrived. At first, I thought it was her manner, to get me relaxed in front of the camera and in the mood, but it has gotten worse as the shoot has gone on and seeing the whispers that travel around the room, I know she is coming on to me. Considering she works with male models often, I expected a little more professionalism and I suddenly admire Willow more because of her strong boundaries.

Any other time, Natasha would do it for me. I know all I would have to do is suggest a wardrobe change, and I could have her bent over the shoe rack out the back before I could count to ten. But my eyes rove over her shoulder to where Willow is watching. I am not sure when it happened or how, but my eyes are now on Willow and her alone. No other woman has the same effect on me like Willow does. But if looks could kill, both Natasha and I would've been dead thirty minutes ago. She is clearly not happy with the situation, so I decide to use it to my full advantage.

"Sure. Why not?" I say with a smirk, looking forward to showing Willow my body again. I also don't miss Natasha biting her bottom lip. "Just tell me what you want," I add, my voice silky and loud enough for Willow to hear. Willow's eyes crease, her mouth pressed into a thin line. She is trying hard to remain professional, but she is about to explode. I can feel it.

"Well, I think your jeans are fine, but let's lose the top. Let's show the women of Baltimore exactly what you are made of." Her hands under my top are already tracing the skin on my stomach, trying to lift it from my body. I stand back half a step to create a little distance, because I don't want to lead her on, even if I do see Willow now coated in a dark shade of green.

"I really don't think we need a topless shot," Willow interjects, stepping up to the set, cell phone in hand. I look at her shooting evil eyes at Natasha, but it is her white knuckles that give her away. She is gripping her phone so hard I am surprised it doesn't break.

"Oh, believe me, his female fans will love it. Even if he just uses it for socials, I can do it in black and white, and it will be tasteful." Natasha is coy and takes a few photos as she steps back to get in position, giving Willow no chance to respond.

Willow looks at me, and I shrug, but my eyes are firmly on her as I grab my shirt from the back of my neck and pull it over my head and off my body. I see her swallow, her eyes raking over my half-naked body as her cheeks redden.

"So hot, Tennyson. You are built from stone or something," Natasha calls out and makes me look in her direction. I tense my abdominals and run my hand through my hair, feeling equal parts like a moron, but also turned on because Willow's eyes are glued to me and I fucking love it.

I turn to face the camera and put my hand on my hips, laughing to myself. This is fucking surreal. Who even comes up with this shit? I have a million things to do at the office. I wonder what my brothers would think if they knew what I was doing right now.

"I think we are done here," Willow says, calling an abrupt end to the shoot. I give her a wink as Natasha comes up to me.

"I think we have it. Tennyson, those suits you had on earlier were amazing, but this, seriously... You need to be on the cover of some magazines, because wow," she says, subtly stepping into my side, right into my personal space, and I see Willow eyeing her closely.

"Thanks, Natasha. Will you have those over to me tomorrow? I want to see what I have to work with," Willow says, remaining professional, but I already know Willow won't use her again.

"Sure. I might even keep one of those last ones for myself, you know, for my portfolio?" she asks me, again biting her bottom lip as she looks up at me. I huff out a laugh. This woman is serious, and if she doesn't stop her shameless flirting, my girl is going to gouge her eyes out.

"Sure," I reply with a shrug like it doesn't bother me, but I know that Willow will never allow it. I grab my shirt and leave the two women to wrap up while I go in the back to change.

YOU COULD CUT the tension with a knife. Willow was quiet the entire drive, so I took the opportunity to reply to some emails, and now as I walk into my office, she is hot on my heels. I can tell by her strut she is upset.

"No interruptions, Melody," I say to my assistant as I walk past, opening my office door and letting Willow in first before I follow and lock the door behind me. I steel myself for her wrath.

"What the hell was that?" she seethes at me the minute my office door is closed.

"What are you talking about?" I ask, acting innocent, when I know exactly what she is talking about. My girl has a jealous streak, and I like it. I walk over to my desk, lean against it, and cross my arms over my chest and wait.

"Flirting with the photographer, have you no shame?" Her hands land on her hips, accentuating her curvy frame, and I clench my jaw as I take her in. Angry Willow is fucking hot. She means business. Not able to help myself, I push off the desk and walk up to her, standing right in front of her, my gaze lowering and tone serious.

"Why can't I flirt with the photographer?" For one, it was harmless, but two, Willow has made it clear that we are not to cross a line. So why should she care?

"Because it is so unprofessional. People talk, Tennyson," she says, stepping even closer, not backing down. I love the fire in her eyes.

"She is a nice woman, pretty too," I say with a shrug, sucking in my cheeks to keep from smirking at the combustible look in her face.

"Pretty? You think she is pretty?" she says, her voice pitching up an octave, again leaning closer. Our chests are almost touching, her breathing rapid, and I can feel her about to come undone. I *need* her to.

"Sure, she seemed to like what she saw too," I say, ready to punch my words in. "Seemed like a woman who knew exactly what she wanted and had no issues in going for it. I like that. Maybe if I—"

"Shut up and kiss me already," she cuts me off with a huff, and I don't hesitate. We fall into each other without a care for what we are doing or where we are.

I pull her to me, my hands grabbing her hips as I smash my lips against hers. Her hands wrap around my neck, pulling me to her, just as my tongue sweeps out and delves into her mouth. Tasting her, having her lips on mine, it feels even better than I remember.

"I feel like I have been fucking waiting an eternity for you," I murmur, our moves frantic, not dissimilar to in that hotel room in New York all those months ago. I'm not lying. I have imagined this moment many times over, but the thoughts don't even come close to the real thing.

"We need to lock the door," Willow pants, her hands already on my belt buckle as my fingers glide up her bare thighs, pulling up her dress.

"Door is locked already. But we need to be quiet, even though I want to make you fucking scream." Her dress now around her waist, my trousers already undone, her hand delves into my briefs. My breath hitches as she palms my cock, feeling all of me, hot, ready, and hard.

"God, I need this, I need you," she says breathily, and I grab her around her ass, turn us around, and sit her on my desk. I have had sex in a lot of places, but my office is not one of them. However, right now, I would fuck

Willow anywhere, my need to have her overcoming any moral sense I have left in my body.

"I need to taste you," I grit out. As good as it feels to have her touching me, I want my mouth on her even more. Dropping to my knees on the floor in front of her, I spread her fantastic legs and run my hands up the side of her thighs. I groan when I see a damp patch on her panties.

"God, you are so wet for me, Willow, so goddamn pretty," I murmur, taking it all in.

"Tennyson, please..." she begs, and I nearly come undone at her tone.

"Fuck." I kiss up the inside of her thigh, my hands on her ass squeezing her muscle and moving her closer to the edge. I don't wait. Pulling her underwear to the side, my mouth is on her in an instant, my tongue swirling, my lips sucking.

"Oh my..." Willow gasps out, her head falling back, and I look up at her from where I am between her legs. I am enraptured by her. Her hair flows behind her, landing on my desk. Her body arching, hands gripping the desk on either side of her. Her knuckles are white as her perfect tits jut out, begging for attention. Legs are wide and open for me, and she has me on my knees. I want to drown in her.

"You are so good at that..." she murmurs, biting her lip as her eyes find mine.

I close my eyes and suck on her bud, feeling her hips rock against my face. I never want this moment to end.

"Tennyson..." Her moaning my name is everything, but then her hand lands in my hair and her hips rock even more greedily. My girl likes my mouth on her, and I am glad, because it is fast becoming my favorite place to be.

"Come for me. Come on my face. Give yourself to me," I groan, my tongue and mouth working together in sync, and I hear her pants increase, her grip in my hair tightening.

"Tennyson... Oh God, Tennyson," she moans quietly before I hear a small high-pitched breath, and she shudders. I growl, feeling her orgasm around me, tasting everything that she gives me. I don't stop. My cock is hard and throbbing and I fucking need more of her.

"You look so fucking hot half-naked on my desk. I have no idea how the hell I am supposed to work here now without thinking about your perfect wet pussy," I grit out, standing in front of her while lowering my pants more and stroking my cock.

"Give me your cock. Now," she demands, reaching for me. All professionalism has flown out the window, her need for me just as high as mine for her. I grab my wallet and pull out a condom, rolling it on, loving her eyes on me the entire time.

She leans forward, her hand wrapping around me, and I grip on to my desk with one hand as my other runs up her body. I open her blouse a little, wanting to see her perfect breasts sitting high and pouty in a black lace bra that I already know is expensive, her scent wrapping around my nose and digging into my chest.

"I'll give you my cock any fucking time you want." I hold her underwear to the side and enter her in one swift movement.

We both moan simultaneously as I fill her. It feels like heaven. When I start to move, her hands grip my shirt as her legs wrap around my waist. I grab her ass, keeping her close to me, my movements now fast, pounding her so fucking hard I can't slow down.

"Are we going to stop pretending now and act like fucking adults?" I grit out to her, slamming into her over and over.

"Only if you promise to fuck me like this..." she moans, biting her lip, her eyes lust-drunk.

"I want this pussy every damn day. It's mine. I want to eat it, play with it, fuck it, make it clench, make it quiver. I want to push it to the edge, then let you explode. One night with you had your body engraved in mine. I want you for days, weeks, months. I want to be with you on the regular. Now let me make you come, Cupcake, because I'm in charge now, and I want to fuck you here on my desk before you spend the entire night in my bed. Do you understand?"

My tone is demanding, matching my movements. I want to own her. This woman who is ferociously independent, smart, sassy, sexy, and fucking managing things in her business like the boss that she is. I want her to beg, to moan, to pant, to come undone every single time I touch her. I want her to be mine.

"Yes, yes, I understand," she says on a moan as I move my hand to her clit, wanting her to come again.

"Are you going to be mine?" I ask, needing confirmation. Needing to hear her say it. My finger circling, teasingly so, holding her body for ransom, wanting her to come undone, but only when I let her.

"Yours, Tennyson. All yours," she says, her breathing rapid, eyes firmly on mine, and I can feel her about to come apart again. I grind my teeth, trying to savor the moment as she explodes. Looking right into each other's eyes, her face flushed, her body convulses around mine. It pushes me over the edge. As I slam into her, emptying myself, feeling her contract around me, I lean forward and put my forehead to hers. The two of us are panting, a light sheen of sweat glowing on our skin. That was the hottest sex I have had since New York, the fire in me that this woman sparks no longer a simmer, but a fucking raging inferno.

"Good girl, Willow. Such a good girl," I murmur before I kiss her like I need her more than air.

"Tennyson," she says, pulling away slightly. Her tone is unsure, our reality seeping back into our minds.

"I meant every word I said, Willow. This is happening. We are happening," I tell her, our bodies still connected, not wanting to leave her yet.

"Now who's being bossy?" she sasses with a small smirk, and a smile takes over my whole damn face.

"Don't you forget it," I say, kissing her again, ready for round two.

22

WILLOW

I'm his. Utterly and completely his. I tried keeping it professional, but all that did was make me want him more. I have wanted him ever since I met him in New York. The fact that I managed to keep my hands off him this long should be awarded. His eyes and mind have been on me and only me from the start. He knew what he wanted; he has been nothing but honest with me from the start, and as hard as I tried, there is no turning back for me now. My business will survive because I am excellent at what I do. But I don't think I could have carried on with life not giving this a chance. Not giving myself to this man. So I did, and now it is like a dam has broken and the water is rushing through—our need for each other is that overwhelming. We barely make it up to his apartment, the two of us mauling each other in the elevator. A private elevator in his office straight to his penthouse is not something I have seen before, but I have never been more grateful before in my life.

"I want to beat our record," Tennyson says, grabbing

my hand and leading me into his space. I have little time to admire it before his lips are on mine again, the two of us only having eyes for each other. The past month since we reunited felt like pure foreplay, as we both now dive straight over the professional boundaries I tried to set. The line I swore I wouldn't cross is now a mere blip in my vision.

"What record?" I ask, my voice almost a moan against his lips, his hands pulling at my dress, trying to get it off me.

"New York. You orgasmed five times," he says as we land in his living room, and he sits on the sofa, bringing me with him. I straddle his waist as he lifts the dress from my body, leaving me in my black lace underwear. His pants are long gone, his shirt already on the floor.

"I remember it vividly," I pant, my lips finding his as his hands trace my curves from my hips, up my waist before he molds my breasts.

"It is burned into my memory. You have already come twice downstairs, and you won't be leaving my bed in the middle of the night, so I am going for at least six." His head lowers as he kisses my chest, his hand pulling down my bra cup, exposing my nipple to him. He encases it, sucking on me, licking and flicking, as my body turns into mush on his lap.

"Promises, promises," I moan, my head falling back, his hands now wrapped around my back and holding me in place as his head is buried in my cleavage.

"Are you ready to bounce, Cupcake? Because I need these perfect tits in my face while you come on my cock," he says, his words making me even wetter.

"I am so ready..." I say, and I see his pupils dilate as a smirk curls his lips.

"Condom is in my wallet," he says, flicking his head to the side a little, and I spot his wallet nearby. Leaning over, his hands continue to roam over my bare skin as I grab his wallet and flip it open.

Sitting straight, he leans back on the sofa, his head falling back. He is relaxed as his eyes look over me, his hands running up and down my bare thighs. He watches me as I open the foil packet, taking out the rubber and slowly lowering it to his swollen head.

"I love you touching me," he hisses slightly as I roll on the latex, my hands gripping him, feeling him hard, hot, and ready between us.

"There is a lot of you to touch," I whisper, referring to his size, my hand not leaving him as I pump him slowly.

"Yeah, I'm all yours too," he says as his breath hitches, his eyes overtaken with desire as his hand sweeps across my hips and finds my center. He rubs me then, the thin piece of lace still between us, as he moves his thumb over my nub, drawing small circles.

"Come here." His fingers dig into my ass cheeks, lifting me and sweeping my underwear to the side, positioning himself under me.

"God, you are big," I pant out, my hands gripping his shoulders as I slowly slide onto him.

"You are perfect for me," he moans as I take him all the way. His hands run up my back to my bra, which he unclips and pulls from my body.

I slowly start to roll my hips. Finding a rhythm, his

hands land back on my ass, his fingers digging into my flesh, and he helps bounce, our skin slapping.

"That's it. Fuck, that feels good," he moans, his torso muscles clenching, his arms keeping me steady.

"I need…" I pant, not wanting to stop because it feels so good.

"What? What do you need?" he asks, attentive, even now.

"The lace. I need it gone," I moan as I rock on him, needing the friction, the lace of my underwear starting to annoy me. I feel his hand move then, my underwear ripped from my body, and he pulls the thin lace from my hips and throws it across the room.

"Now I want you to come on my cock," he says, his voice deep, as his hand grabs my breast and he lowers his mouth, encasing my nipple again, the feeling shooting through me to my core.

"Oh God," I moan, speeding up my rhythm, chasing the high.

"I fucking love your body," he mumbles from where his head is buried.

"Tennyson…" I whimper, about to come, his words, his hands, his desire almost all-consuming.

"I've got you, Willow." His lips find mine, his hand on the back of my neck, pulling me to him.

"Tennyson, I'm going to—" I pant, moaning as our foreheads meet, our eyes glued to each other. The swirl of emotions between us is intense.

"Come for me, Willow, come on my cock," he demands, and I lean back. As his hands land on my waist, he lifts me on and off him like I weigh nothing, my body now humming entirely into another universe, and I do as he asks.

"Tennyson. Oh God…" I pant over and over as my orgasm rushes through me.

"Fuck, Willow," I hear him grit out, then he roars so loud as he comes with me that it echoes around the room, his hands squeezing my flesh as he thrusts into me, giving me everything.

He falls back onto the sofa, pulling me with him, and I lay on his chest. The two of us are panting, a light sheen of sweat on our bodies as we come down from our high. My head rests in the crook of his neck, and I look out his living room window, seeing the cityscape below.

"Tennyson?" I say quietly, the impact of what we are doing now hitting me. This isn't sex. This is more. Much more. I have no idea what it is, having not ever experienced anything like this before.

"I know, Cupcake. I know," he says as his hand runs up and down my bare back, strumming my skin. Our breathing is now synchronized, his hand not wavering, and we sit here with each other, naked, in each other's arms, both of us deep in thought.

23

TENNYSON

I delivered on my target. We are up to six already, and even though it is late, we are both still wide awake. I love making her come. I think it might be my favorite thing to do. In fact, there is a lot I love about this woman. I love a challenge and the fact that she keeps pushing me, whether in my work, in my personal life, or just with her fiery banter. I get off on it. I get off on her.

After making her come on my tongue in the shower, I watch her from where I stand in the bathroom. She lies on top of my bed, completely naked, looking better and better every time I see her.

"You owe me two pairs of underwear," she murmurs.

"Two?" I ask, smirking, walking to the door and leaning against the frame.

"You took my underwear in New York, and you ripped the ones I had on today," she says, smiling at me.

"I'll buy your some more, because I can guarantee you that I will be ripping the majority," I tell her, because the urgency I have around her is surprising. I can hardly wait until she is naked to have her. I lean against the bathroom door, watching her. Enamored.

"Have you ever bought women underwear before?" she asks me, and the question stalls me for a beat.

"No. Never," I say, wondering where this line of questioning is going.

"Never, ever?" she asks, her eyebrow rising.

"Never. Ever. But it sounds like I am about to start."

"Have you ever bought a cupcake for a woman before?" I smile as I think about that lemon cupcake I got her when I interrupted her date.

"No. Can't say I have ever bought that either," I tell her honestly.

"How many times have you flown a helicopter to save a woman from her disaster of a date?" she quips, giving me a little smile, clearly liking this game of researching my previous history with females.

"Only once. Flew it to DC to rescue this girl who is the most beautiful women I have ever seen. She is funny too. And smart. She is a successful businesswoman, yet is perfectly at ease cooking cupcakes in her kitchen. She can run a business meeting with her eyes closed, yet wear adorable fuzzy socks to bed every night," I tell her, unable to help the wide smile that comes to my face.

"Wow, she sounds like a catch," she teases.

"She is, and I am the lucky bastard who caught her. I also don't plan on letting her go."

"Is that so?" she smarts, her eyes lighting up.

"That is a fact." I cement my feelings and ensure she knows. My eyes trail up and down her body, burning this vision of her into my brain.

"What are you looking at?" she asks, her voice sleepy, but I haven't finished with her yet.

"You. Your body. How good you look in my bed. The way your hair flows like water around your shoulders. Your curves, your perfect tits, your amazing ass. All of you. I am looking at all of you," I say, not sure how I've become so addicted to her. But I am.

"Tennyson..." she moans as her hands rub her face. Her cheeks tint, and I smile.

"You keep moaning my name like that, and I am not sure I can be much of a gentleman anymore."

"What do we do now?" I know she is worried. We have both now thrown caution to the wind and are taking what we want, but that doesn't make the reality of our issue any less serious.

"We be together. We don't have to flaunt it, but I am not going to be hiding it either." There is no way I can keep my hands off this woman, so people are going to find out eventually. I hear her belly rumble.

"I'm hungry..." she says, her hand slapping across her bare stomach.

"I have something you can feast on," I offer. I should get us some food, but right now, I am hard as a rock, and I need to alleviate that issue before I get busy in the kitchen.

"Are you ever sated?" I can tell by the smile on her lips she is toying with me.

"Not with you." I watch her naked chest rise and fall rapidly.

"Well, are you just going to stand there all day or

come show me what you got?" she says, and I like sassy Willow. Sassy, sexy Willow.

I throw my towel down and the cool air brushes across my naked frame as I walk toward her and come to a stop, standing at the end of the bed.

"I like you in my bed," I say as my eyes roam over her naked body, having not yet gotten my fill. We have been with each other for hours. The rendezvous in my office earlier this afternoon has now been overtaken by the darkness of the night. My eyes rake over her brown locks, her glowing skin, her long, shapely legs, and her curves. Her fucking curves make my mouth water every time I look at them. Her amazing tits sit high and perky. Her waist skimming in just a little, soft, round, feminine. Her hips dip back out, her ass round and full, and her thighs I want permanently around my neck. They are thick, and I want to bite them to mark her, then suck them to soothe her.

She trails her fingers up over her round hips, tracing her curves before lowering them again. She is teasing me, her eyes alight with arousal that, like mine, hasn't dampened. This woman matches me for everything and takes everything I give her and more. My hand moves to my cock, which despite all the activity, is full and thick, and she watches me as my hand wraps around it. Giving it a few pumps, I see her bite her lip, and I can barely contain the groan that rises from my throat. I ache for her. Physically, I can feel this weird pull in my chest, and I wonder if she will actually give me heart failure.

My eyes are glued to her as she sits up on all fours and crawls across my bed, over to the side where I am standing. Her back dips a little, her hips swaying, like a cat stalking her prey, and the need I have to make her purr is all-encompassing. I keep up the pace of my hand, my dick standing at full attention. As she comes closer and watches the movement, her expression heats.

A little precum leaks from my tip, and she doesn't hesitate. Leaning over, with her ass high in the air, she flattens her tongue, licking my tip, tasting me, and my knees nearly buckle.

"That's my girl…" I murmur as she bends down again, taking the tip of me into her mouth. I move my hand, letting her mouth take over. I have no idea what she is doing to me, but if she keeps this up, I am going to come harder than a teenage boy who saw his first set of tits.

"Fuck, your mouth feels good," I murmur as I caress her back, rubbing my hand up and down her spine, before I grab her ass tight, needing her in my hands. Needing to touch her, feel her, ensure that she is real. My breath quickens with her pace, and she lowers even more, taking more of me into her mouth. It feels fucking amazing. She moans then, her tongue swirling, the sound running down my length and hitting my balls. Her lips and mouth take all of me. I am starting to learn that this woman is talented at perhaps everything she touches. Including the way she sucks me down her throat like I am the best thing to ever touch her lips. I reach around to cup her breast, pulling and tweaking her nipple. They pebble, and I know she is turned on. She has been wet for me all night, our need for each other obvious.

"Good girl. You're a good fucking girl. You've got a fucking amazing mouth, Cupcake," I murmur, between the panting breaths I now need to take. I see her hips squirming, and I know she needs more. My filthy words are doing things to her body that I know she enjoys. As if to prove my point, she licks up and down my shaft, and my hand lands on her head as I gather up her long hair in my fist.

"You taste so good..." she breathes out, and I pull her hair tighter, and again, she meets me, by taking me in even farther, so I touch the back of her throat.

"Just like that. You look fucking beautiful with my cock in your mouth," I moan as my hips start to move a little, and I speed up my rhythm, sliding my length in and out of her warm, wet mouth.

I pull her hair even tighter as my other hand grips the back of her head, keeping her with me. This vision I have of her will never be erased. It is the hottest thing I have ever seen. She is still leaning forward on all fours, her round ass high in the air, as I see her quivering for more.

"Touch yourself. I want you to come with my cock down your throat." She does exactly what I ask her and puts her fingers on her clit as she moans around my cock. I am now setting the rhythm and pace, gripping her head and thrusting in her mouth as she massages her clit and continues to moan around me.

"Fuck, Willow. You look fucking beautiful. Come for me. Fuck your fingers while I fuck your face." As soon as the words leave my lips, she lets go. Her orgasm washes over her, and I feel her throat relax as I move faster before I come too.

"Fuck, fuck. Fuck!" I yell into the room as I come down her throat, and she moans as she swallows, my body and mind now exhausted. My grip relaxes, and I brush her hair away from her face and down her back. I can't stop touching her, and I watch her pull back and sit on her knees, then she looks up at me, her lips swollen, her eyes heavy, her chest heaving.

"Fucking beautiful," I growl again as I lean forward, gripping the back of her neck and pulling her to me, kissing her hard. Our lips don't part as I climb onto the bed, laying her down on her back and peppering kisses from her lips, down her throat and collarbone, and back again. I just came, but I can't get enough. When it comes to her, I am always hungry.

"Tennyson." She giggles, and I pull back with a smile.

"What?" I ask, my smirk fully in place. I am so fucking happy.

"I need food, then I need sleep. I don't think my body has had this much of a workout since..." She trails off, her cheeks blushing slightly.

"Since?" I ask, wondering what she is going to say.

"Since New York," she breathes out, and I feel relieved. Relieved that I am the only man to get her like this. The last one she's had.

"Well, I better feed you, then I will tuck you in tight," I say, smiling, because she is right; as much as I want to be with her over and over again, we need food and sleep. It is late, and I can rest easy knowing that I got her to seven. A new record, and one I hope to beat in the near future.

$\sim$

IT'S RAINING. The sound is nonexistent in my penthouse, but the view out my bedroom window is dark and gloomy, the droplets hitting the glass before they slowly drip down. My eyes are wide, my mind alert, yet my body relaxed as the woman next to me snores softly. I feel content. For the first time in a long time, I slept all night, not waking once. Now my bed is warm, her body is soft, her snores sweet, and I itch to kiss her lips that puff out with every exhale she takes.

"I can feel you looking at me," she says, and I grin. Nothing gets past her.

"Making sure you don't run away again," I say jokingly, although there's a little bit of truth to my statement. Her eyes open slowly, and she looks right at me.

"I'm not running away. I'm not leaving. I could get used to this comfy bed and all the orgasms you deliver," she says, her mouth curving into a smile, and I laugh.

My hand dangles near her shoulder, and my fingers strum up and down her arm, brushing her soft skin. I don't want to move. I have to go into the office today. I have meetings scheduled, and after leaving early yesterday, I am acutely aware that the paperwork I have to do has probably doubled in size.

"How did you sleep?" I ask her, because like me, I think she was out cold.

"Heavy. So good. You?" she asks what is to her an innocent question, but to me, it carries weight.

"Surprisingly well," I say honestly.

"Why surprisingly? Do you not usually sleep well?" I forgot how smart she is. Always picking up on what I don't say rather than what I do.

"No, not really. I think the last time I slept well was in New York." I give her the truth. There is something about lying here, the two of us totally naked, that has me wanting to give her nothing but my honesty.

"Really? Why is that?" she asks, and I shrug.

"A lot on my mind, I guess. Speaking of which, I took your advice," I tell her, my mind running.

"Which advice was that?"

"Singapore. It was a good idea. I have our scouts over there, and they are already teeing up meetings." I'm feeling highly optimistic about this move and one I need to speak to my brothers about.

"That's good? Right?" she asks, a small smile playing on her lips.

"Yeah. So far. I might have to make a trip over there in the next few weeks, to help things along." That is how I usually operate, but suddenly, I don't want to leave Willow for even a moment.

"Well, that will be our focus in the interview with *Business News* that we have coming up. You can talk about breaking new ground and Langford Construction entering new markets. We don't have to go into details, but it will show leadership, innovation, strength, and resilience," she says, and I watch her and can see her mind working overtime right along with mine. Her quick thinking and insights make her look even more desirable, if that's even possible.

"You will be there?" I ask her. I hate interviews and hate being put on the spot, so I would like her to run interference if I need it. That, and the fact that I just want her with me. All of the time.

"Of course. But I do need to get up and go home this morning. My sister comes home today, and I haven't seen her in a few weeks," she says, her hand coming to rest on my cheek, her thumb brushing against my skin. It feels nice lying here like this. I haven't done this before. It is new. I usually jump out of bed, not giving my sexual partners any morning chatter or caresses. But Willow is different. I am different with her.

"Well, before you go..." I lean down and take her lips in mine. I kiss her slowly. Taking my time. Pulling her closer to me, her body melts into mine. I run my hand up and down her naked torso, feeling all of her as she maneuvers her legs, wrapping one around me. My hand lowers down her middle until I hit her core, and I dip my fingers inside. Warm, wet, and ready.

"I'm going for a new record," I whisper on her lips.

"Oh yeah?" she asks, her voice hitching as I rub her clit.

"Yeah. I think we can get two more in before you need to leave." She moans lightly and bites her bottom lip as my fingers find a rhythm.

"I think that sounds like a good idea." Just as her body arches and her breasts hit my chest, I lower my mouth. Hitting my target that morning, making it a solid nine orgasms for my girl.

24

WILLOW

I'm home. Showered and content, even though my body is a little achy in places it hasn't been for a very long time. As I sit tapping on my laptop, I feel the familiar sense of foreboding rise up my throat. I crossed the line. There is no going back. Have I done the right thing? I feel like it is the right thing. I want him. He wants me. We are adults. I smile to myself as I think about last night. How good it was. How good we are together. I let go of the breath I have been holding and try to rid my body of the remaining stress over the situation. Will this damage my reputation? Being with a client? I try to think of other people in similar situations and some have worked out and others haven't, but in all cases, their businesses haven't been affected. Not long term anyway.

I shake my head to dislodge the thoughts as I put the finishing touches on the monthly report. It is hard to believe I have already been working with Tennyson for over five weeks now, and looking at everything we have achieved, I am proud of the progress we have made. No more drunken one-night stands, no more paparazzi photos of him with a different woman or leaving a hotel in the morning, looking worse for wear. The press attention he is getting is all positive, with great photos and inspiring stories about his philanthropy, even touching on the good relationship he has with his brothers.

I add in the social media highlights and go through the email from my digital manager to ensure I haven't missed anything, and that's when I see a small note from her to check his messages. I save the file I am working on and jump into his Instagram, wading through the messages that come up—all from women, some from a few men, none of whom have any shame in what they are proposing. I am sure deleting and blocking them is a daily job for my team, unfortunately. I see a few left for me to review and I click through. I chew my lip as I see a familiar name, Katerina Newcomb. Clicking on the message, she's reaching out this week asking to see Tennyson. That on its own is not anything to be too concerned about, as she made it clear a few weeks ago at the business dinner she was more than interested. But I see two more messages, each one sounding more desperate than the next. I delete them and make a mental note to talk to Tennyson about it. While I don't love the idea of him talking to other women, especially now that we are involved, I am an adult. I can deal with it.

As I finish up, the doorbell rings. I'm not expecting anything, but I rush to the door and see a delivery man waiting.

"Hello?" I say, opening the door.

"Willow Valentine?" he asks.

"Yes, that's me." I smile, thinking maybe Saide ordered something.

"Sign here, please." I sign the digital screen, and he passes me a box.

"Thank you," I say, but the man is already walking away, no doubt in a hurry to get to the next stop.

I look at the box as I close the door. It has my name on the front, but there is no other label that tells me where it is from. Walking to the kitchen, I rip it open to find a luxurious cream box with thick cream ribbon. La Perla.

My heart races as I pull it out and open it. Black lace underwear. A few matching sets in black and red and white, along with a beautiful lace nightdress that feels so heavenly soft, I am not sure I could even wear it. I look further and see a note and pull it out.

I want to rip these off you and kiss every inch of the beautiful body underneath.

As I feel the soft silk in my fingers, a smile comes to my face. I know I have done the right thing. I am done questioning it. It is happening. Tennyson and I are happening.

"Oh good, you're home," Saide says, and I jump, having not heard the front door open. I scurry to put the note away, my palms sweating and my heart racing. How is he even capable of that when he is not even here? The front door slams shut, and I get everything back in the box before her luggage rolls on my floorboard toward me.

"Hey, welcome home. How was your trip?" I ask my standard question and clear my throat, my voice betraying me a little.

"He broke up with meeeee," she whines, and I see my baby sister looking like a hot mess, tears streaming down her face, her eyes swollen and her face red and blotchy.

"Oh, honey," I say softly, rushing over and hugging her, my mind now on her as my top is wet in an instant from her tears. I can't say I am not relieved, but I hate seeing her like this regardless.

"Come, let's sit and you can tell me all about it," I say, keeping my arm around her and leading us to the sofa.

"What is there to say? He broke up with me because his wife is pregnant. He is going to be a father," she wails, and even though I know she saw him often, I had no idea she was this serious about him.

"I am sorry that it didn't work out, Saide."

"No, you are not. I know you are dying to say 'I told you so,' so go ahead, say it," she smarts, still looking miserable.

"No, Saide, I may not have approved, and it was always going to be a hard situation, but I never want to see you upset like this," I tell her, and she starts wailing again. I hug her for a bit and let her get it all out before her tears slow and her sniffles lessen.

"Why don't you go up and shower and change. I am sure I have the ingredients for death by chocolate cupcakes to make us a batch." That's her favorite.

"Can you make two batches? I want to eat my feelings and sit on the sofa and wallow in self-pity for a while," she says, her lips quirking up at the side, and it is then I know she is going to be okay.

"Sure, two batches, and maybe some red velvet as well." She knows I would do anything for her. Including chaining myself to the kitchen for the next few hours to bake and ice her favorite cupcakes. She smiles and jumps up to grab her bag and starts walking to her room.

"Oh, and when I come back, I want you to tell me all about last night," she says, giving me a cheeky look.

"Last night?" I ask her, pretending I have no idea what she is talking about.

"You can't fool me, Willow Valentine. You have that post-sex glow going on, and I want to hear all about it," she says, looking at me and waiting for me to refute her claims, but I remain silent, which tells her everything she already knows.

"And I also want to see what is in that box that has you so hot and bothered," she adds, thinning her eyes at me. I can't keep anything from her. She can read me like a book.

"It's just some clothes…" I wave her off, pretending that it is nothing as my cheeks tint pink.

"I see cream ribbon. La Perla is not just clothes." She looks at me accusingly.

I can't stop the stupid smile as it hits my face and her eyes light up in delight.

"Good. At least one of us is having amazing sex!" she yells out as she walks down the hall, and I laugh, glad to have her back home.

25

———

TENNYSON

I have no idea why I am here. Why do I even bother? Why do any of us do it? I look around the table, and none of us boys seem happy with this. Yet we come and have dinner with my mother every month. We make sure she is alive and try our best to keep her in line. If nothing else, seeing her ensures we are usually on top of anything she has planned so we can get ahead of it and limit the negative media. She usually loves to sprout about her latest foray into society, so we can pick up any little issues before they arise.

"Are you just going to sit there with a sour look on your face, Tennyson, or are you going to eat that prime cut steak in front of you?" my mother almost snarls from across the table. I grind my teeth and look at her. My body is tense, my shoulders stiff, and I need a fucking whiskey.

"I haven't seen you since you left Harrison's business dinner early with that brunette. I can't say I am surprised, but you really should wait until after formal proceedings before you run off with your floozies, Tennyson." She pushes my buttons on purpose, I am sure of it.

My eyes flick to Harrison, and he looks at me and shakes his head, silently telling me that he doesn't care about the business dinner and to ignore her. My teeth grind, my jaw almost cracking under the pressure. Her eyes flick to mine, and we stare at each other for a beat. The more I look at her, the more the memories come back. Keeping my distance from her has enabled me to push everything out of my mind, but I haven't had a drink for over a month. I'm sleeping better, eating better, enjoying life more, enjoying time with Willow. And that means the brain fog I had swirling for years is clearing and the memories I've ignored are starting to surface. I just can't get a firm grasp on them yet.

"Can anyone here tell me why we still come here and sit through this shit?" I ask everyone and no one. My brothers are silent, but their eyes are on me.

"Tennyson!" my mother berates me, and I clench my jaw even harder.

"What, Mother?" I push her. I hear one of my brothers gasp, probably shocked that I am actually conversing with her.

"Do not speak to me in that tone," she seethes.

"Or what? Is that a threat?" We both know it is.

"It's called respect."

"Respect? Respect!?" I raise my voice. She doesn't have the first idea about respect. I go from zero to one hundred when she is around. It is like a natural instinct I have with her. My defenses come up immediately. It is not even a conscious decision at this point. It is like my mind's way of protecting me.

"Calm yourself, son," she warns, thinking she has the upper hand, but little does she know, I am not the same boy I once was.

"Or what, Mother?" I see a little fear in her eyes, but blink and I would have missed it. She now knows I mean business. I am not afraid of her. Not anymore.

"Tennyson Langford, mind your manners," she yells at me, and I have had enough.

"I'm out, fucking done." I push my chair back with such force, it falls onto the floor. I throw my napkin on top of my plate, not touching a piece of food she serves. I don't trust her; she probably would poison it.

Stomping out the door, I hear my brothers yell out for me, but I ignore them all. Slamming the front door behind me, I strut to my car, and I am out of her driveway in a flash. I have never been so on edge to leave her place. I pay no attention to where I am going.

My mind runs on autopilot. Memories flood me, and I rub my eyes, trying to remove the images that filter through my mind, but they remain. They all lead to Nanny Helen. The woman who raised me. The woman I really wanted to call Mom. The woman who helped with my homework, fed me dinner, read me bedtime stories, and patched my cuts and bruises.

I put on the radio, turning it up loud to drown out the noise in my head, grinding my teeth, feeling like I need to punch something. I slam my hand against the steering wheel, once not being enough, so I do it again and again. Zooming in and out of the traffic, snaking my way through the streets and along the freeway, I start to settle. The farther I get from her house, the more my body starts to relax. My phone rings, and I see Harrison's name, but I ignore it. Steering the car around the corner, I drive into the quiet residential street and pull over to the side and park. Turning off the car, I look up at Willow's cute little house, the lights on inside. It looks warm, inviting, safe, welcoming.

I haven't had a girlfriend before, and I am not sure if that is what Willow is. We haven't labeled it, but I know if she dated anyone else, I would kill them. I sit in silence, looking at her door. I sent her a box of her favorite underwear, not just because I have ruined a few, but because I want her wearing something from me every day. That way, even when I am not with her, she has me all over her body.

I sigh and rub my head. I should leave. She was with me all last night. She wanted to spend time with her sister. She would be tired. Probably sore. But right now, my body aches to see her. My phone ringing startles me. Willow's name flashes on the screen, and I don't hesitate.

"Hey," I answer, still looking at her house like a creeper.

"Are you going to come in, or just sit outside like a stalker?" she asks, and I huff a laugh. Why doesn't it surprise me that she knew I was here?

"I didn't know if you were awake or were up for visitors," I say, giving her an out if she wants it.

"Come in. I'm baking. You can be my taste tester." I unclip my seat belt and step out of the car immediately at the invite.

"On my way," I say, ending the call and walking up her path, her door opening before I reach it.

"You okay?" she asks, looking sexy as fuck with an apron on, with her hair tied up in a topknot, a bit of flour on her nose.

"Better now," I tell her honestly, my arms automatically finding her waist and pulling her to me. I bury my head in her neck and suck in her fantastic aroma, the stress, pain, and heartache leaving instantly.

"Good." She smiles wide before I take her smile with my lips. I kiss her slowly, feeling the desire deep within.

"Jesus, wasn't nine enough already?" I hear a woman's voice from behind us, and I pull away from Willow. I cough a laugh, and Willow stares at the woman with lasers shooting from her eyes.

"Tennyson, this is my sister, Saide. Saide, this is—" Willow says before Saide cuts her off.

"The man who delivers more orgasms than an entire army. Yes, I think I caught on to that," she says, waltzing up to me with an outstretched arm. She is smaller than Willow, with long hair too, young, a total knockout, but she doesn't hold a flame to the woman currently in my arms. She is funny as hell, though.

"Nice to meet you, Saide," I say, keeping one arm around Willow and stretching out my other to take in her handshake.

"Likewise. Just in time to get a fresh cupcake before I eat them all." I look down and see a plate of about six chocolate cupcakes in her hand.

"They look good," I say, smiling at Willow, who is now tucked into my side.

"Yeah, well, get your own. These are mine. I need to eat my feelings away," she mumbles before turning and walking into the living room. I see the kid already in there too, and he gives me the evil eye over the top of the sofa.

"Hey, kid," I throw out at him. I don't think he likes me much, but I plan to stick around, so he needs to lighten up.

"Whatever," he murmurs, before shoving a cupcake in his mouth, and he and Saide tune into the show they are watching on TV.

"Sorry, she is a bit out of sorts. Jacob broke up with her," she says, leading me into the kitchen.

"The married guy?" I ask, because that is surprising.

"Apparently, he is going to be a father."

"Shit." I wince. No matter how good a relationship is, that kind of news could hurt. As I walk into her kitchen, I pause and look over everything.

"Errr, do I dare ask?" I say, surveying the room. There are cupcakes everywhere. Chocolate, red velvet, all looking like they belong in a five-star bakery.

"I made Saide's favorite, and then Josh wanted more for him and his mother, so..." She shrugs, and I chuckle.

"Tell me something?" I ask, walking to her, my arms automatically wrapping around her waist again and pulling her close.

"What's that?" she says, looking up to me with a bright smile, her hand running up my arms. I love making her smile.

"What is your favorite flavor?" Because I would hazard a guess that it isn't chocolate nor red velvet. She giggles then, her bright eyes sparkling at me.

"Lemon," she states, and my eyebrows rise.

"The flavor I got you at the small restaurant in DC?" I question. I only got lemon, as it reminded me of her. Bright, sunny, friendly, and a pleasant mix of sour and sweet.

"Yep. It is fresh, tangy, and delicious. Now sit down. Let me make you a coffee and get you a cupcake. If you don't eat them, Saide will, and she will have a stomachache for a week," she says, still looking after everyone else but herself. I take a seat at the counter and watch her move about the kitchen.

"You know the last person I watched bake like this was Nanny Helen," I say, not sure why the thought pops into my head, but I guess I haven't been in a busy kitchen like this since I was a kid.

"Oh yeah? Tell me more about her." I can tell she's interested as she looks back at me, multitasking while making us coffee.

"She was like you, used to love baking. Cakes, breads, pastries..." I say, thinking back to when I was a kid. "I would rush home from middle school and be greeted by the smell of baked goods the moment I walked in the door."

"What was your favorite thing that she made for you?" Willow asks, sidling up to me, pushing the coffee and cupcake in front of me and leaning on the counter.

"Every Friday, she used to make me a classic New York cheesecake. We would both take a slice and sit outside, and I would tell her all about school, my friends, and everything else in between. We would debrief from the week. She would laugh at my jokes, give me advice. It was the best." Staring off into the distance, I take a moment to live in my thoughts. "The last time I ever had that cake was when I was twelve. It was the last time she made it for me before she died." Sadness sweeps over me with a vengeance.

"I'm sorry you lost her. How did she die?" Willow asks, her brows furrowed as her hand reaches over to cover mine.

"If you had asked me that question a few years ago, I would have said heart failure..." I murmur, looking at her seriously now.

"And now?" Willow presses, and I snake my arm around her waist and pull her closer to me.

"I would say I am not sure anymore." I offer her the only explanation I have.

"Did something happen to her? An accident or something?" I can see the confusion in her eyes. But that is the problem. I can't remember all the details. I was young, impressionable, and only now am I starting to remember bits from that day, but none of them add up.

"Yeah, I was young. I can't really remember, but for some reason, my memories are coming back, and I just get a sinking feeling that things are not as they seem," I say on a sigh.

She looks at me for a beat and thankfully drops the subject.

"Okay. Well, no cheesecake here, only cupcakes," she says, pulling away and opening a drawer.

"Well, there is really only one cupcake I love to eat," I tell her with a cheeky grin.

"I heard that!" Saide screams from the living room

and my eyes widen. I totally forgot there were people here.

"Here, put this on." Willow throws an apron at me. I hold it up. It is pink with frills.

"What for?" I look at her as though she is crazy for even suggesting it.

"Because I would hazard a guess that suit you have on is designer and you are about to get busy." She slides some empty bowls across the counter.

"I have never baked anything in my life..."

"I don't doubt it. Here, measure out the milk." Pushing the milk across to me, she gets busy measuring out the flour. I get a picture of what my life may be like with her. The TV blaring in the other room, her being a domestic goddess, and me just trying to keep up. It is complete contrast to my current lifestyle, yet I can't help the smile that is cramping my face.

She makes me happy, and baking is her thing, so I pull on the frilly apron, roll up my sleeves, and get to work.

26

WILLOW

I watch Tennyson in his designer suit, looking every bit the billionaire that he is. He's sharp, his eyes clear and alive, his skin glowing. It's in stark contrast to how he looked when I was first hired. I feel proud of him, of us, for getting him to be the best version of himself. This is why I love my job. This is why I do what I do. Tennyson is right. I love to rescue people, help them and then see them shine.

Tennyson is currently being interviewed by a journalist from *Business News*, this feature recorded to stream to the business community nationwide. It is a big deal, a great opportunity to highlight him as a businessman and also the great work that he is doing for Langford Construction. It will be positive for both he and his brothers, and from watching, I can already tell that this is what will firmly establish him to be taken seriously. This is his moment.

"He looks good," a deep voice says, stepping up to my side where I stand in the dark shadows of this TV studio.

Startled, I look up to see Tennyson's brother, Ben, who's looking equally dapper in his suit, his eyes not wavering from his brother.

"He does," I agree and nod.

"I called his office, and Melody said he was down here. It appears you are a positive influence on my brother. I will admit, I was a bit worried about him. Looks like I don't need to be anymore," he says, looking at me now, giving me a small smile. I appreciate the kudos.

"He is talented, highly skilled, and one of the best businessmen I have worked with." And I mean it. Many see Tennyson for his playboy lifestyle that flashes on the internet. Not the hardworking, successful man who I am trying to bring forward.

"He is," Ben agrees with me, his eyes on me a little longer than necessary. He squints slightly, like he is trying to work me out, like I have a special power or something. "I am glad that the world finally gets to see it. And see him so happy," Ben adds with another smile, one that makes me feel a little more settled.

"Looks can be deceiving." I'm not sure what it is, but I know that Tennyson is battling something. I just can't figure out exactly what it is.

"What do you mean?" Ben asks, his smile now gone.

"I don't know. But he is carrying something heavy." I sigh as I look back at the man who currently consumes my thoughts.

"Might have something to do with the calls my office is getting," Ben says, and my head whips around to him.

"What calls?" I almost demand. The only way I can do my job is to be on top of everything. I don't need surprises; they are so hard to manage. Ben looks at me for a beat, and I already know I am not going to like what he has to say.

"One of his many women is trying to track him down. A woman by the name of Katerina Newcomb." My world stops.

"She has been messaging him on social media a lot too," I say, now deep in thought.

"We may have a potential stalker on our hands, but that is what I wanted to talk to Tenn about today. See what he has to say before we get back to her. I can serve her a protection order, to make sure she stays away from him if he thinks she is going to be an issue. But I also don't want to make it a bigger deal than it is."

"Do you do that often? Push out protection orders?" I ask. From how he speaks so casually about it, it sounds like something he does a lot of.

"More than you would believe," he says on a sigh, like it is painful, so I drop the conversation and look back at Tennyson. He dazzles in the bright studio lights, his face lit up in a smile, charming the pants off the interviewer and no doubt all the viewers at home who will tune in to see this segment when it airs in a few weeks.

We both stand in silence, watching on, admiring how well Tennyson is doing. He is providing great points, doing some deep discussion on the business environment, contributing to some really insightful conversation. Touching base on the expansion plans in Asia, yet not giving anything away. He is articulate, precise, and sits confidently, giving an air of authority I think people will be surprised by when they watch him. He is a natural, at both the interview and the business knowl-edge. By the end of it, I think even his brother is impressed.

"How did I do?" Tennyson asks, walking up to us once his segment is done, but looking straight at me.

"Perfect," I say with a smile as he stops next to me, and the familiar feeling of his hand wrapping around my waist warms my insides. He pulls me to his side, not afraid to let his brother know exactly how close we are. Ben looks at both of us and stills. I should have already spoken to Harrison and Beth about this, but I have been so caught up in my feelings around what is happening it completely fell off my radar. My palms start to sweat as I wait for his reaction.

"Shit," Ben says, and we both look at him as his eyes flick between Tennyson and me.

"So this is a thing? I mean, a few weeks ago on the golf course, I knew it could be, but... shit." My eyebrows rise, and I look at Tennyson in question. We haven't talked about what we are or what is happening. We both, however, have come to the conclusion that we enjoy each other, like spending time together, and both need to succeed at this job together so that's what we will do.

"Golf course?" I ask, wondering what Ben is talking about.

"I knew weeks ago, this was happening, but it just took you a little longer to figure it out, Cupcake," he quips, giving me a wink before looking back at his brother. I ease my shoulders a little, knowing that Tennyson has already prepared them so it won't come as such a shock.

"There a problem?" he asks, and I am not sure if he means with me or something else.

"Maybe. Who is Katerina Newcomb?" Ben asks as the three of us huddle in the dark corner of the studio while the crew packs up around us. I feel Tennyson stiffen slightly, and Ben's looking at me, unsure. I remain impartial, even though inside, I am flaming. Jealousy coils in my stomach, my memory flashing back to when I met her at that business dinner. Pretty, beautiful actually. Confident, clearly not hesitant in going after what she wanted after she came straight up to Tennyson and acted like she was his. I would imagine his dismissal of her hurt, or at least hurt her ego.

"An old acquaintance," Tennyson says, leaving it at that.

"Well, she is calling my office, trying to get to you. Know anything about that?" he asks again.

"Shit," Tennyson says, running his hand through his hair, but his other hand on my waist remains, keeping me close.

"She has been calling my office as well, but I get Melody to field the calls," he admits.

"She has been sending messages across social media as well," I add, and Tennyson looks at me, confused.

"Why?" he asks, looking at Ben and me.

"Money. They always want money, Tenn," Ben says, again breathing out his words like they are painful. Like he knows from experience. "Just talk to her, see what she wants, and then we can deal with it. Call me later once you do," he adds, pulling his phone from his pocket and checking it. "I've got to run. Looking good up there, brother." He smiles and slaps Tennyson's arm in what can only be described as brotherly love.

"Thanks, Benny Boy," Tennyson says, his smile small, but there just the same.

We watch Ben walk away, and I turn around, standing in front of Tennyson and looking up to gauge his expression. My mind is racing, stomach churning, and my skin prickles as my spider-senses ricochet off the charts. Something doesn't feel right. Not one bit. I need space. I need to collect my thoughts. I need to get ahead of this, because I have a feeling I'll need to have all bases covered.

"Don't worry, Cupcake. We are fine," Tennyson says, obviously attune to my feelings already. I wish I could take solace in his words, but I don't.

"I need to go. I have a new client I need to meet with. Call me later?" I ask him, plastering a fake smile on my face, positioning my work front and center where it should be. His jaw tightens, not happy that I am leaving.

"I will," he says, pulling my body to him, kissing my forehead before I step away, straighten my shoulders, and turn to walk to the exit. I take deep breaths as I head toward the bright lights of the day, maneuvering around the crew, stepping over the cables and dodging the many people who flit around this studio. My steps quicken, the air feeling thinner than it did ten minutes ago, but I push it to the back of my mind. I need to get to this next meeting, then go home and review the interview from today and approve it for the studio. I need to work. I'm married to my job, and I need to remember that.

27

TENNYSON

It's been a day since I've seen Willow, and I hate it. The minutes feel like hours, the hours feel like days. When this change in me occurred, I can't pinpoint, only to say that I am not the same man I was before New York. There is a line in my life now. Before Willow and after. And I am a much better man after.

The vision of her walking away from me at the studio yesterday is my last memory. I prefer the ones I have of her naked, squirming underneath me, a moaning mess on my cock. My dick's already getting hard just from thinking about her. But she worked late yesterday, and I had calls with Asia all night. The two of us had little time to chat apart from a quick call when we were both almost asleep within minutes.

"Tennyson, there is a Katerina Newcomb on line one." Melody's voice breaks through my thoughts, and I still. I didn't call her yesterday like my brother asked. After he chased me down about it this morning, I decided I wouldn't, but I would answer if she called again. I will just tell her not to bother calling. I am not interested and not available. I can barely remember her face and have no recollection of her or that one night we spent together. If I hadn't seen her at Harrison's business dinner weeks ago, I would go as far as to say that I have no idea who she is. The fact that she is the daughter of my nearest competitor is slightly unnerving, but insignificant just the same. Not remembering her is not necessarily something I am proud of, but it is the truth.

"Thanks, Melody," I say as I pick up the call. "Tennyson Langford." I put on the best senior boss voice I can muster.

"Tennyson, it is Katerina Newcomb," she says, her voice different from what I remember.

"How can I help you?" I ask, remaining professional.

"I'm pregnant," she blurts out, and I wait for something more, but nothing comes.

"Congratulations?" I say in question, having no idea why she is calling me about that.

"It's yours. This baby is yours." In an instant, my palms sweat and my heart almost stops in my chest. *That can't be right*. My mind races, thinking about when our night together was, the day a blur. It must have been six or seven weeks ago. The only thing helping me to remember is that I saw Willow the very next day. That day is burned in my memory.

"Impossible." I fake the confidence in my voice as I grab my cell in my other hand, my hand shaking as I quickly type in 911 to my brothers group chat.

"You are the only person I have had sex with in the last few weeks," she spits out.

"I used protection. We used protection," I grit out. Even though I was always drunk when I was with women, I always remembered to wrap myself. That little act is ingrained in me from my father's antics. I have never had sex without a condom.

"What can I say, it didn't work." Her voice changes again. One that would match a very satisfied smile. Vomit feels like it is going to crawl up my throat at any minute. This is what happened to my father. He was with so many women, we couldn't keep up with all the monetary demands in the end. After he died, so many women came out of the blue, demanding money to pay for children they said belonged to him. The fact that Ben and his legal team investigated every single one of them and none of them were a DNA match did little to settle any of our nerves.

"My lawyer will be in touch," I say, slamming down the phone as I start to hyperventilate. This can't be happening. This can't be fucking happening. I look at the small bar at the side of my office, the decanter of whiskey looking at me. Sparkling in the lights, the vintage timber cupboard it sits on almost pleads with me to walk toward it. I need Willow or whiskey, and I am not sure the first option is a good idea right now. I push back from my chair and stalk to my liquor cabinet and grab a glass.

"Fuck it," I say, reverting to my old behavior as I splash a small amount into the crystal glass, one finger at best, and then throw it down my throat. The burn is nearly unfamiliar since it has been a while, but it has the desired effect.

"What happened?" Ben pushes open my door, Eddie

hot on his heels. They look at me, their steps paused as they take in my stressed state and the empty glass in my hand. It helps that all our offices are in the one building, and our penthouses take up the top four floors. We are close, both in terms of our loving relationships with each other, but also in terms of logistics.

"Fuck," Eddie says, and my eyes ping to him. He is dressed casually today. Too casual, almost in workman attire, like he has been fixing something, although given he lives behind a desk and not in a workshop, I have no idea what he has been doing.

"What's going on?" Harrison races through the door next. We have had enough 911s in our group chat to warrant the panic.

"I spoke to Katerina Newcomb," I say, looking at Ben and his face contorts, already knowing it isn't good.

"Who the fuck is Katerina Newcomb?" Harrison asks as he closes the door to my office, and my brothers crowd around me near the liquor cabinet.

"One of Tennyson's many one-night stands," Ben grits out, waiting for the bomb to drop.

"Daughter of Geoffery Newcomb," Eddie says almost simultaneously. Harrison scowls.

"She's pregnant. She says it's mine." My three brothers look at me first in shock, before it morphs into disappointment, and I have never felt more like a fucking failure than I do in this moment. I have let them all down. I have let myself down. And I know, without a doubt, that once Willow knows, I will let her down as well.

"Don't you use protection?" Harrison seethes, stepping up to the cabinet and pouring himself a whiskey, throwing it back in one fluid motion.

"Get me one of those," Ben murmurs.

"And me," Eddie says, before Harrison just grabs the entire decanter and four glasses and motions for us all to sit on my couch.

"I always wrap it. I have never had sex without a fucking rubber." I pace my office, trying my hardest to think about that night and coming up empty. Rubbing my head, I will the incoming migraine to retreat before I run my hand through my hair and pull on it roughly.

"Then we will get a test," Eddie says, and I start to feel a little more settled. Sure, there is a possibility it is mine. But there sure as hell is a possibility that it isn't.

"Paternity tests can be done at around ten weeks. How far along is she?" Ben asks, as Harrison lines up the four glasses and splashes a healthy amount of whiskey in each of them.

"I don't know. I didn't ask," I say, feeling even more like shit. I wish I could erase the past fifteen minutes of my life entirely.

"What, you don't remember her? When did you fuck her?" Eddie asks, his eyebrows rising, surprised that I can't remember the night.

"It was the night before I met Willow again at the estate," I say to them. Willow is my only guiding light in all of this.

"That was about eight weeks ago, I think," Ben murmurs, obviously thinking about that weekend since we were all at his estate with the kids.

"Fuck," Eddie sighs, as we all pick up our glasses and

throw back the liquor. The burn feels good, but I can't say I enjoy it like I once did. I side the empty glass back on the coffee table and continue to pace.

"God, my head is a fucking mess. I have enough going on with dealing with the memories of Nanny Helen," I say without thinking, pulling at my hair, my mind so busy I have no idea how to calm it.

"Nanny Helen?" Ben asks, looking at me as though I am crazy.

"Yeah. I have no idea why, but she has been popping up in my mind for weeks. Ever since I met Willow."

"Speaking of Willow, we need to get her in on this. She needs to be aware of it," Harrison says, changing our conversation back to the topic at hand.

"I'm not sure she is going to be too receptive," Ben murmurs again, his eyes flicking to me.

"What? Why?" Harrison asks, his eyes narrowing.

"It will hurt her," I say, feeling sick to my stomach about that fact. What kind of woman would stick around with a man she just met when he is going to be a new dad? I shake my head to dislodge the thought. It isn't my baby. It can't be.

"She is a professional. I am sure she has come across this before," Harrison says as he stands, and I take a breath.

"Willow and I are..." I start, my voice trailing off as Harrison comes to a stop in front of me, his face in a scowl.

"Fuck," Eddie says, sitting back, running his hand through his hair.

"Well, it didn't take you long!" Harrison barks, looking at me sternly.

"We have a history, and we reignited it." But he already knows this. My jaw clenches as I re-explain myself to him.

"So what, you're dating? Or just fucking?" he asks, and I do not appreciate his tone. Especially talking like that about Willow. I know he is only worried about me, but I don't entertain his comment with an answer.

"That is really unprofessional of her," Harrison spits out, and I know he is stressed. He likes Willow, they all do.

"Fuck off, like you can talk, fucking your events manager for months before anyone knew. You, of all people, know how these things happen. And don't worry, she is the most professional person I have ever worked with, and besides..." I say, my words falling off again as emotions take over.

"Besides what?" Eddie asks, my three brothers looking at me, waiting.

"Besides, I think... I am in love with her," I say, holding my breath. They look at me like I am crazy, before their looks morph into acceptance and then sadness and remorse.

"Love?" Ben asks, his eyebrows rising.

"She cooks me cupcakes, she buys me bed socks. She is smart, sassy, sexy, and funny. Her best friend is a twelve-year-old kid with attitude who hates me; she takes in stray cats; Bob fucking loves her; Melody wants to be her best friend, and I think I want to marry her." The admission whips out from me, almost leaving me stumbling. I grip on to the desk with one hand, half bent over as I pant. I'm turning into a man with feelings, and it's making my chest burn, the remorse I feel from my actions beyond painful. *God, is this what it feels like? Is this what love feels like?*

"Shit," Harrison says, before he picks up the decanter and pours another four glasses, and we remain in my office all afternoon, finishing off a bottle of fine Whiteman whiskey.

28

WILLOW

With Saide out tonight, dancing the night away with some friends to try to forget about her sinful affair, and Josh with his mom, I take the rare quiet evening I have and run a warm bath. My body is still sore, my muscles tight, and as I lower myself in the tub, I feel a sense of calm take over. Sinking into the water, I inhale a deep breath, smelling the lavender oil I put in, hoping it helps me relax.

Life has been busy. My mind is not only focusing on work, Saide's heartbreak, Josh, Betty, and everyone else, but suddenly also myself. I look at my naked body underneath the water. I used to hate it. The rolls, the cellulite. The curves were fine, they were just big. I rub my stomach. I've been feeling good lately. Not a lot of bloating. Not too much period pain. I take in a breath and let it go slowly as I think about the conversation I will need to have with Tennyson. It feels weird bringing this up so soon, but if children are part of his future, then he needs to know that it is not something I can give him. I have no idea what his thoughts are around the topic. But for a woman who has struggled her whole life, I have never once felt sexy in my own body, especially with what I feel I'm lacking.

Until Tennyson.

That night in New York was magic. I never thought I would ever feel like that again. A wanted woman. A desired lady. Now Tennyson makes me feel like that every day of the week. He can't keep his hands or eyes off me. The sexual desires he has awakened in me, the need I have to have him all to myself growing. It feels almost selfish. I have always thought of others first. Always looked after everyone else, then myself. But now I want to run full steam ahead, and it is freaking me out, because that is not like me at all.

I hear the doorbell go off, and I sigh. I wasn't expecting Josh tonight since his mother is home, so I locked the door. No doubt he wants some ice cream or something, although it is late, and he should be in bed already. I jump out of the bath, wrap a towel around me, and run, knowing that the ringing won't stop because nothing stands in Josh's way of a tub of Ben and Jerry's. My body is dripping, and I leave wet footprints on the floor as I race down the stairs to the front door, hoping to let him in and dive back into my warm bath before I catch a chill.

"Josh, what are you..." The words die on my lips as I see Tennyson leaning against the doorframe. His eyes are red and half-closed. His clothes are crumbled, shirt buttons undone at the neck, his tie loose. His hair is a mess, like he has been pulling at it. And he stinks of whiskey.

"Tennyson?" I have never seen him drunk before, and as his large frame stumbles into my place, nearly knocking over a vase, I wonder if I can handle him.

"What are you doing here?" I ask, opening the door wider so he can get in. He looks sad. He is clearly intoxicated, and I am not sure what is going on. I shut the door and pull my towel around me tighter, now regretting not putting on my robe.

"I wanted to see you," he slurs. Whatever he has had to drink, he has had a lot of it.

"You're drunk!" The shock is now wearing off, and my voice grows louder and accusing. Disappointed in him. It's not like he can't drink; he doesn't have a problem or anything. But he should limit it and not drink to excess. This is clearly excessive.

"You're cute when you yell, Cupcake," he says with a smile as he staggers toward my living room.

"I'm not yelling!" I say even louder, following after him, now just proving his point.

"Getting cuter..." he singsongs as his legs nearly trip over each other, his hands landing on the back of my sofa.

"Tennyson!" I huff, frustrated, as my hands find my hips, my anger at this situation starting to build.

"So fucking cute," he murmurs, his hand reaching out to cup my face. His touch is warm, and it feels nice, but his eyes are hazy. He isn't focusing on me; he has no idea what is going on.

"I cannot believe this." I shake my head, but his hands hold my gaze on his.

"Why aren't you dressed?" he asks, suddenly taking in my appearance, like he is looking at me for the first time. My hair is high in a bun, the towel tucked in tight under my arms, barely covering my butt.

"I *was* having a relaxing bath," I state, but he just looks at me lovingly, his eyes almost slitted.

"Oh great, I will join you." He kicks off his shoes and takes off his jacket, throwing them all across the floor.

"Wait. What? No!" I say, my mind jumbled, as he starts unbuttoning his shirt.

"So fucking adorable." He flashes me his grin, and I melt a little.

"Tenn, why did you drink so much?" I ask him, using his nickname for the first time. This man just digs into my chest further and further every time I see him. He struggles with his shirt. My anger subsides a little as I watch him trying to rip it from his arms like a raging toddler.

"Oh, I'm going to be a dad, and I can't even remember the mother..." he says, and I jolt.

"What?" My eyes wide, my heart starts racing, and I wonder if I heard him right.

"Adorable," he mumbles before he loses his footing and falls onto the sofa behind him.

"I don't understand," I say on a shaky breath, walking toward him, looking down at him as he lies on the cushions, his feet bare, hanging over the edge, his shirt off and his belt half undone.

"I love you, Willow. Don't ever leave me," he murmurs before he is out cold.

I'm scared to move. *Is this happening? Is this real?* Dread swirls in my stomach as I slowly think about his words. *A father?* Tennyson is going to be a father? I have never seen him this drunk, and I know then and there that what he says is the truth. Tennyson is going to be a father. I grip the sofa so I don't fall into a mess on the floor.

Because father is a title that I can never give him.

29

TENNYSON

I hear noises. The sun is bright against my eyes, and I squint them to keep them closed. My head thumps, and I feel like there is a jackhammer against the front of my skull. I try to swallow but can't. There is no moisture in my mouth, and I stick out my tongue to lick my dry lips, the exercise completely futile.

"Hmmmm," I mumble as I feel warmth on my chest, and I think of Willow tucked up next to me. I try not to move too much, not wanting to wake her. I feel short, sharp jolts on my forehead and lift my hand to rub it away, something grabbing my finger as they pass over my skin.

"What the..." I say as I open my eyes and immediately regret it with the bright sun streaming in. I know I am not in my bed, that much I can tell, so I try to gather my thoughts to figure out where I am. I take a breath and I smell baked goods and come to the conclusion that I am at Willow's. Lowering my hand, I reach out to her. I'm hard and I can think of nothing better than delving into her warm, wet center, but as my hand reaches for her, I get a handful of fur. Another ping hits my forehead, and I open my eyes, trying to understand what is going on.

"You need to leave." My eyes flick to the kid sitting in the armchair opposite me. Currently holding an industrial sized staple gun in the air, aimed in my direction.

Ping.

"What the hell?" I say as I get a sharp sting to the forehead again. He's shooting me with staples. *What the fuck is wrong with this kid?*

"What did you do to her?" he demands. He looks upset, and I look to my side where I thought Willow was and see Betty, whose nails are starting to come out as she stretches, the prick of them marking my skin on the underside of my arm. It burns, and I pull away from her quickly, which has her launching up, arching her back before she attacks my bare bicep.

"Shit! Betty!" I groan, pushing the cat away, my skin now coated in red scratches. She hisses at me like it is my fault before she jumps from the sofa and runs to the kitchen. *What the hell is going on with everyone this morning?*

Ping.

The sharp prick hits my forehead again, and I turn my head sharply, too quickly, the pain shooting in my temples. Rubbing my head, I try to ease the sting, and as I pull my hands away, I notice blood.

"What the fuck. Stop it, punk," I grit out to the kid, my head now throbbing and my heart feeling heavy.

"Oh, I haven't even started..." the kid warns. His eyes are evil as he looks at me sharply. I wonder if he has watched too many Marvel movies. My eyes lower to the gun, and I see him clench it, and I wonder how he knows how to hold it like that. Strong and steady in his hand. The staple gun is still raised, and he fires another shot, hitting me right between the eyes.

"Kid. Quit it!" I say louder, grimacing at my own voice as it rattles my brain.

"You need to leave," he says again, firing another shot, turning his head on a slant. He looks like a gun crazy godfather, even though he is preteen.

"You got a problem with me, Josh?" I ask, sitting up, noticing that I am bare-chested, but still have my pants on. I'm trying to remember last night and why I am on Willow's sofa instead of her bed.

"You are my problem," he sneers, firing another shot. His lips buck up at the ends like he is a cowboy in a western. Do all twelve-year-olds act like this? What the fuck happened to respecting your elders?

"Listen, I have had a late night and you are starting to become a pain in my ass," I mutter, sitting fully, my bare feet touching the floor, before I immediately pick them up the minute I feel the sting.

"What the hell..." I say, looking down, the floor littered with staples. "Where the hell did you get that staple gun?" He looks at me furiously, like the descendant of the devil himself.

"This? It is hospital grade. Top of the line. The staples are extra sharp. The kind that pierce skin," he hisses, and my eyebrows rise. Who the hell raised this kid? What the hell is he doing with industrial grade weaponry?

"I will say it one. More. Time, because for a business-man, you are really slow. *You need to leave.*"

"Or what!" I challenge, my eyes slitting, matching his evil look. *Two can play at this game, motherfucker.*

Sitting in the armchair, he lowers his weapon and leans back. I sigh and smirk at him. *Yeah, back down, motherfucker, I won this round.*

He pulls out a big shiny red apple from his pocket, along with a sharp knife that looks like it would do a good job of gutting me. Our eyes remain glued to each other as he slowly slices the apple, the piece peeling off smoothly, the knife razor-sharp, before he puts the piece to his mouth and chews. I think Willow needs to move. I will talk to Melody about getting in touch with my real estate agent and seeing if we can find Willow a new house. This kid clearly has anger management issues. Our eyes remain on each other, in a stare-off challenge, my eyes burning, but I refuse to blink first, as he continues slicing a piece off at a time. I swallow. He looks as scary as fuck.

"What are you? The godfather or something?" I say, blinking, my eyes now watering. The bastard won.

"Or something," he says, his eyes still not leaving me, looking deranged.

"What time is it?" I have no idea where my phone is, and I want to get out of his gaze. Who knows what he has in his other pocket.

"Nine a.m.," the kid answers, slicing another piece of apple and popping it into his mouth. He chews slowly. This kid is fucking getting on my nerves.

"Why are you up so early?" Kids usually sleep in on the weekends, don't they?

"I'm an early riser. It appears you are too?" he says, pointing the knife right at my dick, where it presses hard against my zipper. My morning wood is now bigger than ever since I met Willow. As I think of her, I get a vague recollection of seeing her wrapped in a towel.

"You need to go," he says again, drawing my attention back to him. He moves the sharp knife in his fingers, almost twirling it.

"I'm not going anywhere. I think *you* need to leave," I push back, because this kid is not kicking me out of my girlfriend's house.

"You don't want to know what I am capable of, Ninja," he says, tilting his head again like he is in a mafia movie.

"Probably coloring in and Legos," I snigger.

Ping.

The staple gun appears from out of nowhere and shoots me in the temple, barely missing my eye.

"What is your problem!" I hiss.

"You are my problem. Now leave."

"I'm not leaving. Where is Willow?" I ask, looking around, my eyes now accustomed to the light, and I see it streaming in the window. I stand, trying my best to dodge the staples on the floor, feeling a few prick into my feet.

"Oh, I am going to have so much fun bringing you down..." he threatens, and I walk past where he is sitting, but he gets up and walks behind me quickly as I follow the noise I hear in the kitchen.

I stop mid-walk at the entrance, my eyes wide. The kitchen is a mess. There are cupcakes everywhere.

Chocolate ones, red velvet, vanilla, marble. I even spot some pink ones cooling on the dining table. There are bowls, flour, trays, spoons, icing, and patty pans scattered over every flat surface. I can't see a spare, clean area at all. I look at her then. Willow has her back to me. She is wearing jeans and a white t-shirt, her hair pulled up haphazardly on the top of her head. She looks amazing, like she always does, but her shoulders are high, her stance tight. She stands at the kitchen counter, a large bowl under one arm, a big wooden spoon in her opposite hand, stirring the contents like it is her dying wish.

"Willow?" I ask timidly, taking a small step toward her. She stops abruptly but doesn't turn.

"You're a dead man," I hear a whisper from the kid who is watching me from behind. My head flicks to him, and he lifts the staple gun again, firing another shot, this one hitting me in the chest before he leans against the wall, watching me. I scrunch up my nose at him, giving him an evil look. I am not letting some twelve-year-old punk push me around.

I turn back to Willow who is still standing there, and she slowly places the bowl on the counter and turns around. She is stressed, not meeting my eye, and I rack my brain to try to think about what has happened, before dread flows over me, along with the memories.

"Willow?" I croak, the pain in my chest now spreading, opening my chest cavity wide. A pain I haven't felt in a very long time blooms.

"I called Harrison. He will be here in five minutes to pick you up," she says, her hands by her sides gripping on to the counter. Her knuckles are white, and I see her swallow, her chest rising and falling rapidly.

"Willow. We need to talk." Looking at her, I see her professional mask slip on, and the pain inside me explodes. I don't want professional Willow, I want my Willow. My sassy, sexy Willow. This can't be happening. I need her. Can't she see I need her? Panic fills my veins as I rub my head, trying to get a handle on this situation.

"I have my team blocking any paparazzi, as they are camped at your apartment. It seems Katerina has already gone to the media. She got a quick jump on us. Lucky for me, they don't know you are here. Harrison is taking you to Ben's estate. You will stay there for the next two weeks. You won't use social media, and you won't be seen anywhere." She gives the orders like a boss, but not my girl. She is straight down the line.

I'm losing her. I can't lose her. Not now. I have only just found her.

"Willow, I need you," I beg, stepping closer to her, my heart in my throat. My voice is almost breaking. It's like I can feel her pulling away, and even though I reach for her, I can't catch her.

"My team and I are here for anything you need. We will deal with the press, and we will assist Ben with the legal ramifications, if there are any." My knees start to feel weak, and I swallow roughly because she still won't even look at me.

"Willow! Goddammit, look at me!" I am about to get on my knees. I will do anything. *Anything.*

"I can't!" she screams back, and I still, shocked for a moment at her outburst, but even though I don't like to hear the pain in her voice, at least I know she is not a robot. I hurt her, but I can fix hurt. I can't fix anything if she blocks me out.

The doorbell rings. *Fuck. Harrison is here.*

"You need to leave," the kid says, pushing off the wall and coming to Willow's side. I might hate the kid, but I can't hate that he protects her. I can respect him for that.

"It was before, Willow. It all happened before you came back into my life," I say desperately, looking at her, and she gives me a nod, but her lips are thin. She is hanging on by a thread too.

"I know. I just need to do my job now, Tennyson. And you need to let me." I see her take a big shaky breath. I hate myself. I hate that I did this to her. I hate that I did this to us.

The doorbell sounds again. I look to the side and see my shoes, shirt, and jacket hanging neatly near the door. Washed and pressed to perfection. When I look back at the kitchen, understanding washes over me that she must have been up all night. To bake like this, wash my things, and to also have her team already in action, along with my brothers. All while I was blackout drunk on her sofa. I slowly walk over and grab my things.

"Willow..." I say one last time, and her eyes flick to meet mine. I pull in a sharp breath at the pain there. I've fucked up a lot in my life. Disappointed many people, but hurting Willow like this is by far going to be my biggest regret of my life. I remain silent and so does she. Giving her a nod, I retreat to the door.

I will do everything she asks of me. Because I never want to feel like this again.

30

—————

WILLOW

I sit on the sofa quietly. The house is now empty since I sent my bodyguard home to his mother and left Betty outside. I sigh. I, of all people, know how things turn from wonderful to damaged in an instant. It is what makes me good at what I do. It is what makes me so in-demand with my skill set. But I ignored the signs. If I wasn't so caught up in Tennyson and our outrageously amazing sex life, I would have figured this out, and I could have mitigated all of it. It is my fault that I now have a client in lockdown. It is my fault that his whole reputation is back in the toilet. The local media is having a field day. My only blessing is that no one outside of Baltimore seems to care too much, meaning the Langford name isn't too tarnished, and Tennyson's business interests remain unaffected. But I am sure Katerina's father isn't going to be happy, and if I know anything about business, it is that it is a dog-eat-dog world, and he will use this crisis to his full advantage. I have prepared for that, though.

Now, after thinking about it for the past hour in the quiet of my home, I knew there were signs. Katerina at the business dinner a few weeks ago should have been my first signal, given that Harrison has since told me she wasn't even invited. Something I probably should have investigated at the time. The constant social media harassment from her. I should have picked that up straightaway. A familiar name, an ongoing daily barrage of messages. Sure, it could have been nothing, but it warrants some digging. And I didn't do that either.

I slump on the sofa and cuddle the cushion. I smell him, his scent mixed with whiskey. No wonder he had a drinking session with his brothers. Finding out that you are going to have a child is a big deal. Harrison explained it all to me on the phone while Tennyson was passed out on my sofa. I sat in the armchair and looked at him for half the night, disappointed I let him down, disappointed that he could be a father of a child he didn't plan to have. The deep pain in my gut at the last thought sears me the worst.

"I came home as soon as I heard!" Saide says as she pushes through the front door and eyes the mess in the kitchen. She was out all night and no doubt had a similar fate to that of Tennyson and probably slept on her friend's sofa. But she looks refreshed.

"You didn't have to," I say, pushing my shoulders back, determined to make this right. Professionally, at least. Personally, I have no idea where I stand with Tennyson or what to do. All I know is that I can't focus on that until this mess is sorted.

"I saw the news on social media this morning. Are

you okay?" she asks softly, coming to sit next to me. We have always been close, but it is usually me who does the mothering. This side of Saide is completely new. But I need it.

"I will get it sorted. I am sure I can get this to blow over in a couple of days, a week tops, and then have him back to being a poster child in no time," I say, not looking at her, but nodding, reinforcing it all to myself. I can do it; I know I can.

"Willow..." Saide says, and I can't look at her, so I remain quiet, staring straight ahead.

"Willow, look at me." My eyes immediately find hers at the gentle tone of her voice.

"It's okay to be upset."

"I'm fine. Stupid, but fine," I mutter.

"You are not stupid," Saide says, flabbergasted.

"I let my guard down. I could have stopped this. There were signs that this woman was up to something, and I missed all of them!" I say, exasperated with myself.

"Willow, are you even listening to yourself? Maybe you could have, maybe not. But I am not talking about work now, Willow. How are you and Tennyson?"

"He is having a baby with another woman. How do you think we are?" I say with a bite, not meaning the venom. Her lips purse a little, and I feel bad for a moment.

"I understand your pain, but it was before you two even got together, wasn't it?" She makes a good point, and that is what I can't reconcile. It makes sense that, yes, it all happened before I met Tennyson, but it doesn't make the pain in my chest ache any less. The sane part of my brain knows that these things happen, and he probably needs me now more than ever. But the hormonal part of me wants to slap him, eat a tub of ice cream, and drown in my tears.

"You know I can't give him that," I mutter to Saide and see pity in her eyes.

"Maybe he doesn't even want kids. Maybe he is not father material?" Saide offers.

"But if he does, I can't give him that. I will never be able to give him that." Pain intensifies in my chest as the reality sets in.

"You don't know that for sure," Saide says angrily.

"I know I may be young on the outside, but my insides are so traumatized that nothing can survive in there. The doctor said it was a one in a million chance," I reiterate what she and I already know. There is no way in hell I can have a baby, or even if I am lucky enough to conceive, chances are I can't carry to full term. PCOS is debilitating, at least it was for me, and although I feel more settled now, on good medication, and have a healthy lifestyle, the dark cloud always hangs over my head.

"But there is still a chance," Saide says, her eyes glassy. We have talked about this many times before. She knows how badly I want kids. Ever since I was one myself, we always played moms and dads at home. I was always looking after everyone. I have always been maternal.

"You live in fantasyland, Saide. No one is that lucky. Now at least Tennyson has that chance to have a family with someone. I mean, this pain was coming for me eventually."

"That's why you don't date, isn't it?" Saide says, like she is coming to a known conclusion.

"Don't be silly. I date," I say, scoffing off her accusation.

"Oh my God, I can't believe I didn't see it before. You don't date. You are a workaholic. You bury yourself in making other people happy and successful because you don't want to meet the man of your dreams and—" I cut her off.

"Disappoint him? Tell him I am barren and can't give him the very thing that, deep down, we as humans are put on this earth to do?" I finish for her, and her lips thin.

"Surely, a man who gives you nine orgasms in as many hours can put a baby in you," she quips, and I huff out a laugh.

"Somehow, I don't think that is enough, Saide. If this baby is Tennyson's, then it is his chance to have a family. I don't want to stop him from achieving that. This woman was a one-night stand, but so were we, and we nearly made it work. Maybe he can make it work with her," I offer, coming to the conclusion that whatever Tennyson and I had needed to stop eventually.

"I can't believe you. It is clear as day that you have strong feelings for him. I am reasonably confident that he feels the same. What if he doesn't even want children? Have you thought of that? Because he is just as big of a workaholic as you, it appears, and given how much sex you two have, I don't think either of you would have time for kids anyway!" Saide protests, and I roll my eyes.

"Want some ice cream?" This conversation is going nowhere and we are both exhausted. I know she is still hurting over the pain of her own relationship failure, even if he was married and she should have known better.

"I can't believe we were both with men who are now having babies with other women..." Saide remarks, and I sigh.

"I will get two tubs." I walk to the kitchen, grab two tubs of ice cream, spoons, and a blanket from the cupboard on my way past.

"*Titanic*? Leo never lets us down," Saide asks, flicking through the movie choices.

"Sounds perfect," I say, slumping next to her, and we both get comfortable. Under the blanket, with our ice cream, we get lost in Rose and Jack and their true love story that was never meant to be.

31

TENNYSON

I have been working for twelve hours straight. My eyes blur, they're so dry. I haven't slept in days, I've lost my appetite, and my body burns for Willow. It has been a week since the bomb exploded in my life. Ben and his legal team are dealing with Katerina, and I haven't spoken to her again. Everything goes through Ben and the firm. We have hired independent doctors, me wanting to get this paternity issue sorted ASAP and Katerina being hesitant to allow anyone to conduct tests. She is saying it is too early and might harm the baby. I am calling bullshit.

As I send off another email to Singapore, firming up our expansion plans, I look around Ben's library, which I have now overtaken as my office. I spot a tub of books and toys in the corner. A pink box overflowing with Rosie's things that she loves to play with. All high sensory toys, noise makers, and tactile toys she can feel and touch and immerse herself with. I sigh and lean back, staring at the box. I still can't believe I *could* be having a kid. A child of my own. I scrunch my face and rub my eyes. It is the last thing I want. I just want Willow.

I hear footsteps and look up, spotting Harrison as he struts into the room, looking like the leader of the free world that he is meant to be. I haven't seen him for a few days, as his work has only gotten busier. It has been Ben who has been managing me and Eddie who has been keeping me sane. But Harrison calls me every day.

"I'm surprised to see you," I say, my eyebrows rising as I lean back, watching him. It is just dusk outside, and the two of us should be somewhere either having dinner or with our women, but here we are. Locked inside because that is what my sexy reputation manager is telling me to do.

"Willow told me we need to have at least one of us boys near you at all times. Help keep you sane while you are locked up in here," he says, taking a seat and looking at me. "She is a drill sergeant. She is so good at her job. I knew she was, of course, but seeing it in action, I am astounded. She not only gets everything handled, dots every 'i' and crosses every 't', but she does it three times just to ensure it is right." He gushes the words so fast they tumble out of his mouth.

My teeth grind as I listen to Harrison tell me exactly how wonderful my woman is. I have called her. Multiple times per day just to hear her voice. She always answers, tells me updates, gives me direction, but it is all professional. The few times I have broached the subject of us, she stops me. She needs to focus. I get that. But I need her.

"If I run for president, I will need her working on my campaign," Harrison adds, and my chest warms with pride for her. Willow would be excellent on his team. He would win, for sure.

"I didn't hamper your opportunity then?" I ask him, because that was a major concern of mine too. I didn't want my fuckups to impact his opportunities.

"No. Willow says this news is contained to Baltimore at the moment. Depending on the paternity of the child, that will determine if it reaches further afield. My run for president is still a few years away, so we should be okay. Are you sure you used a condom?" he asks me, hope in his question. He has asked me this almost every day, and my answer remains the same.

"One hundred percent certain. The only issue is if it broke and I didn't know." I have thought about this. I have thought over and over about that night, trying to remember it. But I can't. All I can think of is Willow.

"Good. Willow has it handled. Beth said she was good, but I didn't know how good until I worked with her this week," he says, still admiring my woman.

"You've seen her?" I sit forward, eager for any information he can give me.

He looks at me and nods. "Every day." It is now my turn to be surprised.

"Every day? What do you mean every day?" I push. *Why can my brother see her, and I can't?*

"We are having a touch-base meeting every day, trying to not only get a handle on this situation, but also get in front of it. It isn't easy out there. Willow is getting phone calls and messages; your social media is running rampant. It feels like Dad all over again." The air in my lungs leaves me. When Dad died, the amount of work us boys had to put in to stop the media, their stories, their lies, was astounding.

"Shit. I didn't know..." I murmur, as the familiar feeling of failure wraps around my throat again.

"It's fine. Willow is containing it. I wish we had her for all Dad's affairs. It would have been much easier." Harrison sits back and looks at me.

"How is she?" I'm almost scared to know. Hoping she isn't baking every day and is taking care of herself.

"She looks about as shitty as you, if that's what you want to know. The fact that the public isn't aware of your relationship is a blessing, really; otherwise, she would be struggling, I think. But she remains laser focused. She said she has only failed one client in the past and has no desire to make it two. Her commitment to you is unwavering." Harrison's voice is full of confidence, any hesitation he had about Willow before now gone. She has yet another Langford who wants her in his life, albeit professionally. Thank God Harrison is already taken.

"She hasn't failed," I murmur, my brow furrowing, not liking her thinking that way.

"She thinks she has."

"Bullshit. She is amazing. I am the one who fucked up, not her." I may have made a huge mistake, but I own it. I'm not perfect, nor have I ever claimed to be.

"She is taking it personally." Harrison watches me like a hawk.

"I knew that she would, married to the job and all that."

"What if it is yours?" Harrison asks the question everyone seems to dodge.

"What do you mean?"

"What if the baby is yours, Tennyson?" he reiterates firmly.

"I don't want to think about it." I dismiss him, really hoping it isn't.

"But you need to."

"I don't even want kids. Don't get me wrong, I hold the trophy for best uncle to Rosie, a title I plan to carry over onto your kids whenever you and Beth get there. But I am not father material. I wasn't wired that way. I am happy to look after them, feed them sugar, and hand them back, and that is the extent of my desire," I say with complete honesty. Having kids was never my mission. If it happened, I would deal with it, but it was never something I wanted. I am happy without that level of responsibility. If nothing else, having Bob to look after these past few weeks has taught me that. I quickly look out the window and spot him digging up the new posies in the garden. Emily won't be happy, but at least Rosie will get a laugh. She loves that dog already.

"Maybe you will feel differently once you see a baby and it is yours," he offers with a shrug.

"If this is my baby, I will do the right thing. I will pay all expenses. I will spend time with it. I will do everything I can and be the best father I am capable of being. But I am not marrying Katerina. This will never be a perfect family situation. I will never go against any of her parenting wishes. She can raise this baby as her own. I will love it, of course I will, but there is no happy family here."

"Why are you so against having kids?" His brow crumples at me, trying to figure me out.

"Mom and Dad were not the best example," I mumble, pretty sure I don't need to explain that one.

"But you see Ben and how happy he is now?"

"Yeah, but you also feel the pain when your parent dies," I snip. Harrison's eyebrows shoot to his hairline.

"I think of Dad often too." He nods, watching me carefully.

"Not just Dad, but Nanny Helen," I admit.

"Helen?" The look on his face is one of bewilderment.

"Yeah, I have been thinking of her a lot lately."

"I am surprised you even remember her."

"She was more of a mother to me than Mom was." Our mom was no mother. Just a woman who was around the house growing up.

"Yeah, but she died so long ago." All us boys had nannies, and I am sure that both Harrison and Ben both still visit theirs, funding their retirement completely. Something I didn't get the opportunity to do.

"You know, I feel like there is something weird about it all," I say to him, finally voicing the things I have been thinking about.

"What do you mean?"

"The night she died."

"You always said you couldn't remember," he says curiously, now sitting forward on his seat.

"I never could, until Willow got my heart beating

again after years of ignoring the world and my feelings. She had me assessing everything about my life from the first moment we met in New York, and I haven't stopped since. I have this one memory of Helen that I can't see properly, but I think..." I tell him, my brain scrambling to pull it all together.

"What?"

"I just think she didn't die of heart failure." I sigh. "It is all I have. A feeling. I wish I could grasp it, but I can't."

"Maybe look into that day. Talk to her family. Maybe that will help you get through the mental block. Seems like it weighs you down and you have enough going on right now. It could be good to clear the old clutter completely," Harrison offers, and he is right.

"I think I might need to go to Singapore for this deal," I put it out there, then look at Harrison, seeing when the penny drops.

"Maybe you should. Take Eddie with you and stop over in Indonesia on the way? It may help you to see her family in person." I nod. My Singapore deal is going through rapidly. Things moved quickly once I had a clear vision, the right contacts, and no competitor standing in my way. Even though the media locally is having a fucking field day about my sperm count, it doesn't even make the news in Asia. So it is full steam ahead on that project.

"Willow said the *Business News* interview will go out in a week or so after the media storm blows over. This deal in Singapore is happening regardless of your sex life antics, so maybe you should fly out tomorrow?" Harrison says, and I take a breath.

"Maybe I should fly out tonight." I look at him for confirmation that I am making the right decision, and he nods. So, I make the calls to Eddie and Melody and pack a bag.

It's time to do the right thing.

32

WILLOW

I sit on the sofa and take a deep breath. It has fast become my new resting place. I have been working ridiculous hours for the last week, and the only chance I get to stop has been when I have taken five minutes just to sit, right here on this sofa.

Things are calming down. But I am still on edge. It is not totally out of character for me. When any of my clients has a hiccup such as this, I work all day and all night to mitigate it. And now I see the dust settling. Even though there is still an interest and an air of intrigue, the local media have spun this story to death already, and with no updates or additional information, they have started to move on to other topics.

Of course it helps if other people offer themselves up for scandal and the media jump on them instead. Disgraced baseball player and former Maryland loveable jock, David Taylor Smith, apparently has new charges against him, something about tax evasion and misman-agement of business funds. My business might be about solving my clients' battles, but I have a healthy relationship with many journalists, and so I have used that to my full advantage this week.

While we are now over the big issue and no longer the hot topic, there is still uncertainty lurking around the paternity of the child. I speak to Tennyson almost every day, and his stance has not wavered. He swears he used a condom and doesn't believe the child is his. Katerina, on the other hand, is adamant and is stalling on the medical requirements regarding paternity. It is one hot mess of a situation. We can't force her, and we certainly don't want any harm coming to the baby. Her being stressed at this situation, her doctor tells us, is not helping. As newly pregnant, she needs to remain stress free. But whether we know now or in eight months' time, we will have an answer eventually.

All that is left for me to decide is where that leaves Tennyson and me. I have thought of not much else but him this past week. Saide and Josh have been around but have kept a wide berth from me, knowing that I need to focus and have mental clarity at a time like this. But in the dark, quiet times, when I am lying in bed and unable to sleep, I think about him. I think about how I am in love with him. I am not sure when it happened. But it did.

Can I overcome this situation? Can I move forward with him with this cloud over us? He told me he loved me that night he drunkenly fell asleep on my sofa, but I doubt he remembers. And people say a lot of things when they are under the influence of alcohol. But I can feel it. When we are together, it is a happiness I have never known. And I know he feels it too.

So what if he is having a baby with another woman? It was a one-night stand, before we were even together. There is no love there. It is not her bed that he is in, not her phone he is calling. I am adult enough to understand that these things happen and to be honest and deal with the outcomes that come from it. But I can't deny the anxiety that swirls inside of me when I think about telling him I can't bear his children. That if he wants me, then a baby is not in our future. I need to be strong enough to tell him I can't give him that and I need to be strong enough to let him go if it's something he wants.

My phone startles me from my thoughts, and I grab it quickly, my adrenaline not calming for a second. It is an unknown number, but I pick it up regardless.

"Willow Valentine," I say professionally.

"Willow, it's Beth," her voice soothes down the line. We have spoken a few times this past week. She is such a good friend.

"Hey, sorry I didn't recognize the number."

"I'm in the office, on the landline. How are things going?" she asks, and I launch into work specifics.

"Media is calming, the story is blowing over. I am sure you are aware of the legal and paternity issues," I say.

"Yes, I am aware of it all, but how are you? Harrison mentioned that Tennyson is missing you terribly." I hold my breath for a beat. While Beth and I have spoken, I haven't delved into the personal nature of my relationship with Tennyson.

"I'm fine. It was a shock, obviously. There was a lot of work to do to get a strategy in place and I feel bad that I let this happen on my watch. But personally..." My voice drifts off, and Beth stays quiet, waiting for me to finish. "Personally, I think I am okay now," I say, resolve in my tone, and I almost feel relief at admitting it out loud.

"You are a strong woman, Willow. But I know Tennyson is hurting too. I hope you guys are talking?" she asks, and that is Beth, always looking out for everyone else too. I smile even though she can't see me.

"We will. I'll speak to him tonight." And we will. I'm resolved to figure this out with him.

"Okay, well, I need to run. Let's catch up in the next few days when you are ready?" Beth asks, but I know her calendar is busier than mine, so I huff a laugh.

"I would love that," I say before we say our goodbyes, and I sink back into the sofa. The phone rings again immediately. It is another unknown number, and I laugh.

"What did you forget this time?" I say to Beth with a laugh. But it isn't Beth on the phone.

"Is this Miss Valentine?" a stern female voice says from the other end of the phone.

"Yes, this is Willow Valentine," I say, sitting up, now on high alert.

"This is Diane Langford. I believe you are managing my son's affairs?" My eyebrows rise. This wasn't a phone call I was expecting.

"I am working with all your sons, Mrs. Langford." Harrison is already recruiting me to be on his team. Ben and I speak to each other about five times per day, and Eddie calls me every morning and every night just to check in.

"Yes. Well, I need you to stop," she says, and I still.

"Excuse me?" I must have misheard.

"I need you to stop. Tennyson is very vulnerable right now. He is going to be a father, and he needs to be with the mother so they can raise this baby together. Be a family. Do the right thing." With every word, my heart feels heavier.

"There is a very real possibility that he is not the father of this baby, Mrs. Langford."

"So?" she snarks, and my stomach clenches at what that could mean.

"So, we need to wait for paternity before we can—" I start to say, but she cuts me off.

"Tsk. There will be no paternity test. Tennyson will be the father of this baby. Please make it happen." I smile in disbelief. This woman is unbelievable.

"Mrs. Langford—"

"Just listen to me..." she says, her voice now almost hissing. "Katerina Newcomb is one of the wealthiest business heiresses in the country. Tennyson *will be* the father of this baby. No paternity test is needed." I feel sick. I have heard about Mrs. Langford, but I didn't expect this. How can a mother do this to her son? Set his life up merely for public display rather than for love. Why the hell would she want to throw her son to the wolves to live a life that is not what he wants? No wonder he needs me. He doesn't even have a mother who cares. In this moment, I swear to myself that I will talk to him and make things right. He doesn't deserve this. None of it. I take a deep breath as the anger starts to swirl. This week has been a mess and now I have had enough.

"No, you listen to me," I bite out, feeling a little bad to be taking this tone, but I know enough about her to not have her boss me around. "There is a firm strategy in place for Tennyson and all the Langford brothers. I am not privy to communicate that strategy to you, as I work with your sons. I would suggest that if you are trying to manipulate this situation, like you tried with your other two sons, then you back down now, because you won't be successful." My heart picks up pace. I can't believe this is Tennyson's mother.

"How *dare* you—" I don't let her finish.

"No, how *dare* you, Mrs. Langford!" My voice rises, my body burning in anger.

"Well, I have never been spoken to like this in my entire life! Do you have any idea *who I am*!" she screeches, clearly not happy.

"Oh, I know exactly who I am talking to right now. But the question you need to ask yourself is, *do you*?" I am not taking her bullshit. Someone has to stand up to this woman, and that someone appears to be me. I will protect Tennyson from her, even if it is with my last dying breath.

"Why you—" I hang up before she can finish. I have had enough, and there are not any more words that can be spoken rationally. I toss my phone onto the sofa and jump up, needing to move my body. I pace the living room, my blood boiling. What an evil, evil woman. She obviously doesn't know that we are connected romantically, because if she did, then I think the phone conversation would have gone differently. Or at least, I'd hope so.

Like it has all week, my phone now rings again, and I march to it and snatch it up. If this is another private number, I am going to throw it against the wall. But

Tennyson's name lights up my screen, and I take a deep breath, relieved.

"Hey..." I say into the phone as I slump back on my sofa. *God, I miss him.*

"Hey... You okay?" he asks, sounding concerned. I guess I am not covering my stress very well.

"Yes, sure," I say, pushing a smile onto my face, trying to sound more chipper. There is no way I am telling him about his mother's call just now. He has enough to worry about.

"Look, I know you don't want to talk about us. I know you need to focus, but—"

"I'm ready. I'm ready to talk," I say too quickly, sounding keen, because I am. I am so ready to just try to move forward now that I have a handle on things.

You are?" he asks, surprised.

"Yes, I am. I am sorry, Tennyson. I am sorry for not talking earlier, for making you leave my house last week. I am sorry I let you down with this." Tears prick my eyes as the sorrys come thick and fast.

"Willow, stop. There is nothing. *Nothing.* You need to be sorry for. It is my past behavior, and it is all occurring because of me."

"Do you want to come over so we can chat in person?" I ask quickly, wanting nothing more than to see him right now, to hug him.

"Urhhhh," he groans. "I really want to, but I got a late flight tonight to Singapore with Eddie. I was just calling to let you know. I didn't think you would want to see me yet, but I can cancel it," he says brightly, and I know he would actually prefer that from the hope in his voice. But we have to stick to our plans, especially where work is concerned.

"No! No. You go. Singapore is important and getting away from the local media and making this big business deal will be a good step in the right direction. Your *Business News* interview is going live in the next few days, so it will all actually tie in really well. We can talk when you get back." As much as I want to see him and talk to him properly, Singapore is an opportunity that might disappear if he waits too long.

"Willow…" he growls like a moaning teenager, and I laugh. I haven't laughed all week, and it feels so good.

"God, I miss you," he murmurs, and I already feel lighter. This is my Tennyson.

"I miss you…" I reply quietly. "When will you be back?"

"I was going for a week, but I will be back in a few days now." I laugh again, tears stinging my eyes.

"Get Ben to drop Bob off here. I will watch him while you are gone," I offer, because I know Bob is tearing up Ben's beautiful estate, the gardens getting shredded.

"Okay, three days tops, and then I will come straight to your place as soon as I land." I nod, even though he can't see me.

"Three days," I say, and I hear commotion behind him.

"I've got to go. I just pulled up to the jet." I imagine him in his flashy town car, pulling up to his private jet, ready to travel to the other side of the world.

"Okay, be safe. Get the deal done." I already miss him even more.

"I'll be back before you know it. And then we have a lot of catching up to do," he says, and I can hear the relief in his tone. "See you soon, Cupcake," he adds sweetly, and I sigh.

"Bye, Tenn," I say, *I love you* on the tip of my tongue, but it doesn't pass my lips. That is something I want to reserve for when I see him. Our phone call ends, and I lie on the sofa, taking a few breaths. My body feels battered, my head hurts. I have been juggling so many moving parts, I am utterly exhausted. So I snuggle in, and within a minute, I fall into a deep sleep.

33

———

TENNYSON

It's so hot, my shirt is sticking to my chest, and sweat drips down my back. Eddie and I have spent the last two days in Singapore, and the project is now all signed.

A few meetings, a fancy dinner, some handshakes and signatures, and I just contracted the most expensive and largest construction development in the Asia region, bigger than any other Langford Construction have ever done before. Eddie will oversee managing the tenancy and leasing arrangements. Willow's advice about Singapore is now all cemented, with the best location, best builders, and best team. We break ground in a few months, and this whole project is more seamless than any other I have had. Seems everything Willow touches flows like gold through my life.

"It's fucking hot as balls," I say to Eddie as we both look out of the car windows.

"I feel like I am swimming in sweat," Eddie acknowledges as we pass rice paddy field after rice paddy field. It is a beautiful part of the world, but it's just not where I want to be right now.

We landed in Indonesia two hours ago. The jet is waiting on the tarmac for us. The urge I have to get back to Willow festers on my skin. As the car pulls up outside a shanty on the outskirts of a small city in the southern region, I see kids playing on the road. Not with scooters or bikes, but with sticks and what looks like a very well-used soccer ball. The sight of which reminds me of Josh and his mean right kick. *Little punk.*

"This it?" Eddie asks, looking out at the street.

"I think so," I murmur as I step out of the car. My stomach feels heavy. Like it already knows that this conversation is going to take a lot out of me. I have no idea what, if anything, I will find, but I feel like it is the right thing to do.

"I'll take a walk around and come in later. Give you guys some time," Eddie says, slapping my arm and walking off down the road to play soccer with the local kids. Now that is a guy who wants a family. He doesn't even have to tell me he does.

Walking up to the house, people in the street look at me suspiciously. I am obviously not from around here. My shirt and suit pants, shiny black shoes, sunglasses, and expensive car make me stick out among the rocky road. The houses are separated by rice fields so green and lush, it's a wonder they are even real. Although hot, the sky is a rich blue. It is beautiful.

I don't get a chance to knock, as Helen's husband opens the door, expecting me since I had Melody contact him while I was in transit. He offers me a big, warm smile, one which I immediately return.

"Come, come," he says, ushering me inside the small home. I need to duck as I walk through, the doorframe smaller than I am used to, and as I stand just inside the door, I get a vision of the entire place. Heaviness overtakes my heart at the conditions he lives in, but his smile is bright as he looks me over. I give him a smile of my own, remembering that he is happy, healthy, and this is his life.

There is a small shrine on the far wall, and my shoes click on the cracked tile floor as I walk over to it. A few photos of Helen are propped up with fresh flowers and incense burning. He must miss her, and my heart bleeds. She looks just how I remember.

"Please sit?" He waves his hands toward the sofa, and as I take a seat in this cluttered living room of Nanny Helen's home, I feel equal parts welcome and out of place. Inside is quiet, with no traffic noises. Only a few squeals of laughter float in from the kids outside, the fan blasting us with warm air, not taking away the stifling heat at all, but I am grateful for it. Helen's husband sits beside me and pulls out an old photo album, seemingly knowing what I need without me even verbalizing it.

"This is the last time she came home before she died." He points to a photo, and I look down at Nanny Helen's smile. I am too big for this small sofa, and I take up almost the entire space, but I hunch over and look at the photo in the album with a sigh. Helen came to our family straight from Indonesia when she was young. When she started, I'm told she could barely speak English, but by the time I was eight, she was fluent. Looking at her now, a flood of memories come back, mainly of me laughing, and her smiling, constantly feeding me, and showering me with love.

"How was she when she came back for that holiday?" I ask. She came back for her annual Christmas holiday for a week. Enough time to see her family and spend time with her husband. As an adult, I am not sure how she did it, but she was the sole breadwinner, the kind of woman who lived off very little because any spare money she had she sent home to her family. He looks solemn. He lives by himself now, as he and Helen had no children because she was too busy being paid handsomely to look after someone else's.

"She was beautiful. Radiant. Full of energy. Talked about you nonstop," he says in broken English with a laugh. "She would be so happy to see you now, all grown up." His smile is genuine, looking at me proudly. I give him a small smile and a nod, my lips pursed. It feels nice to know she loved me. At least someone did.

There is a small knock on the door, and we look up and see Eddie. His soccer game with the kids must've been short-lived. I make the quick introductions and Eddie sits at a stool opposite us as I get back to learning more about Nanny Helen.

"Does heart failure run in her family?" I ask, because she was young, fit, and happy. But the cause of death on her medical certificate is heart failure. I have read and reread that certificate numerous times these past few weeks and have come to the conclusion that unless she had a secret addiction of some kind, then she must have had a family history. There is really no other explanation.

"No. Her parents are still alive. As are all her siblings. Each of them as healthy as the day they were born." I can't believe he is so calm. My insides are tangled, my stomach in knots. *God, I need Willow.* I flick my eyes and meet Eddie's as he looks at me. A mix of confusion and suspicion is on his face, and I look back to Helen's husband, needing to know more.

"So she had no ailments at all?" I ask, frowning, because that doesn't make sense.

"Only her allergy," he says, flicking the page in the book to show more photos of Nanny Helen on her final trip home that Christmas.

"Allergy?" I look at him in surprise. *I can't remember any allergies.*

"Nuts. She was highly allergic to nuts. All types, tree nuts, seeds, you name it." I see Eddie run his hands through his hair, the look on his face one of uncertainty.

"I don't remember that," I murmur as I feel nausea clawing at my stomach.

"Neither do I," Eddie says, and we share a silent moment, knowing that pieces are starting to come together, but it isn't the full story yet. We continue to look over the beautiful, smiling photos of Helen, and we work through a second album, then a third, but my mind is not settled. It is like my memories are coming together, and I can feel the answer to my questions right at the surface. I just can't grasp them yet.

$\sim$

"So, what are you going to do about the information?" Eddie asks me. He slept for most of the flight home. The heat and kids in Indonesia had him soaked by the time we got back outside after spending time with Helen's husband.

"I had no idea she had an allergy! Why can't I remember these things?" I growl, frustrated at myself. I am itching to see Willow. I jumped off the plane and into our waiting car so fast, Eddie struggled to keep up.

"I think you are placing too much pressure on yourself. You were only twelve. I am surprised you remember anything." He looks at me, concerned. My younger brother is the nice Langford boy. He has women follow him everywhere like all of us do, but he is a bit softer than the rest of us. He hates the billions we have. I am sure he would prefer to travel the globe and get lost in communities all over the world, volunteering and helping others. But he has a role to play in our family business, and we couldn't do what we do without him.

"She gave up her entire life for me, Eddie," I say to him, still not comprehending that a woman who wasn't my mother did that.

"It is the life many women lead. They leave their home countries to make money abroad and send it back to their families. It is common. You can't feel bad about that. You never had a say in it all anyway." His brow crumples as he looks at me.

"I have been having flashbacks. Memories pop up and then disappear just as quick."

"How long has this been going on for?" he presses.

"A while, but they have become more vivid this past

month or so. She has always been on my mind, but I think I blocked it out. As a kid, I was shipped off to boarding school so fast that I barely had time to think about it. Then girls started paying attention, and partying became my go-to."

"That was when you started working with Willow, right?" Eddie asks curiously, and he is right.

"Willow has really opened my eyes to a lot of things, but I think the biggest thing she has done has helped me clear my mind and clean up my lifestyle, which has allowed all these old memories to flow." I smile, thinking about her. She was hired to help my reputation, but she doesn't even know how much she has helped me. I rub my head, itching to see her. "I have a headache thinking about everything. Anyway, are you all good with this Singapore deal?" I ask him. He loved Singapore. He had some good meetings himself.

"It will be a big project, but I think I can handle it," he says with a smirk, one I match.

The car slows as we pull onto Willow's street. "I'm out. Are you good?" I ask him, already grabbing my things to jump out of the car.

"I'm going to look over the maintenance at Harborside. Go get your girl," he says, waving me off. I have so many questions about why he spends his time maintaining a building we own, when we have a whole raft of maintenance men, but I know it is his way of de-stressing. He actually enjoys working with his hands so I leave him be.

I grab my bag from the driver and don't even wait for the car to retreat before I take the few stairs on Willow's porch two at a time. I raced here straight from the airport. I need a shower, I need food, I need sleep, but I need Willow more. I lift my hand to knock, but as always, she is a step ahead of me and opens the door.

"Hi," she says sweetly, and it is enough to leave me breathless. She leans against the open door, looking up at me. Her hair is down and wrapped around her shoulder. Her white t-shirt that dips into a V at her chest. Her jeans are rolled up to her ankles, her feet bare, her toenails painted light pink. I swallow the growl that is begging to come out.

"Hey," I say, my voice sounding hoarse.

"You're early," she says, stepping back, opening the door wider.

"I wanted to be quicker," I say honestly as I walk in. I reach for her automatically, my hand finding the familiar curve of her waist, and I sweep it around her back and pull her to me. My lips land on her forehead as her hands slide around my waist, and together we stand in each other's arms. I feel her body soften in my embrace, and I close my eyes and take a deep breath. *It feels so good to have her back in my arms.* We have a lot to talk about, but I never want to let her go. Bob's loud bark interrupts my thoughts, and my eyes ping open at the same time as Willow steps away from me, my body feeling cold again.

"Come in, I have a surprise for you," she says with a small smile playing on her lips. I follow her into the kitchen, the rest of the house quiet. My attention flicks to the sofa where I spent my last night here, and I run my hands through my hair. *I'm never drinking with my brothers again.*

When I spot Bob outside, my smile widens. Surprisingly, he has grown on me, and I will admit, I think I missed him too. I walk over to the glass door to look out at him. Willow has set him up with a few balls and toys, and he is currently pushing one around with his nose in a big circle, keeping himself very entertained. It makes me happy that he feels at home here just as much as I do.

"He hasn't touched your garden?" I ask, looking at her in question, because her garden beds still look immaculate.

"No. I got him some toys, and he has been too busy playing to bother with my garden."

"You've been busy?" I spot a few containers with cupcakes piled high on her kitchen counter.

"Yeah, I will give them to Josh's mom to take to the hospital. The nurses love them." She laughs, and I feel warmth run through my body at the sound. It is like I have been out in the cold for days and now I am slowly defrosting.

"I've missed you," I say, turning to her, and she smiles.

"I made you something." Pulling away from me, she opens her refrigerator. I take a few steps toward her, and the sting of her not saying she missed me is short-lived when I see what she places on the kitchen counter. My body stills. My heart pounds as I look at the large New York cheesecake that sits there. It's perfect. It is exactly like Nanny Helen used to make. Every Friday without fail. *Today is Friday.*

"I hope you don't mind. I spoke to Harrison, and he told me what it used to look like. I wasn't sure if—" she says, but I cut her off.

"It's perfect." I'm still in a state of shock as I continue looking at the cake before my eyes land on her. I strut toward her, wanting her in my arms again, but she stands firm, putting her hands up to stop me. I frown, not liking the distance she creates as she takes a step back.

"There is something I need to tell you. Something we need to talk about." She looks stricken, and I feel sick. *Has the paternity test been done, and she is telling me the results? Has something else happened?* I have no voice, but I nod at her to continue.

"Let's take a seat," she says, and my body fills with dread.

"I have been sitting for hours. Willow, what is going on?" I ask, panicked, because she looks a little pale. She takes a seat at her dining table, her hands wringing together in front of her.

"Please, can you sit? I need to talk to you about something." I scurry to the table and pull out a chair to appease her. I feel like I want to vomit.

"I know there is a lot going on. Maybe it is too early for us to have this conversation, but..." she starts, and I see her swallow, struggling with the words. My heart races as my mind fights through different scenarios.

"What is it? Just tell me," I plead with her, feeling whatever is coming is not going to be good.

"It's just, if we are going to move ahead with us, then you need to know. You need to be aware..."

"Willow, just tell me, please," I growl, wishing she would just say it already.

"Tennyson, when I was younger, I had a lot of medical issues, a lot of minor surgeries and various medical procedures on my uterus and ovaries. Because of this, I can't have children. I wanted to tell you this now, because... because while the paternity test hasn't been performed, if you want children, then I need you to know that it isn't something that I can give you. We are new, just starting out, and my feelings for you have grown. But if a big family and lots of babies is something that you want in your future, then maybe Katerina and this baby—" I have to stop her before she can say anything more.

"I don't want kids. I never wanted kids. I told you that first night we met in New York that I am not marriage material and that also extends to kids. I love kids. I love being the fun uncle. I love to hang out with Rosie and play with dolls for a while, then walk away and leave her to her parents. Kids are not a part of my future that I ever envisioned," I tell her quickly, hoping she takes me seriously. Willow looks at me, her eyes glassy, her chest moving rapidly.

"But, Tennyson, if you change your mind, I can't..." I'm not able to fight the smile that starts on my face, and relief sweeps through my body.

"I won't change my mind, Willow. It is something I have known for a very long time. Willow, you are more perfect for me than if I actually made God a list and he produced exactly that. You are everything I want in a woman. You are strong, independent, career-focused, loving, the best cook, amazing friend and sister. You are destined for great things in your business, and I love everything about you. Even your psycho crazy twelve-year-old best friend."

I watch her swallow, taking in my words.

"But if you..." she says again, and I see her shoulders start to lower, her voice sounding a little more hopeful. I feel like jumping in the air and doing a happy dance. She is perfect. So fucking perfect for me.

"I'm not changing my mind, Willow. We were destined, you and me. You were put on this earth for me. Now get your sweet ass over here before I go crazy from not touching you." I need her to meet me halfway. I am serious; there is no changing my mind. Kids are not something I ever really wanted. But Willow is someone I really do want. I wait a beat, wondering if she is actually going to come to me, my heart feeling like it is in my throat as my breathing is shallow.

"Bossy much?" she mumbles before a big smile comes to her face, and she jumps off her seat, launching herself into my arms. I catch her with ease, feeling her legs wrap around my middle, and my hands immediately grasp her round ass just as I take her mouth with mine. I feel her body relax on contact. Relief sweeps through both of us, my heart expanding even more, knowing that we have just pushed through some of the biggest boundaries we are ever going to face as a couple. We are on the same page. We've cleared the air and can finally be together just how I have always wanted.

"God, you feel good, Cupcake," I moan against her lips. Now that I have her in my arms, I am not putting her down. My hands are glued.

"I missed you so much," she says, and I taste a tear as it falls silently down her cheek. I pull away for a moment, looking into her glassy eyes. Another tear falls, and I lean forward, kissing it away, and she huffs a laugh.

"I will catch all your tears, Willow. Today, tomorrow, the next day. I will catch them all."

She leans her head to rest on mine, our eyes glued to each other, as her hands run through my hair, before landing on the back of my neck and pulling me closer. Our lips meet, and I kiss her slowly. Purposefully. Deliberately. I take my time, wanting to savor her. She tastes like sweetness and seduction all rolled into one. We are soft and wanting, our tongues tangle, and I relish having her lips on mine. Her hands continue to massage my scalp, which is soothing and almost my kryptonite. My hands flex on her ass, and I pull her hips tight against me, meshing our bodies together. As exhausted as I am, I want to sink into her, my dick already standing at attention in my pants.

"Are you telling me where your bedroom is, or am I going to fuck you right here on your dining room table?"

34

WILLOW

"Top of the stairs to the left," I pant, feeling whole for the first time in over a week. He came back. He is here. He is with me, and I can't believe it. I had worked myself up so much that I was sure he would turn and walk out the door the minute I told him my news. I practiced what I was going to say all day. I repeated the words over and over to ensure I got them right. It took me a moment to comprehend what he was saying back to me. Having children and starting a family is a general norm for most people, so when Tennyson admitted that wasn't something he wanted, it was a surprise. It took me a few seconds for it to register, but then I felt relief, then ecstatic happiness. Now I just want to feel.

I frantically tackle the buttons of his shirt while he holds me tight in his arms and runs up the stairs. He looked exhausted when I first opened the front door, probably due to the long flight and lack of sleep, but he is full of life now. With me glued to his front, he bounds up the stairs and struts straight toward my bedroom. My sister is out with Josh, but even with the house empty, he kicks the door shut before we fall onto my bed.

"You are beautiful, so fucking beautiful," he murmurs, his lips leaving mine momentarily as they drag down my neck and cleavage. "Sit up," he demands, and I do. He pulls at the hem of my t-shirt and lifts it straight off my frame, throwing it across the room. His mouth immediately lands on my shoulders, peppering my skin before he lowers my bra straps from my shoulders. He feels so good, his lips on me making me melt. Kneeling on the bed between my legs, his hands mold my breasts, pulling the cups of my bra down. He exposes my nipples, which peak at his touch, before his hands trail around my back and he unclips my bra.

"God, I missed your tits," he mumbles as he lowers his mouth, taking one between his lips. He rolls his tongue around it and bites it a little, tweaking the other nipple with his hand.

"I need you," I say, not recognizing my own voice, the pleading sounds new, but I have never wanted anything more in my life than this man naked right now. With his shirt all undone, my hands tackle his jeans, unbuttoning them as he pulls his shirt from his body. I lower his zipper and pull his jeans down, taking his underwear with them and watching as his cock springs out already hard, ready and waiting right in line with my face. I wrap my hand around it and massage, eliciting a growl from his chest.

"Mmmmm, I missed your hands on me," he says, looking down at me as both his hands work magic on my breasts.

"What about my mouth?" I ask innocently, then lean forward, taking the tip of him in my mouth. I moan at the taste, at having him back, at our connection.

"Mmmmm, your mouth is one of my favorite things about you," he moans, my eyes flicking up, and I see him looking down right at me, so I swirl my tongue teasingly and take him deeper.

"Did you miss my cock? Did you miss me fucking your face, Cupcake?" My body quivers. His dirty talk is something I love, and I immediately squeeze my thighs together. "You need me between your thighs, baby?" His hips start to move in time with my mouth. "Is your warm, wet pussy craving my cock, just like your pretty little mouth?" He is panting now, and I need to come. As he pulls away, I take a deep breath. He grabs my hips and throws me back farther on the bed, then his hands are unbuttoning my jeans in an instant and he pulls them down my legs along with my underwear in one rapid movement. His eyes are watching me closely as he pulls his jeans off and throws them to meet mine, our clothes now all in a puddle on the floor.

"Are you just going to talk about it or show me some action?" I push him with a sly smile, and he laughs.

"Oh, you are so fucked. I am going to eat this pussy until you are a moaning mess in my mouth, then I am going to fuck it so hard, your screaming will cause the neighbors to come running." His hands run up the inside of my thighs, and he lowers himself, ready to start on the first promise. His face meets my thigh, and I feel his tender kisses before his tongue lashes up to my center. He buries himself then, his mouth meeting my skin, his tongue lapping at me, sucking my clit, finding a rhythm.

"Ohhhhh, I missed this," I moan, my body already twisting, the feeling almost too much. I lean up on one elbow as my other hand rushes to the back of his head. My fingers dig into his scalp and pull his hair. A growl vibrates across my skin, and my fingers automatically massage his head as my hips grind against his face.

"Oh, Tenn..." His hands now firmly grab my ass cheeks, squeezing them and pulling himself in deeper. My head falls back, and he sucks harder and harder, his warm tongue then hitting my core, and I combust. My breath pauses, the air getting stuck in my chest, and my muscles contract as he continues to suck my clit hard until I'm shaking.

"Tenn!" I yell out into the room, my body now liquid as I relax back onto the bed. But his mouth's not yet finished as he continues licking and kissing my center before he moves up my body, his tongue trailing up my skin, latching on to my nipple, sucking and groaning some more.

"If I can do that every day for the rest of my life with you, I would be a very happy man, Willow Valentine," he says as we come face-to-face, our noses nearly touching.

"Hmmmm, I think I would like that very much, Mr. Langford." A wide smile now stretches across my face, one that he matches.

"Now, though, I want to fuck you till you scream. Think you can handle that? Because I need you hard and fast. It is going to be quick and dirty," he quips, and I laugh.

"Do your best." A large, barking laugh that carries around my room sounds from him before it lands back into my chest.

"I love you, Willow," he says, still smiling, his eyes twinkling, and my heart almost bursts. My breath stops at his statement, the two of us lying here, completely naked, a light sheen of sweat on our bodies, him looking right into my eyes. It's perfect.

"I have totally and completely fallen in love with you, Tennyson," I whisper my truth, and he leans down, taking my lips with his. His lips don't leave mine as we spend a moment relishing our new words, being together and touching each other endlessly.

I see him looking around, and I realize that he is looking for a condom.

"Tenn... we could go bare..." I suggest, wanting to feel all of him now. He looks at me with slightly widened eyes, pausing his movements.

"I'm clean. I haven't been with anyone else but you for a very long time, and well, we have already established that there are no babies coming either," I add, raising my eyebrows.

"I'm clean. You saw my medical records. I've never had sex without a condom, Willow," he states with so much conviction, I have no doubt. All I can do is nod because I did see his health check. As part of his paternity requirements, he had to give over a DNA sample but also had a full sexual health exam at the same time.

"Fuck, Willow, I have never been bare before," he says, crawling over me, smiling. I can feel his anticipation building.

"Okay, well, then all you need to do is make me scream," I tease, and he smiles.

"Challenge accepted," he says at the same time he slams into me. I hang on to his shoulders, because he wasn't lying, his pace is frantic. His thrusts are fast, hitting my clit with every quick movement, the feeling running through me instantaneously as my hands claw at his body.

"Fuck, this feels fucking amazing," he moans, lost in the new sensation.

"Oh my God..." I feel him giving me every emotion. Every stress, every bit of tension, every feeling that he has inside, he is giving to me. He is powerful, his desire for me intense, and it is all I can do to hang on for the ride.

"I need you... I need this," he grits out and pulls out quickly, sitting back on his knees and grabbing my hip. Turning me over in one sweep, so I'm face down, he grabs my hips and lifts them up, pushing into me from behind.

"Ohhhh, Tenn..." I whimper, the sensation new. His pace continues, his hands squeezing my hips, and I feel him deep, taking and giving all at the same time.

"You feel so fucking good, so fucking good, Willow," he moans as my fingers grip the bedsheets, and I curl them around my hands, struggling to hang on, the pleasure overwhelming. We are not cementing our feelings. We are engraving them on each other.

"Come here, baby." He changes our position again. Pulling me up, sitting me on his lap, my back still to his chest. His hand lowers to my clit, his finger circling, matching the pace of his thrusts, sweat now covering both of us, the slap of our skin traveling around my room.

"Tenn..." I cry out like a woman possessed, never having felt anything like this before. He has total control over my body, and he knows exactly what to do with it. I lean my head back on his shoulder, my arms up and around his neck. He buries his head into my neck, sucking my skin as his fingers continue to circle, the other hand molding to my breast.

"This feels so fucking good. I am never fucking you with a condom again. So good, baby, such a good fucking pussy you have," he whispers in my ear, and his words send me over the cliff.

"Tenn!" I scream. "Tenn... Tenn... Tennn!" I'm panting to catch my breath, my orgasm feeling like it comes over and over, one after another, after another. His hold on me tightens as his hands move to my hips, him bouncing me on top of him, and then I hear him roar.

"Fuckkk, Willow..." My name leaves his mouth on a yell, as I feel him pulse inside me, his orgasm just as intense as mine, before we both fall onto my bed in a tangled mess.

We are still for a beat, trying to catch our breath. Tears prick my eyes at how intense that was, how connected we felt, how amazing we are together, before I look at him and smile.

"Now that's what I call a *welcome home*, Cupcake."

IT IS DARK OUTSIDE, and Tennyson and I have hardly moved, apart from a very quick shower and when I ran downstairs to grab the cheesecake and two forks. We are now perched in my bed, the cake almost half-eaten between us. Both still naked, we have talked for hours about everything.

"So how was your trip?" I ask, our conversation only now just getting to the last few days.

"Singapore is done," he says, a small smile dancing on his lips.

"Congratulations! That is awesome. I'm so proud of you." But from the look on his face, I can tell there is more.

"I stopped in Indonesia on the way back." My brow crumples in confusion.

"It is where Nanny Helen was from. I went to see her village," he offers, and now I am intrigued. He has talked about his nanny a few times, and I know they were close, but it feels like there is something that is not settled within him about her. I just don't know what it is.

"Tell me more about Nanny Helen," I encourage, feeling full, but taking another small scrap of cheesecake on my fork. I just can't stop eating it, it is so delicious.

"She came to our house when I was a baby. From an agency originally, I think. She was with me from just after I was born until she died when I was twelve," he says, looking off into the distance, lost in his memories.

"When she first came, she barely spoke English, but she came to the United States to make money to send back to her family. We had a small cottage at the back of our place where she lived. I was her life, and she was mine." I have noticed that he talks about her a lot. Now with the faraway look in his eyes, his demeanor changes, and he looks almost sad.

"Did you speak to her family? Friends?" I ask, hoping that they are all well.

"I spent an hour with her husband, just going through old photos and talking about her." His eyes become glassy, and my heart breaks. I know this wound is deep. I am just not sure how deep it goes.

"That's nice that you got to see him. Spend some time with him and talk. I am sure it brought him some comfort to see you after all these years," I offer, and he turns slowly to look at me.

"It brought me comfort too. I still think about her a lot," he admits.

"She was a big part of your upbringing; it is understandable to think about her."

"Is there something I can do? For her husband, do you think? He is poor. She was obviously sending money home, and while I don't think he is the kind of person to want much, I just feel like there is more I can do for him. I mean, I took his wife from him for twelve years and then returned her in a box," he says, almost looking choked up.

"Why don't we start a fund of some kind? Maybe helping Indonesian nannies or the kids from the region where she lived? Maybe something to support him in another way?" I suggest, my mind already racing. There are a lot of opportunities to support.

"Hmmmm. Let's think about it some more, but I like all those ideas." A small smile lights his eyes.

"It is a nice thing to do, Tennyson. You have a big heart." I see it. I see him.

"And it is all yours, Willow Valentine," he says as he leans in, taking my lips with his.

35

TENNYSON

I t's early. It must be about six, and I lie naked with Willow tucked into my side, snoring. I slept well for the few hours we had. It was good to talk last night. We got everything out in the open, and there is now nothing Willow doesn't know. I feel fresh, like she has breathed new life into me, and now I am just as starving for her as I have been for weeks. I run my hands over her naked torso, feeling her under my palms.

"Mmmmm, what time is it?" she moans, making my already hard dick weep.

"Time for me to show you exactly what you mean to me," I say quietly. Her sister came home at some point last night, so I know we are no longer alone in her place. I pull her to me gently and position myself between her legs.

"Have I told you how beautiful you are lately?" I whisper to her, hovering above her head, my lips pecking hers. Her hair is ruffled, her cheeks slightly pink from our warmth, her lips more pouty than usual.

"Hmmm, not today…" she mumbles, still half-asleep.

"Have I told you that I love you today?" I tease a little, not able to contain my smile. I have never told anyone I loved them before and now I can't stop. No other woman has even come close to hearing those words.

"Not in so many words…" she says, starting to rouse, a small smile dancing on her lips.

"Have I given you any orgasms this morning?" I ask, my mouth latching on to her naked breast as I lower my hand down her soft tummy, finding her warm center. I start to circle her core, letting her know my intentions.

"Tenn…" she moans, her back arching a little, and I move my lips up to meet hers. We kiss then. Soft, sultry kisses. I take my time, not rushing, wanting to savor every moment, to do this right. I want to make love to Willow this morning.

Our lips move together, our tongues tangling in time. She tastes like sweetness and savory all rolled into one. A perfect package. My other hand delves to the side of her face, cupping her cheek and keeping her with me, as my fingers continue to circle her below.

She moans, the sound so sweet I want to add it to a personal audio library so I can listen to it all the time. Her hips move, her nipples peak, and I pull my lips from hers so I can watch her face as I push inside of her. Her mouth opens, her eyes focus on mine, and her breath hitches as she takes all of me. I am slow, my dick so hard that I feel like I will erupt at any moment. It feels like fucking heaven. She is so warm, so soft, so wet.

"God, this feels good, Willow. So fucking good," I whisper to her, my lips on hers again, our breathing becoming rapid. I have never felt sex without a condom. Ever. And if I had known it was this good, I may have not been so sexually safe.

"So good..." she moans, the two of us quiet, our hips doing all the talking. We move in synchronization, our bodies working as one. I know what she likes. I know what makes her moan and gasp, and as I watch her bite her lower lip, my grip on her hip tightens, never wanting to let her go.

Leaning up on my elbows then, I cage her in, looking directly down at her. I move my hips slowly, grinding, swiveling, savoring this moment, feeling every thrust, taking my time and enjoying watching the emotions dance across her face. The way she bites her lip a little, the way her eyes close slowly in ecstasy. Her hips move in time with mine, her hands skirting up my back, her fingers dancing on my skin before they dive into my hair. I fucking love her hands on me.

"Tenn, I'm going to come..." she pants into my mouth, our lips barely touching, our eyes locked.

"Come for me, Cupcake. I want to feel you come," I moan out, long and loud. I love sex, hard, fast, different positions, different locations. But I have never made love like this before. It is special. Her head pushes back on the pillow, and her mouth opens, a gasp falling from her lips. I lower my mouth, catching her orgasm in a kiss.

I swallow her moans, her cries, her high pitches as I feel her body shudder around mine. She sends me off, and I grind into her, burying myself deep. The growl in my throat low and deep, vibrating my throat as I lower my forehead to her chest and catch my breath. I feel a connection that I have never felt before. Her hands run up and down my back as I ease my body down on hers, careful not to squish her, but wanting to stay connected to her as long as possible as we both take a moment to catch our breath and come back to reality.

"Do we have to get up today?" I murmur, my lips automatically finding her neck, tasting her skin, kissing her, biting her. My body feels completely exhausted, I have never come so much or so hard as I have with Willow this past day. Yet I can't stop kissing her. I will never get enough.

"Yes. Your interview is going live this morning, so we should get up and get ready. I am sure there will be some things that we need to address once it is live." I can see her mind starting to whirl, her work brain taking over, and I know we need to get up and shower and face whatever this day will bring us.

"WHAT ARE *YOU* DOING HERE?" the devil child from next door asks as I walk downstairs after I've showered and changed. Willow's house is small but cute, and I feel at home already.

"The question is, what are *you* doing here?" I mumble, fixing my shirt. This punk has had it out for me since day one and I have no plans to go easy on him. Looking around, I spot Willow's sister outside playing with Bob.

"I'm having my breakfast. Willow always makes me breakfast every weekend. It's *our* thing," he hisses, giving me a death glare over the top of his spoon full of Cheerios. I match his stare, thinning my eyes at him, not giving him an inch.

"Well, I stayed overnight last night. That is *our* thing," I say back to him, sounding even more juvenile. I stare at him for a beat, wondering how to get rid of this kid who is a giant pain in my ass.

"Hey, coffee is on the counter. TV is on. It's nearly time," Willow says as she breezes into the kitchen, grabbing her cell and some paperwork from the kitchen counter before striding out again. I run my hands down my face, hoping the interview goes well and praying it is a success in the eyes of the public. To be honest, it could go either way. They may edit it to showcase me in a light that is unbecoming, positioning me into the careless playboy asshole persona the local media have tried to establish this past week. A few months ago, they wouldn't have been wrong. But my life has changed. Significantly. I am not the same person, nor do I want to be. Or it could be an intelligent conversation about business and my expansion plans, all of which have now been cemented in Singapore, and Geoffery Fucking Newcomb will choke on his morning coffee.

The thought of him brings back my other reality. His daughter and her lack of willingness to have a paternity test... the whole thing is smelling off. She is lying; I just have no proof and no way to show it. I can't force her to undertake the tests required to prove paternity or even prove she is with child. So she could very well drag this out for the next seven months until a baby appears.

Which I don't want. I want answers now. I want this all cleared up, and I want to forget about it.

"Are you deaf as well as dumb?" Josh says to me, and I throw him an evil look. He has now finished his breakfast and walks his dishes to the sink. "Here's your coffee." He pushes the cup that Willow prepared for me along the counter, but not before I see him lick his finger and dip it into the hot brew, stirring the coffee like he is using a spoon. "Still warm, *just for you.*" He plasters on a fake smile, encouraging me to take it. But I balk. Who knows where his fingers have been? Probably up his nose, for all I know.

"Hey, rock star," Willow's sister, Saide, says as she comes in from the back garden.

"Saide, how are you?" I ask her, trying to be polite as Josh stands behind her, giving me the middle finger and sticking out his tongue. *I could buy his house next door and force him to move.*

"Better now that my sister is happy. Glad you got your shit together, hotshot. Let's go and see if you keep it together in this interview, shall we?" she says, raising her eyebrows, almost in a challenge. I should have expected it. Of course she would be a little protective of her sister. It isn't a good situation for anyone to be in. Saide walks past me to go into the living room, Josh following behind her, but not before he checks me with his shoulder on the way past. He is shorter than me by far, so his shoulder digs into my torso, making me lurch a little, hitting me right in the stomach. *I think I will buy up all the houses on the entire street, just to be sure.*

For a short kid, he has a strong shoulder, and I rub my

side, wondering what his problem is. Ignoring the snot-infested coffee, I follow behind them closely, seeing Saide perch herself on the armchair, Willow on the sofa right in front of the TV, typing on her cell. Josh walks in and immediately sits next to her, leaving the only space for me on the other side of him.

"Willow, you are coming to my school presentation this week, aren't you?" Josh asks in a sweet voice that I have never heard before. I raise my eyebrows at him, as he looks at me with a sly smile.

"Of course, I wouldn't miss it!" she says, and his smile at me gets even wider.

"Actually, why don't I bring Tennyson too. I am sure he would love to see you get your award," she says, her head still buried in her phone, paying no attention to either of us. Josh's smile is wiped from his face, and a smile immediately comes to my lips.

"That would be great, Cupcake. What is the award for? Passing elementary school?" I tease him, knowing full well he is already in middle school. My words grate on him as he gives me a scowl.

"He received a science scholarship into high school," Willow answers, and my eyebrows shoot to my hairline. The kid is obviously a genius, and I had no idea.

"I know how to blow stuff up, Ninja," he whispers in a threat, and I swallow. Great, now I have to bomb proof my entire life. Our eyes remain locked for a beat before the intro of *Business News* comes on, and I take a seat as Willow turns up the volume.

We are all quiet for the entire show, listening to every single word that is said. I crack my knuckles and grind my teeth throughout. I am tense, but I need not be worried. It is perfect. I look good, I sound confident, and the entire thing is focused on business without any statement about my personal life, except for a small mention of the current situation in the outro once the credits are already rolling.

"That was perfect," Willow says quietly in awe. I look over at her, and she's already looking at me, almost stunned. Her eyes are wide, relief on her face.

"No, Willow. You are perfect." Without a doubt, she is the one making this happen. Our eyes connect over the top of Josh's head, and we look at each other for a beat, before both our phones start going crazy.

36

TENNYSON

My brothers and I sit around the large timber dining table. The polish is so thick on it, our paperwork slips at every opportunity.

"So with the expansion of the construction business in Singapore, we are expecting to see a threefold increase in our finances over the coming three to five years," I state, giving all my brothers and my mother an overview of the new contract. We do this every quarter. While the businesses are ours, our mother has a silent role in our family trust, and as such, she needs to be informed of the paperwork, the finances, and our tax position. In return, we continue to pay for her lifestyle. I am sure she would rather be shopping or lunching with her friends, but it is what Dad set up for us to do in his passing, and like the four idiots we are, we continue to do what our father tells us to do. I look at my watch, mindful that I need to be across town at Josh's school ceremony this afternoon. I am not sure which meeting is better. Sitting here with my mother or sitting at a school with the kid who I think may be a borderline psycho.

"I heard all about this on *Business News*. The entire interview was all about you. No mention of your brothers or *me*," she says, obviously unhappy that she didn't get airtime. Our reputation is very important to our mother; it always has been.

"My publicity manager set up the interview for me, for Langford Construction. Why would we mention you?" I ask her, my eyes squinting at her. I am pushing her just as much as she is pushing me. The anger between us is getting hotter by the day. My brothers all look at each other, Harrison watching us both like a hawk.

"You only talked about Singapore. I have no idea why Asia is a place you want to work in. It is so far away. So dirty." She scoffs like I am ridiculous for even thinking about expansion in Asia.

"That's what you thought about Helen, wasn't it, Mom?" My brothers' heads snap in my direction, looking at me with their eyebrows raised. I usually don't converse this much at these meetings. I also haven't brought up Nanny Helen lately with anyone but Willow, so the subject matter is probably surprising. But my life has changed now, and my feelings are surfacing. After ignoring them for the better part of nearly two decades, they simmer on the surface.

"What does that poor excuse for a nanny have to do with it? Are you just trying to throw barbed words at me, Tennyson?" She stares right at me. She is on edge, I can feel it.

"Umm... why don't we get back to business..." Eddie butts in, but Mom and I can't break from our conversation. Our eyes are glued to each other, flames flicking from both of us.

"Why is Helen a barbed word for you, Mom? She raised me better than you did." I push and see her face contort in anger.

"I will not have you talking to me like that!" she bellows, and like a lightning bolt, my memories come back in a flash.

Me reading a book quietly in the library, then hearing a loud noise. Running to the kitchen to see Helen lying on the ground, clutching her chest, my mother standing over her.

"You have no idea what you are talking about. You were a child," my mother spits.

"You were standing over her that day. I remember now. I remember it clearly." My nervous system starts to get out of control, and I clench my fists under the table, trying to stop them from shaking.

"You have no idea what you are talking about!" Her voice rises another octave as she looks frustrated, angry, and guilty all wrapped into one.

Me running, kneeling next to Helen, watching her face contort in pain. Tears coming to my eyes, not knowing what to do. Looking up at my mother, begging her to call someone to help.

"There was a bag of peanuts on the kitchen bench. I remember seeing a bag of nuts! Did you know she had a nut allergy, Mom?" I seethe as I sit forward on my seat, adrenaline coursing through my body as my leg starts to bounce, my jaw clenching. I hear Eddie take a breath as he connects the dots as well. Of course she knew. Nanny Helen would have had a full medical exam before she even stepped into our house.

"I have no idea what you are talking about. I called Dr. Wilson that day. He confirmed her death as a heart attack and wrote up the report himself! Now stop being so stupid." She throws the words at me, but I don't believe them.

"Dr. Wilson? As in, the man who was always at our house when Dad was out of town?" Harrison asks, looking like he is fitting puzzle pieces together in his mind. Being the older one of our family, he has his own recollection of things.

"Oh my…" Ben whispers, his eyes wide. *Was my mom having an affair with Doctor Wilson?*

"Wait, Dr. Wilson was at our house?" Eddie asks. As the youngest of us boys, he wouldn't remember the doctor being around so much.

"Did you kill Nanny Helen?" I ask, not holding back any more punches, my breath catching on the words.

"What the hell has gotten into you all?" my mother says, looking at each of us, our eyes glued to her.

"Mom, tell me you didn't. Look me in the fucking eyes and tell me you didn't give Nanny Helen any nuts that day." Slowly standing, my nostrils flare. We both know she did. I have no idea why, but I know she did.

"You can look at the death certificate yourself. Heart attack. Now sit down," she says with venom, and it is not lost on me that she didn't deny it. She is not meeting my eye, but I feel her fury rolling off her.

"I can't fucking believe it." Glancing at Harrison, I see

him swallow. Ben looks white as a ghost, and Eddie just looks confused.

"Rather than dredging up the past, shouldn't we be talking about your current issues, Tennyson?" she snides. "You are all quick to judge my parenting, but now look what has happened. You have the potential to have our whole business crashing by fucking your way around Baltimore!" I bite my tongue, because if I don't, all hell will break loose. I know what she is doing. She is deflecting. Changing the subject, not wanting the heat on her anymore.

My heart is broken. Nanny Helen deserved so much more than what we gave her. What my mother did is shocking. How or why she did any of it, I have no idea, and the sad fact is that I know I never will. Doctor Wilson was close with my mom. Too close by the sounds of things. Both of them now complicit in this situation. But it was so long ago, I have no proof; I just have the flashbacks in my mind from when I was a kid. Even I know that is not going to do anything to warrant any investigation. I feel like shit. I want to vomit. I want a drink.

She looks at me as she sits back in her chair, her eyebrows arched like she has a checkmate.

"I am not a parent, and I don't plan on being a parent; therefore, I have no parental responsibilities," I grit out to her. I lean forward and balance myself on the table, my hands white-knuckled as I grip the timber. The last thing I need is her to weigh in on this paternity issue, but I should have been prepared for it.

"I shouldn't expect you to do right by the girl. Just like your father, bedding every woman in the state, yet taking no responsibility for it. You must marry this girl," she pushes, shaking her head with disgust.

"The baby is not mine," I seethe.

"Of course the baby is yours," she half yells, her voice rising.

"Mom, we don't have paternity yet," Ben grits out from the side, and I can tell by the way he is holding the table himself, he is just as angry as I am. This is the only time he sees our mother now. At these quarterly business meetings. He has banished her from his life after what she did with Emily. Mom's eyes flick to him momentarily before landing back on me.

"At least your publicity manager seems to know what she is doing, even if she shows me absolutely no respect at all," she quips, the change of topic so quick, I nearly stumble. But now she has my full fucking attention.

"What are you talking about?" I demand, not liking her talking about Willow at all. The hairs rise on the back of my neck, and my eyes flick to my brothers, now understanding how they both felt when she involved herself in their relationships. I don't like it, not one bit.

She eyes me warily. "She is very protective of you. But I will not stand for her to talking to me with such disrespect." I am upset she is harassing Willow and Willow hasn't told me. But a sly smile comes to my lips, knowing that Willow didn't cower to her.

"What do you mean?" I ask, tilting my head in question. God, I couldn't love Willow any more than I do right now.

"She is a horrible, disrespectful woman, who didn't even attempt to take into consideration my thoughts on the issue," she says, huffing, not happy about not getting her own way.

"She is the smartest one out of the lot of us," I murmur, looking at my brothers. We all nod to each other in silent agreement that this meeting is now over.

"I'm out," I say, itching to get out of this house and away from my mother. I need to get to Josh's school, then I need to talk to Willow. At some point this afternoon, my brothers and I all need to touch base on what the fuck happened here today.

"Me too," Ben says just as quickly. He was over it all before he even arrived today.

"I'm done," Harrison says, also standing, gathering his things, and us three boys stand, looking at Eddie. It isn't fair that he doesn't have even half of our memories. By the time he was old enough, he had a great nanny, a reasonable relationship with our parents, and even though they never got along, I feel like Eddie was always the apple of Mom's eye.

"Let's call it a day," he says diplomatically, and I don't wait any longer, hearing Mom rant behind me as I walk out of the room and out of the house, never once looking back. She and this house are now dead to me.

37

WILLOW

Driving out of my place, I rush to buckle my seat belt when I am already on the road. I have exactly fifteen minutes to get to Josh's school, find my seat among all the parents and caregivers, and see him get his award. With his mom stuck at the hospital, unable to miss her shift, I didn't hesitate to attend today to support him. I am so proud of his achievements. My phone is charged and ready to take too many photos of the moment.

As I drive down my street, I look at the cars parked to the side. They are a new addition to our neighborhood this week. Black SUVs with dark tinted windows. Tennyson and I are now public knowledge, and the media have been circling. They have kept their distance for the most part because of the relationships I have with many of them, but that doesn't really stop the paparazzi from trying to get a shot. I expected it, so I have plans in place. Police drive-bys occur often just to have a presence, and neighbors have all been notified to limit concern.

While things are relatively calm and steady for Tennyson's reputation, paternity is still not sorted, and both parties are at a stalemate. The baby's health is the priority, so we can only move as quickly as the mother allows. Which, at the moment, is no movement at all. She hasn't even been examined, so we are just taking her word for it that she is, in fact, pregnant. Given the date she and Tennyson were together, we estimate her to be around ten weeks along now.

"Damn," I say as a car darts around me. Speeding past me, I slam on my brakes, not wanting an accident to occur because of me, and let it pass. I was driving to the limit, but I see a camera flash from the back window and know the paparazzi do this type of activity all the time, trying to get a shot of me with anger on my face, to portray a story that just isn't real.

"Assholes," I murmur as I slowly pick up my pace again, turning off the main road, taking the back streets and hoping to miss both the traffic and the media.

My eyes flick to the time, and I should be fine. I will get there just as everyone is taking a seat. I have been to a few of these before, and I know the principal will talk and welcome everyone for about twenty minutes before the awards begin. I hope Tennyson can make it today. I feel like he and Josh got off on the wrong foot. From their first meeting with a soccer ball to the head, to Tennyson being in my home, taking over Josh's title of the man in my life. It was always going to be an adjustment, but I hope that Josh can see both Tennyson and me in the crowd today and know that he isn't losing me, but gaining Tennyson. Without a father figure in his life, his mom does it all, and

I feel that Tennyson and Josh would actually be good for each other.

I slow down as I approach a red light and take a breath. I am making good time. I just need to slip down the right avenue and I will nearly be there. As I am lost in my thoughts, I hear a loud screech of tires as a car skids right next to me. Looking up, I see a large black Escalade close by my side in the other lane. I sigh heavily. The media are so intrusive sometimes. The car doors open, and I put my head down, looking at my lap, and my hair falls across my face, shielding me. I don't want to look their way and get my face on camera. But within seconds, they are pulling open my door, and I curse myself for not locking it when I got in, too preoccupied trying to race to the school on time.

"Hey, stop! You can't do that!" I yell as a big guy with dark clothing opens my door wide and leans right into my personal space. I slap at his arm, which is thick and solid and unflinching as he unbuckles my seat belt.

"Stop. This is against the law!" I yell again, having never experienced paparazzi like this. I hear him growl, then he grabs my arms and pulls me out of the car like I am nothing more than a doll.

"Ahhh!" I scream, and my fists continue to hit at his chest.

"Shut up and get in the car," the man growls again, and I still. This is not the media. Blood pumps in my chest. I try to take a step back and twist my arm, attempting to get out of his hold, but his grip tightens.

"Let me go!" I scream, hoping to get someone's attention, but on these back streets, it is quiet. I should have stuck to the main roads.

"Get in the fucking car!" he roars, but I continue to wrestle, not staying still. I have no idea about self-defense tactics, but the more I move, the less likely he will get a good grip on me.

"No! Help! Somebody, help!" I yell before a fist flies to my face, my body reeling back, slamming into the side of my car. My face throbs, and I taste blood. I've never been hit before. The pain is instant; it feels almost like a burn, then a woozy feeling comes over me quickly. I blink, fighting the tears that threaten, and as I slowly come back, I start to scream.

"Help! Help!" I have no idea what is going on, but my instinct is to run. I push off my car and take a step, my car still running, keys still in the ignition, my driver's side door fully open. I can hear my cell phone ringing from where it sits in my bag on the passenger seat, but I need to get away. I take another step and am about to dash around the trunk to run to the nearby houses, but I feel a grip around my wrist before my body is yanked back hard. I slam into his chest, the solid wall of muscle hard on my bones, and the air is pushed from my lungs so violently I struggle to catch my breath. He is so big, my head barely reaches his chest, and he holds me to him tightly as he lowers his mouth to my ear.

"I said, get in the fucking car, you fucking bitch." His voice sends a shiver down my spine as his hands roughly wrap around my waist and he picks me up as though I weigh nothing, throwing me over his shoulder. I kick my legs and thrash my body, my fists thumping into his back, doing anything I can to make him drop me, but his hold is strong, too strong for me to fight against.

"No! Stop! Help me!" I yell, not giving up. I kick my legs so violently, my heels fall from my feet. I have no idea who this is or what they want, but I have little time to think about that before my body is thrown into the back seat of his car, my head hitting on the doorframe on the way in, my world turning black before my body even hits the seat.

38

TENNYSON

I stand outside the school, calling Willow, but she still doesn't answer. Looking around, I see smiling parents, grandparents, and teaching staff, all having the time of their lives as they wander around, shaking hands and smiling. Their life appears calm and serene, while mine is in total turmoil, and I can barely figure out what the hell is happening.

I have a million other places to be, including debriefing with my brothers after the shit show at my mother's this morning. But I promised Willow I would come today to support her psycho bodyguard. His mom is working at the hospital, and he doesn't have a father around so it must be hard. The fact that it is Willow who comes to these things cements to me that maybe Josh has a less than ideal family situation. *I know all about how that feels.*

As I see everyone moving inside, I decide to go in, saving Willow a seat so she can glide in unnoticed, because I know she won't miss this. Josh is very important to her, and with no one else here to support him, she knows she needs to be.

I move around the families and grab two empty seats halfway down and to the side. A few people give me the side-eye. Probably because I seem so out of place here in my suit and with a don't-talk-to-me look on my face. One older woman looks at me with pursed lips, not too happy to have me here, and I flash her my pearly whites.

As proceedings start, I send Willow a text telling her where I am sitting and asking her how far away she is. The principal starts talking, welcoming the crowd and outlining the school values, my ass already numb from this hard wooden seat. I look over the group of kids standing at the front and try to find Josh among them. It doesn't take me long. He is the only kid looking right at me like he wants to gut me from head to toe. He wasn't happy that I was coming today. I give him my biggest *fuck you* smile, and he rolls his eyes. *One point for me.*

As the afternoon rolls on, I keep looking over my shoulder, but Willow still isn't here. I text her again, but still no answer. I start to feel agitated. This is so unlike her. Something feels off. Panic starts to fill my body. I am deep in thought about where she might be when I hear Josh's name called and I look up. He looks at me with his eyebrows raised in question, but I shake my head, letting him know she isn't here, and I visibly see his shoulders slump. My eyes don't leave him as I watch this young boy walk across the stage with a lackluster clap from the crowd to collect his certificate.

I do something then, something I didn't think was possible. I put my fingers to my lips and let out a big whistle before I yell "Go, Josh!" out to the crowd. Lifting my phone, I hit record to start taking video, knowing that Willow will want to see it later. He looks up at me, startled, and I give him a thumbs-up, and he shockingly gives me a small smile. When he takes his final steps across the stage to meet the school principal, he is now standing a little taller, his shoulders not as rounded, and his small smile remains.

"You are such a good father. It is so good to see you support your child today," a woman says from beside me, and I look at her and smile, except the smile was already there, and I didn't even know it.

I keep filming until he is off the stage, and I turn off the camera. I watch him for a beat as he joins the group of kids again. A few of them give him high fives before he looks my way again. I give him a nod, one he returns, and I wonder if we now have a truce or if I need to make my life bomb proof ASAP.

I STAND out in the sun at the front of the school again, my head buried in my phone.

"C'mon, pick up, Willow," I murmur to myself as her phone rings yet again.

"Hey," a voice says from the side, and I see Josh standing there awkwardly.

"Hey, punk," I say. "Good work up there."

"Where's Willow?" he asks, looking a little upset.

"I have no idea. I have been trying to call her, but she isn't answering," I tell him, my stomach feeling like lead. I wasn't too worried before. But now I am. She was meant to be here two hours ago and is not picking up my calls or text messages. This is not like her at all.

"She said she would be here," Josh says, and I can tell he is really disappointed.

"She must have gotten caught up with something," I offer, not wanting him to worry. Meanwhile, my insides are churning, and I am barely keeping it together in front of him.

"Do you know where Saide is?" I ask Josh, because maybe the two of them are out doing something.

"She went to Connecticut for the day," Josh says, taking a few slow steps toward me.

"Maybe something happened with Saide and Willow had to help her out?" I remember Willow telling me Saide's married boyfriend lives in Connecticut, so maybe Willow went to support her with something.

"Can I call Saide?" Josh asks, and I nod. I don't admit my concern out loud, but I have a feeling he knows. I watch as he pulls out his own cell and calls Saide. I frown as I listen to his end of the conversation. It appears Saide is on her way back from Connecticut already, with no idea where Willow is, and has been calling her all day herself. A sinking feeling overtakes my body, and I swallow harshly. *What the fuck is going on?*

"Let's go, kid," I say to Josh as I pace toward my car.

"Where are we going?" he asks, trailing me just as quickly.

"Tell Saide we will meet her at home. Something is not right." Josh relays the message before he pockets his phone. My car is right at the curb. A few of the dads stand around, admiring it. Like most men, I enjoy cars and have a healthy collection. This one is my sports car, good for zipping around the traffic and getting to Willow quickly. Josh looks impressed as we both get into the car, and I roar the engine and speed from the school to the looks of horror from who I assume are the PTA ladies who stand and stare at us from the sidewalk. And I think I see a small smile on Josh's lips.

"Willow! Willow!" I yell the moment we walk into the house.

"She isn't here. Her car is gone, though," Saide says, running down the stairs, looking concerned.

"Let me call her again," I murmur, grabbing my phone.

"She still isn't answering," Josh says, lowering his phone, constantly calling her too. His eyes almost plead with me, like I have all the answers.

"Let me call Beth; she might have talked to her." I kick myself for not thinking of it before. They are friends, so maybe Beth has her doing something. I rush and punch in her number as I start to pace. The need to move, talk, do something festers at my skin.

"Beth, have you seen Willow?" I bark out before she even has time to answer my call. My hands are already in my hair, pulling it, needing the pain.

"Nice to hear from you too, Tenn," she smarts, and I try hard not to yell. I am on the edge.

"Willow is missing, Beth. I'm at her house with her sister, and we haven't seen her since this morning. She didn't turn up to meet me today when she was supposed to. I am worried," I say, pacing the small kitchen, seeing

Josh continue to call her phone like he is possessed and Saide texting everyone they know. The feeling in the room has thickened.

"Sorry, no, Tenn, I haven't seen her. I last spoke to her a few days ago before you left for Singapore." I can hear her walking now. "Let me ask Harrison." I pause, hearing their low murmur before she comes back to the phone.

"No, he hasn't spoken to her either. He is calling your brothers," she says, and the hairs on the back of my neck stand up.

"Something doesn't feel right. This is not like her at all. She would not have missed the meeting this afternoon," I state, my pace purposeful as I ruin Willow's floor with my trail.

"Let me call the police headquarters. Text me the details of her car. Maybe they have something on file; they can at least see if it was involved in any accident," Beth offers. *Accident. God, no.* We have just come full circle. She can't be hurt... what if she is lying in a ditch somewhere?

"I will text you now," I say, hanging up, and my fingers move at lightning speed, texting her a description of Willow's car. Just as I send the text, a call comes through from an unknown number. I don't usually answer these, but I am stressed and not thinking so I pick it up.

"Hello?" I answer, looking at Saide and Josh, who both watch me with hope on their faces.

"Tennyson," the male voice states on the other side. I know the voice.

"Geoffery, I don't have time to chat right now." I'm about to hang up, as stressed doesn't even come close to the feeling I have running through my body, and I certainly don't have time to talk business with this asshole.

"I have Willow." I have a brief moment of relief, even though I find it completely odd.

"What do you mean, you have Willow? Why? Where is she?" My words tumble, and Saide and Josh move closer, looking at me with wide eyes.

"She is alive, a little battered. Purple really isn't her color," he snides, and my insides drop.

"What the hell are you talking about?" I question with a bite, meanwhile my body is trembling.

"I am going to offer you a deal, Tennyson," he says like he is talking business, and I clench my jaw.

"What offer?" I say, knowing that unless I play his stupid games, I won't get the answer I want. He has always been an asshole. He is ruthless, and his business has been built from always taking, never building anything of his own.

"You sign half of Singapore over to me, marry my daughter, and raise the baby in a perfect family unit, and I will return Willow." My world stops. *He has taken Willow to get back at me? To blackmail me into marrying his daughter?*

"And if I don't?" I look at both Saide and Josh, and I see the panic on their faces. Now, it's warranted.

"Then you will never see her again. You have an hour," he says, before the line goes dead and my world falls apart.

39

———

WILLOW

My head's fuzzy, my mouth dry. Then the thumping starts. It feels like my brain is on fire, the burn running across my temples, making my eyes water and my cheeks hot. *Is my face swollen?* I open my eyes, a light from the side so bright, I scrunch them together again. Pain shoots through my skull even more, and I blink rapidly as it takes me a while to focus.

"Awe, sleeping beauty is awake," I hear a woman with a twang say, and I try to focus my vision at the figure in the room. My heart races, and as I come to, panic fills my body, and I can feel my hands behind me start to shake.

"About time," I hear a male voice, somewhat familiar, say from beside her.

"Where am I?" I groan, trying to sit up from where I am lying on the dusty hardwood floor. I struggle, not being able to move my arms, and my wrists burn. They are both tied together at my back. My breath quickens as I take in the situation. I look down at my clothes. I am a mess. There are rips and tears in my dress, my shoes are missing, my face feels hot and dirty, like I need to wash it, my skin scratched, my legs battered and bruised.

"Who are yo—" The question stops on my lips as their faces come into my vision. Katerina and her father, Geoffery Newcomb.

"Hello, Willow, glad you could finally join us," Katerina says in a fake sweet voice, reminding me of a Southern belle, but I now know her to be anything but. I remain still and quiet, wondering what the hell is going on, willing my brain to start functioning as my hands behind my back start moving, trying to undo the rope in my panic.

"Cat got your tongue, baby girl?" Geoffery says, looking down at me, and I want to slap the smirk right off his face.

"What am I doing here?" I ask, my voice getting stronger as I take in the air I need. There is something wrong here. This is not a situation I was expecting. I look around the room. Tall timber ceilings, straw in the corner, a water trough. *Am I in a barn?*

"Well, you didn't think I would let you stay with Tennyson while I was having his baby, did you?" Katerina says, and my eyes meet hers.

"What?" I ask, confused. *Tennyson. Josh. Oh God, I missed his school presentation.*

"You are the only thing standing in my way of becoming Mrs. Tennyson Langford. One of the country's only billionaire bachelors. The very man who, if he joined forces with my father's business, would give us the potential to be wealthy beyond our wildest dreams. So you need to go," she quips before looking at her nails.

"Go? What do you mean go?" This woman is batshit crazy.

"You need to not be earthside anymore. Isn't that right, Daddy?" Her voice pitches up, almost in a baby tone, her words making my heart race.

"What Daddy's little girl wants, she gets," Geoffery says, nodding, although looking over me in a way that makes me vomit a little in my mouth.

"You are delusional." How the hell I am going to get myself out of this situation? The two of them look like this is a normal weekday afternoon. My wrists burn, the pain almost excruciating, and when I look out the small window and see blue skies and green trees, it is then I realize I have no idea where I am. The last thing I remember is being in the car, before being manhandled.

"Why don't you go inside, Kitty Kat, and get ready. We need to call Tennyson soon," Geoffery says, and I swallow as I fill my body with confidence. I need to get out of here.

"Okay, Daddy. Love you." She gives her father a peck on the cheek before twirling on her stilettos and walking out of the barn. She looks like she walked off a fashion runway, not someone who is in a barn with dust, dirt, and straw strewn about.

"Tennyson knows I'm here?" I ask, feeling positive that he might know where I am. I look around, trying to work out an escape route, moving my wrists a little more to see if I can get these ropes off my hands.

"Not in terms of location, but I have made him an offer." Lowering down, he grips my elbow, lifting me up. I look at it, knowing I can't trust him, but I am at a disadvantage on the floor, so I accept his help as my wobbly legs try to support my weight and I start to stand.

"What offer?" I ask as I move gingerly. My limbs cry out in pain, my head feeling like a balloon. I am sure my hair must be everywhere if my clothes are anything to go by. I look like I have been dragged through the forest backward, and everything hurts. At least they didn't tie my ankles, probably because I have no idea where I am, with no footwear and no idea where to run to.

"I told him I would let you go, if he gave me half of Singapore and married my daughter," he says, looking at me. Dread fills my chest. I already know Tennyson will do it. I watch as Geoffery looks over me again, and I can't believe I thought this man was dapper. His eyes run from my face, down my chest, to my toes and back. He looks different from that night I met him months ago. At the business dinner, he was in a suit, his salt-and-pepper hair styled, looking every inch a handsome silver fox. Now he is currently in worn jeans, a threadbare bare t-shirt, looking all of his years and then some.

"But you know, the more I look at you, I am thinking I wouldn't mind keeping you for myself." My body stills, as I feel his hand wrap around my hip. I want to headbutt him, but I need to play the strategic game. I need to be smart about this.

"I don't think you would want that..." I say, not liking him touching me. Not liking him near me. But starting to play along, I can outsmart him. I know I can.

"Ohh, but I think I would. Wouldn't you like that? Stay out here at my ranch with me?" he asks, and I wonder for a beat if he is mentally well. Although, he isn't, because no healthy person would kidnap a woman and leave her in a barn with bruises and torn clothes. I begin to wonder what day it is and how long I have been here because I have no sense of time at all.

"My home is in DC," I state, making it clear that I am not interested.

"Yeah, but I would look after you. It has been a long time since I had a lady friend out here." Panic rises more as he steps closer. I can't move. My feet are glued. I am scared stiff because I have no idea what he is capable of and no idea what he will do next.

"What about Katerina? I don't think she would like me around," I offer, looking up at him through my lashes. Trying to play coy, a little flirty, which is so far out of my comfort zone at the moment, and I wish I had a bit more of Saide's sultry moves right about now.

"Ohhh, Kitty Kat will move to Baltimore to be with Tennyson. Perhaps buy a big family estate just like his brother, make lots of babies, and live the life of a socialite. His mother has already reached out to her. They have a ladies' lunch planned later this week." I grit my teeth. Of course Tennyson's mother would be somehow involved with this crazy family already. He stands right in front of me then, his body so close to mine, I can smell his sweat. I clamp my mouth closed so I don't vomit, even though my head is still spinning.

"How about it, Willow? Do you want to give yourself to me, or am I just going to take what I want?" he says, his head moving down to my ear, his lips brushing against my cheek.

"What is it that you want?" I ask, my body now shaking uncontrollably, but I downplay it, needing him to undo my hands so I can at least put up a fight.

"Well, you can either spread these beautiful legs for me..." he says as his hands lower over my hips, down my thighs, before they come back up, tracing the sensitive skin on my inner thighs, lifting my dress up on the way. "Or I can take you any way I want to." I hear his breath shake, see his chest rise and fall quicker, and I can feel him hard on my belly. He is aroused, clearly wanting something from me that I am not prepared to give.

"I don't think you want to do that..." I whisper, my eyes looking everywhere but at him. My wrists burn as I move them more, trying like hell to get the ropes off me.

"Oh, but I do want this." His hand travels up my inner thigh to my center, cupping me, and I gasp, clenching my hands, my nails biting into my palms. I grit my teeth as a shiver runs through me in fear, but I feel his lips peck my jaw, and he hums in appreciation, obviously thinking I am into this. His fingers start to move on the outside of my underwear. He is rough, his touch not something I want.

"You want to touch my cock, baby girl, because ever since I saw you that night in Baltimore, I have thought of nothing but you. It will give me great pleasure to fuck the woman Tennyson Langford loves." I grit my teeth tighter, tears burning the backs of my eyes. His hand continues to move on my center, my nails indenting my palms. I bite my lip to the point of almost bleeding. I could run, but he would catch me. I could scream, but no one would come.

I could fight, but I know it will be futile. My hands are tied, I have no shoes, I have no idea where I am.

"If I untie you, you will be a good little slut, won't you? You will let me pull this dress from your body and fuck you right here in my barn?" he says, his voice croaking like he is struggling to control himself. My brain fires; he said his barn, so at a guess, I think I am in Kentucky. *I don't know anything about Kentucky.*

"Is that what you want to do?" I murmur, again trying to sound sexy as his lips find my chest. I look up to the ceiling, wanting to knee him in the groin, but I need my hands untied.

"Ohhh, it is one of many things I want to do to you." His hands circle around my back, and I feel him tugging the rope from my wrists. Now is the time. I am not going to get another opportunity. I need to surprise him and do it as soon as my hands are free.

I feel the rope go slack, and I wait for a beat until I see it hit the floor at my feet, then I immediately start to hit and scratch him before I turn and run. But it is short-lived as my bare foot steps right on a sharp nail sticking up from the barn floor.

"Arghhhh!" I cry out, the pain shooting up my foot excruciating. And I start to hop about, gripping my foot as blood gushes from it.

"You little bitch!" he yells, striding toward me, his hand on my arm firm as he swings me around to face him. I lose my balance a bit and let go of my foot, putting it back onto the floor, immediately regretting it.

But I don't get out another scream before his hand

lands in the collar of my dress and he pulls, the clothes ripping slightly, baring my chest to him.

"No!" I scream, the sound not familiar. It is almost guttural as it leaves my chest. I pull my hand back and slap his cheek so hard my hand stings from the impact, and I try to hobble away from him again.

"You are mine, whether you give yourself to me or if I take you by force!" It takes him two big steps before he is on me again, the bright-blue sky out the window the last thing I see before his hand connects with my face.

40

TENNYSON

Willow's small cottage is full of people. The normally quiet and serene escape is now full of people talking on phones, walking in and around the house to find a quiet spot to talk. Bob is barking like crazy in the backyard, clearly aware that something is happening, and Betty sits right next to him. Any other day, my eyes would bug out of my head at the two of them getting along, but today my mind is elsewhere.

All my brothers and Beth are here, each of them on the phone calling in numerous favors. Harrison is talking to the police, and Beth is talking with her press team so they can get a handle on this early. Emily is talking with Saide in the kitchen, the two of them making coffee after coffee that no one drinks, yet both needing to stay busy. Meanwhile, Josh sits next to me with a mix of fear and anger on his face. He hasn't left my side, stuck like glue to me these past few hours. It is like he hates me, but I give him a strange comfort as well.

"It's because of you she has been taken, isn't it?" he spits out as we wait here for the police to show, but they are taking their time. Time I know I don't have. I thought I felt bad about my playboy history before. I thought the paternity test and the potential of being a father to a one-night stand I don't remember was the worst that could happen to me.

Turns out, I was wrong.

"Yes. Yes, it is." I'm honest with him. He's a smart kid; he doesn't need me to sugarcoat it for him. It is all because of me that Willow is gone, in danger, probably hurt, in pain. My stomach clenches and my chest aches. It reminds me of the feelings I had when I looked at Nanny Helen all those years ago. I feel useless, not able to help, not able to get to her, fight for her.

"Why didn't you protect her? Why didn't you take some of your millions of dollars and have security following her? Why did you come near her at all?"

He is getting upset and I am surprised it took him this long. He has been pretty quiet all afternoon, taking in all of us adults as we strategize and discuss what to do. He is right, though. I should have. My head has been so busy focusing on myself—my reputation, my business, and the expansion into Singapore—I missed focusing on the number one priority in my life. Willow. As a general rule, I don't have security. I've never needed it. Harrison and Ben both have it. At their place, following them every day. But I always thought they had good cause for it since Harrison has his new role as governor. Ben has been through so much with Emily, I don't think he will ever let his guard down. Their security is tight, always following them. But not for one second did I ever think Willow would become a target. I didn't think that Geoffery Newcomb or his daughter would be dangerous. To me or my family. I should have known better. Everyone wants something.

"I can't stay away from her. I can't. I love her," I say to him, my voice cracking as I speak, feeling heartbreak at knowing that I did this to her. It is because of me that she is God knows where, no doubt hurt, hopefully still alive.

"Tenn," Ben interrupts our conversation, and I stand quickly, knowing he has news. My brothers and I step to the side as Josh eyes me with venom.

"Turns out Geoffery Newcomb has a bit of a history. He has been up on assault charges before, against his ex-wife about a decade ago. She hasn't been seen publicly for the past five years. Also, he has been in court for speeding, drug possession, and pornography charges more recently," Ben offers. My eyes thin. I knew he was an asshole, but I didn't know how bad he really was. Again, I wasn't paying attention.

"Pornography?" Harrison asks.

"Believe me when I tell you, you do not want to know the details," Ben tells us with a shake of his head.

"Fuck…" Eddie says, rubbing his face.

"Have we called the sheriff in Kentucky?" I ask, looking at them all.

"I've made calls. You were right. Newcomb has a large ranch in East Kentucky. I have the local sheriff driving there now to make a welfare check. But, Tennyson, it's in the middle of nowhere. It will take the sheriff's office a couple of hours to get there, and then Newcomb may not even let him enter the property, stalling it all even more," Harrison says.

"Jet is on standby," Eddie says, looking at me.

"Let's take the chopper." I need to do something. We already have Geoffery's confession that he has her. "I can fly us straight there. Eddie, can you navigate?" I ask my younger brother, because he is the best at directions. The other two are hopeless.

"Are you okay to fly?" Ben asks, concern lacing his features.

"I need to do something. I can't just sit here," I grit out.

"You need to answer Geoffery's call," Eddie says, being the more reasonable one.

"He said he would call in an hour. That was three hours ago!" I can feel myself getting worked up again. My emotions run from anger, to sadness, and everything in between today.

"Something must have happened," Ben says, deep in thought, and fear wraps around my throat.

"She is a fighter. She will fight." I swallow roughly as I think about Willow and what is happening to her right now.

"You guys go. I will stay here and talk to the police. They are due to arrive any minute. See if I can't get them to hurry up. Lord knows, our family has provided them with enough work these past few years, so surely, they can start being a bit quicker and smarter with their output," Harrison says, looking over at Beth, and I see her nod at him, their silent communication astounding. His hand lands on my shoulder, giving me a squeeze.

"I will get the team to put a rush through on any flight permits and clear things with the Kentucky air control. I will call them in transit," Ben says as Eddie and I are already getting our things.

"Where are you going? What's happening?" Saide asks, walking in from the kitchen, seeing us move. Her face is panic stricken, and her hands rub her upper arms like she is cold. Emily comes to stand next to her, putting her arm around her in comfort. I see her pleading with me with her eyes. The weight of expectation that rests on my shoulders is heavy. Ben gives Em a quick kiss before he and Eddie walk out the door.

"I'm going to get her," I grit out, before my eyes move to Josh, who comes to Saide's other side. He looks at me, his nostrils flaring.

"I'm going to get our girl," I repeat to him like it is a promise, and he nods to me in understanding before I run out the door. I move quickly. Eddie already has the car going, and I jump in, joining my brothers, the three of us speeding out of the usually quiet street. Eddie races us to the nearby airport where my chopper has been stationed and fueled within the last hour, waiting for us. A few paps follow, but I know they will get no further images, as the airport is private. Not a visual of us or my chopper will be seen from outside the security zone.

I sit deep in thought. I would give him all of Singapore and marry his daughter in a heartbeat. I would do anything to have Willow safe and alive and home. But Geoffery never called back. And that makes me unsettled.

Something has happened. Something not to his plan. I just hope that Willow is safe and unharmed and can hold on until I get there. My brothers and I are on our way.

Because experience tells us the law is too slow, we need to do this ourselves.

41

WILLOW

As I peel open my eyes, I feel the familiar burn immediately, my wrists and now ankles feeling like they're on fire. Coupled with the excruciating pain in my foot, I nearly vomit as my head spins. I move around, panic starting to set in again, my bare foot covered in blood. I wiggle my toes, ensuring they still work, and feel searing pain shoot up my leg.

"Ugghh," I hiss as I roll over and try to pry my eyes open even more, digging my forehead into the hard wooden floor and gritting my teeth. I take in the now familiar sight of the barn. From where I am lying, the floor is warped, uneven, with a thin coat of dust. As my eyes skirt across the floor, I see the footprints that run from the door to where I am, along with a long line, which I imagine may be from my body being dragged across the floor since I am now positioned even farther from the door than I was originally. My breathing is shallow and rapid, my lungs struggling with my weakness. I feel like I have done ten rounds in a boxing ring, without the taste of success. The smell of straw and animal shit combine and infiltrate my nostrils to the point that I wonder if I am covered in it.

"Daddy really doesn't like rejection," Katerina's voice says, making my head move to the side as I try to breathe through the pain that is running all over my body. I don't know what happened to me when I was out, but the throbbing is running over my torso and every limb. My chest and ribs pull with every breath I take.

"What happened?" I ask, needing the details. The sun is still bright, so I can't have been out of it for too long.

"He tied you back up. He should have just killed you already like I asked him to. But he wanted to wait. Wait to see if you would go to him willingly. Now you have made him feel like a fool, so he has left me in charge while he went inside to cool off. Slapping around a woman who had already passed out on the floor wasn't much fun for him." She walks in her red-soled shoes across the wooden floor, her hips swaying to an imaginary beat. Her accent crawls up my throat, almost choking me with the anger it is laced with.

"This must be stressful for the baby?" I ask as I take in her appearance. High heels, tight dress, she looks like she is going to a nightclub, not holding an innocent woman hostage in a barn. She isn't showing, but at only ten weeks, I'm not sure if she should be. She cackles then. Her laughter booming around the empty space, sounding like a witch around a cauldron.

"Since you will be dead within the hour, I have no problem telling you that I am not pregnant. But as soon as Tennyson is back in my bed, I plan to be," she says, her red glossy overinflated lips stretching out into a smile, looking exactly like the Joker in a *Batman* movie. *I knew it. I knew something about the situation wasn't right.* I feel sick as I think about these women who circle him. Katerina, his mother. None of them wanting the best for him, both of them eager to sink their poisonous claws into him.

"I know what Tennyson likes. I can seduce him again, and I have been taking hormonal injections to make it easier to fall pregnant. That is why I am so bloated," she says, rubbing her nonexistent tummy. "So the next time he fucks me, we will do it raw, and I will have his baby, and you will be nothing but a distant memory." She flicks her hand out like she is swatting a bee, acting like she has it all figured out and without a care in the world.

"Sounds like you have thought about this for a long time, considering you only met Tennyson a couple of months ago?" I ask, wanting to keep her talking as my mind slowly starts working. My hands and feet are tied tight, and the fight starts to leave me a little, knowing that I can't get out of the ropes on either of them. With my foot damaged, there is no escape for me. Unless I roll out the door, but I have a feeling even Katerina in her teetering heels will be able to catch me.

"My father and I planned for me to be with Tennyson for years. I grew up knowing that the only way for my father to have global success was to tumble Langford Construction. The only way to bring down their business was to take out their owner. Or make him mine and combine our businesses in one large family holding. We were close too, until you walked into the picture. My dad has his eyes on you, though, for some reason. Maybe because you look a little like my mom when she was younger. Apparently, he wants you to stay here with him. He saw you at that business dinner and has talked of nothing else since. But I don't think I want to call you 'Mommy.' I want you gone." I watch her walk to a small cupboard on the other side of the room.

"What are you doing?" My adrenaline pumps up as I see her pull out a large jerrycan. The battered tin is in complete contrast to her designer outfit. It must be full to the brim because I see her struggle with the weight of it, and I can hear the slosh of the liquid inside. My panic rises. There is only one liquid that the jerrycan holds, and I know it isn't water. Heart racing, I get a last-minute spurt of adrenaline coursing through my body and I try to sit up, my head spinning as I move like a mermaid out of water, shuffling toward the door on my butt.

"I'm burning this barn to the ground. With you in it," she says simply, the look in her eyes now wild. She looks like a totally different person, one who has pure evil in her veins. She flings her arm out, splashing gasoline along one wall, and then around the corner to the next one before the can is empty. The smell is strong, burning my nose hairs, my throat almost choking in the fumes.

"No. No. You need to let me go. I will walk away. I will move from DC. I will move far, far away. Please. Please don't leave me here," I beg her, not able to stop the tears now as they fall down my cheeks. I move my hands and feet like I am already on fire, the rush in my limbs to push myself free of these restraints now frantic. *This is not it. This is not how this ends. It can't be!*

"You look like a frightened rabbit caught in a snare," she says before cackling again. And then I hear it. The noise is faint, but familiar.

"He's here," I say, in shock and awe. My body stills, and I try to listen again, ensuring I am not hearing things. The familiar sounds of helicopter blades. A feeling of relief sweeps across me briefly. I know it is Tennyson. His helicopter is one of his favorite toys. I hear the noise get louder and louder the closer it comes.

"Well, he is too late," she says as she flicks open a lighter.

"But if you light this barn, he will hold you responsible. You will never get him then," I say quickly, trying anything to stall her. To stop her.

"Maybe not. But if I don't get to have him, then neither do you." Looking at me wickedly over the small lighter flame, she throws it across the room and runs out of the barn.

My body jolts as large orange flames ignite immediately, running up the wall quicker than I can prepare for and straight across the ceiling, almost covering me instantly. The roar of fire is deafening, blocking out any helicopter noise I thought I heard, and smoke billows around the walls, blocking the window, plunging me into darkness. I shimmy closer to the door, no longer able to see a foot in front of me, guiding myself from memory rather than sight.

Smoke fills my lungs, my throat dry, and I cough, not able to cover my face, my hands still tied. My eyes burn, water coating my cheeks, and I try to hold my breath as I shimmy along the floor on my butt. It takes all my energy to move even an inch, so I lie down instead and try to roll. The movement's faster, but as the flames get hotter and the smoke gets thicker, I realize it is futile. For the first time in my life, I have no idea how to get myself out of a bad situation.

42

TENNYSON

As I fly over the forest below, I see a small trail of police cars racing down the road. Looks like the governor got a hold of the right people, because it isn't just one car. There are many. Even from where I am in the sky, I see their blue and red lights flashing. The few cars driving on these quiet roads pull over to the side immediately, probably never having seen a motorcade like it before in their life.

"Two minutes out," Eddie says from beside me as he looks at both his map and GPS. I have been flying at top speed the entire journey. My eyes have been focused on where we need to get to, and I have concentrated on getting us here as quickly as possible. I have given little thought to what I will actually combat when I get onto the ground. We don't even have weapons with us.

"Look!" Ben says, pointing to the side, and we see a clearing ahead. In it lies a large house, with a huge barn not too far from it. Various other smaller outhouses are scattered around. There are a few horses and not much else, aside from a helipad that is wide open for me.

"Heading in," I say as I fly the chopper down, seeing the landing right in front of me. I feel antsy, on edge. I need to get Willow and get the fuck out of here. I turn sharply, pushing the helicopter harder than I ever have, my brothers gripping the handles next to them to keep them steady. My grip on the controls is tight, my heart pumping hard in my chest.

"Shit. Look!" Eddie says in a rush, pointing out the front window, and my eyes snap quickly to the barn, where I spot big, bright flames flickering from the roof. I know without a doubt Willow is in there.

"Hang on," I say as I fly the chopper and land quicker and harder than I ever have before.

"Go. I got this," Eddie says and I don't wait. I duck out of the door and leave Eddie to power it down. The noise from the blades is almost deafening as I run faster than I thought possible toward the fire, without any consideration for myself or anyone else.

"No! No! No!" I hear screaming to the side, and I see Katerina stumble out of the barn, looking at me in shock. She is waving her hands to get me to stop, but I don't. In a tight red dress and sky-high heels, she looks at me like a spoiled toddler, upset that I have taken her toy away, her face a little lopsided. I pay her no attention, my feet continuing the thump on the grass underneath.

"What the hell is going on!" I hear Geoffery yell, and I turn my head to the other side of the property and see him running out from the large house. But my legs move at a speed not known to man as I continue to make my way to the barn.

"Right behind you!" Ben yells, and I know he and Eddie are on my tail. I push through the door and see nothing but black smoke and instantly feel heat on my face. The smoke is thick, my hand automatically coming to cover my face. My eyes burn as I squint and try to see in front of me, but I can't. Sirens scream louder, letting me know the police are here.

"Here!" Ben shouts, grabbing some rope lying at the door and quickly tying it around my waist. "Go!" he screams, and I don't wait. I run in, my hand covering my face, trying to shield me from the heat.

"*Willow!*" I scream, hoping she is alive and that she can hear me above the noise of the crackling timber. "*Willow!*" I scream again, the smoke infiltrating my lungs as I take a deep breath to scream again. I choke, my chest burns, but I hear muffled screams and move forward. I trip over something and fall to the floor, my lungs pained, and I rub my stinging eyes. I feel the rope tug, but I am not ready to go out yet, so I pull back on it, silently telling my brothers I am okay.

"*Willow!*" I scream again where I am on all fours. The physical pain is high, but the pain emotionally almost carves me in two. Smoke continues filling my lungs, and I try to push back up on my feet and stagger forward some more, and it is then I feel her. My hands reach out, and I would know her curves anywhere. She is lying on the floor, not moving, and I pull her to my arms and yank on the rope again as I try to stand and stagger back the way I came, holding her tightly. I can't see; I just follow the pull of the rope, taking small but steady steps quickly, hoping I don't fall. The ceiling of the barn creaks, timber slats start falling around me, and I know we are about to be buried. I try to quicken my pace, stumbling with every step, praying to whoever's listening that my girl is going to be okay.

I see the blue sky finally come into my hazy vision as I put one foot in front of the other and push myself toward it. Willow is heavy and a dead weight in my arms. I have no idea if she is even breathing. Eddie runs toward me, putting his own life on the line, and grabs Willow from my arms and runs back out. Ben pulls on my rope, the movement enough to keep my legs moving before I crash into him. He grabs me around the arms and runs me out to the grassy patch, farther and farther away from the flames. My feet are heavy, my lungs burn, my eyes are stinging, and I can't breathe. But I watch Willow like a hawk as Eddie lays her on the grass and steps back, turning his head to not look at the blood coating her as the police take over and do CPR.

Geoffery and Katerina are both shrieking, and I see the police handcuff them and push them into separate cop cars, slamming the doors on their noise. Then we all hear an almighty roar as the ceiling of the barn collapses. The large structure is entirely engulfed in flames. Sparks and smoke billow out as the barn is reduced to pure orange. There are shouts and screams as the few police who are here all jump on their radios, calling for support. A few of them run to the nearby water tanks and hoses appear. They water the ground around the barn, ensuring the fire doesn't spread and take hold of the entire property. The heat is overwhelming, but my eyes remain on Willow as the man continues to pump her chest and breathe into her mouth. Ben splashes water bottle after water bottle over my head, and my feet slowly give way and I fall to my knees. I kneel on the grass near Willow. My clothes are black, my chest hurts, my hands are a charcoal mess. But all I care about is her.

"Breathe, Cupcake. Please breathe." The words fall from my lips in a whisper, and it isn't lost on me that I am on my knees and begging next to her body, just like I was with Helen when I was twelve. The pain of losing one woman I love is immense, and I can't go through that again. *Please let her live. Please God, let her live.*

Then she coughs and splutters and relief fills my bones. My body sags against Ben's and Eddie's, the two of them holding me as I crumple. Pain starts to shoot through my body now that I know she is alive. An oxygen mask is fitted to her face from a paramedic who has now just arrived, and with Eddie on one side and Ben on the other, I sink into my brothers' embrace, and I cry.

43

WILLOW

I wake up, and the first thing I feel is my throat. There is no moisture in my mouth. My lips feel chapped, sore, almost sunburned. Then I smell it. Smoke. My eyes snap open, and I start to panic.

"It's okay. You are all right. You're in the hospital, but fine," a whisper of a voice says from beside me, and I feel a soft touch to my arm. I look up to see my neighbor and Josh's mom in her full nurse's uniform, giving me a warm smile.

I don't speak, still in fear and shock, having no idea what I'm doing here. My eyes trail down the starched white linen, where I see my hands are pink, and there are bandages on my wrists. I have one foot jutting out from the blankets, wrapped thickly with gauze bandages, and I wiggle my toes, my memories flooding back. *The barn.*

I gasp for air, the oxygen mask on my face helping me, my eyes feeling stale and gritty, almost like I have pink eye. But I remain quiet, looking at my surroundings. I feel my heart thud in my chest, and I try to swallow as

Josh's mom removes the mask and offers me a glass of water that I happily sip. On one side of the bed, I see Saide spread out on a chair, her hair everywhere, one leg protruding out, the other flung over the arm of the chair. She looks a mess, although probably better than I do.

As Josh's mom takes the water and replaces the oxygen mask, she then checks my pulse, and I turn my head to the other side and see Tennyson. His eyes are staring right into mine. He sits silently, watching me. His jaw works overtime, his eyes black with lack of sleep. He is dressed casually, in jeans and a long-sleeve t-shirt, his sleeves pushed up. I notice his arms and hands have small plasters, a small bandage on one of his hands. His eyes are red and watery. We both remain quiet and just look at each other. Almost silently acknowledging the events we went through, even though they are still hazy in my mind. On his lap lies Josh. Too big to sit on anyone's knee, but curled up just the same.

"Hey..." I croak. My voice does not sound familiar to my ears.

He remains silent. I watch him, our eyes anchored, and I see a tear slip over onto his cheek. My own eyes glass at the sight. My heart breaks for him and what we have had to endure.

"Cupcake?" he whispers, like he doesn't believe his eyes. They widen then, as he realizes that I am, in fact, awake.

"I'm okay..." I whisper. Josh's mom moves quickly to pick up her son and puts him softly back in the chair Tennyson vacated as he stands and rushes to me.

"You're okay? Are you in pain? We can get the doctor.

Do you need—" His words start to rush out, his hands finding my own and holding them delicately.

"I'm okay. We are okay," I say to him, a little in disbelief, as my memories start to flood back. "How did you find me?" The last thing I remember is hearing his chopper.

"I will always find you," he says, leaning in and taking my lips, giving me a sweet kiss so gentle I wonder if I am dreaming it.

"Katerina?" I ask, not wanting to say her name, but needing to know.

"Not pregnant. Lying the entire time. Police took her and her father, blackmail and attempted murder only two of the many charges that will be laid on them. Ben is working on keeping them in jail. We are rejecting any suggestion of bail." His hand cups my cheek, our lips remaining so close I can feel his breath on my own.

"What happened? I just remember the barn. The flames?" I ask, my voice wavering. I can't believe I made it. We made it.

"Katerina set the barn alight and left you there. She fucking left you to burn," he says, clearly still angry and upset. His jaw is tight, his teeth clenched. He rubs his eyes as though he is in pain, and I grab his hand, brushing it with my fingers, trying to give him reassurance that I am okay.

"But you got me..." I say in wonder as I lift his hands, inspecting the damage. A few pink marks, a few more small heat burns on his hands.

"Willow. I will always get you. I will always be there

for you. I am never leaving your side, and I am never letting you leave mine. I love you. I love you so goddamn much, it hurts," he says, his eyes searching mine, ensuring I understand, and I do.

"I love you too," is all I can choke out before he kisses me again.

"Any chance you can stop kissing now so I can hug my sister, rock star?" Saide's voice rings out at the side of the bed. Tennyson pulls back gently, then he pecks my forehead in his signature kiss and leans back.

"Hey..." I say to Saide and see her take a breath.

"I hope you charge this fucker danger money. I have never known you to put your life on the line for your job before. Surely, there is some cash coming our way for that?" she asks, jutting out her hip in sass, giving Tennyson an eyebrow raise in question. She is joking, of course, trying to lighten the mood.

"Hmmm, good idea, I will add that to my final invoice," I mutter and smile, letting her embrace me and sighing at the warmth of her hug.

"I am going to buy us an island and we are going to move there. I will also buy the water surrounding it so no fucker can get to us without us knowing about it," Tennyson mumbles, and I smile, thinking he is joking, but the look on his face tells me he is seriously considering it.

"Willow?" I hear Josh's voice, full of emotion, and Saide pulls back as I look at him. Standing next to my bed in front of Tennyson, his hair is messy, his eyes half-asleep. Tennyson's hand rests on his shoulders like a supportive parent, and my heart melts at seeing the two of them like this.

"Hey, bodyguard," I say with a smile and watch him crumple right in front of my eyes. My strong, smart, and usually full of confidence little neighbor, drops his head and weeps. I reach for him, taking him in my arms, his tears coating my shoulder.

"It's okay, champ. She will be okay," Tennyson says, rubbing his back, and I am glad he speaks because I can't, too choked up at the sight of these people getting weepy at my bedside.

My eyes water, even though the lighting is dull, and I want to move, but my body is heavy, hurting, and I am so, so tired.

"You need to stay in for observation for a few more days. You have stitches in your foot, so you need to take it easy and stay off it when you get home. The smoke will completely clear out of your lungs in the coming days. You will probably still smell it for a while, even after you bathe. It tends to stick around in your nostrils and hair for a while," Josh's mom says.

"I will look after her," Saide, Josh, and Tennyson all speak at the same time. Josh's mom laughs.

"Perhaps take turns?" she offers as the three of them look at each other like they want to kill the other.

"I am sure I will be fine in no time," I offer, already feeling better.

"You are not leaving the house," Saide says.

"You are not cooking any cupcakes," Josh says.

"I am not leaving your side. Ever," Tennyson says,

trumping them all, and I see Saide and Josh both roll their eyes.

And as crazy as they all are, I love them. No matter how damaged we all are, they are my little family.

EPILOGUE - TENNYSON

"Take it easy, just slowly sit, and then you can lie back," I say, cautious of Willow as I lift her onto her bed at home. A few days in the hospital was too long. I plan on keeping her here in her bed right next to me, where I can make sure she is comfortable and safe.

"I'm fine, really, no need to fuss," she says, but I see her wince a little, her foot still giving her some trouble. I grind my teeth as I look at her bandage. I have Ben and his firm working overtime on building the case against the Newcombs. It is one thing to try to blackmail me into being a father of a fake baby, but it is a whole other level to kidnap my girlfriend and leave her to die in a flaming barn. I swallow down the anger that festers, knowing that they won't see the light of day again. Or at least not for a very long time.

"I have your favorite movies. I have told Betty and Bob to be on their best behavior, and even though you can't wear them yet, I got you a new pair of fluffy yellow bed socks and a matching set for me," I say, watching the animals as one jumps up near Willow's head, the other slinking near her feet.

"Tennyson. I'm fine," she says, smiling, rolling her eyes at me.

"She said she is fine, stop crowding her," Josh says to me as he elbows me out of the way, delivering her a plate of her favorite lemon cupcakes. I picked up a few boxes from the local bakery she likes, knowing that she would enjoy them. While there, I also spent way too much money on upgrading all her bakery supplies and have a new oven on order from Germany. One of those deluxe models that has different compartments so she can cook cupcakes and bake a cheesecake at the same time.

"You boys are already giving me a migraine. Josh, come and help me downstairs," Saide says from where she stands behind me, leaning against Willow's bedroom door. Willow and I smile at her, knowing that she is giving us a bit of space, that I am on the edge, really wanting to ensure Willow is okay.

"Fine," he grumbles and walks off as I plump Willow's pillows and help her get settled.

"Have you spoken to your mother?" she asks me, and it is a question I have dodged from her the past few days, preferring her to concentrate on getting better, not thinking about my horrible mother.

"Not really. Before the accident, I had it out with her," I mumble, now only telling her the whole story.

"What do you mean? What happened?" she asks, her eyes running over me with concern. This is what I was trying to avoid. She needs to concentrate on herself, not me.

"We had a family meeting. She started pushing me, and I started remembering things..." I say, sitting on her bed next to her, needing her close.

"Remembering what things?" Willow pushes me, like she always does.

I blow out a breath. "I just have a vivid memory of Helen and how she died. I have no proof, and I was only twelve, so I have nothing else to go on, but I am reasonably confident that my mother had a hand in her death," I say to her and still as I wait for her response.

"Oh my God. I can't believe it," she says, her eyes wide in shock.

"Unfortunately, I can. I need to speak to my brothers about it, but like I said, no proof, no evidence, just the inconsistent memories from when I was a kid. None of that will hold up in a court of law," I say, grabbing her hand and strumming her soft skin with my thumb. Her skin is pink and glossy where the medical ointment has been applied. On a lot of her body, she has hot spots, where the flames flicked a little too close. Nothing that will cause scarring, but the soft pink flesh is still tender.

"Sorry, I didn't tell you, but she called me," Willow says, and I look at her sharply.

"Yeah, Mom mentioned that." I say, my body stiff. I don't want her anywhere near Willow.

"It was the day you left for Singapore. She called to tell me to talk you into going to Katerina. That you had to marry her and raise the baby as your own," she says, her eyes looking at me with sorrow. I would like to say it doesn't hurt. That my mother's complete disregard for my life and my happiness doesn't even register for me. But it does. It cuts deep.

"It won't happen again. She is not to contact you at all," I growl, wondering what I can put in place to prevent that from happening.

I lean over and kiss the top of her head, feeling her body next to mine, and take a deep breath.

There is still a lot to do and a lot to work out, but I feel more settled now than I have in a very long time. Relaxing back, I pull her close, letting her rest on me. This is the first time in days we have been allowed to connect and be this close, and as I hold her gently, I feel like I was merely a shell of a man before I met her. Broken. Damaged.

But now the future is full of potential, with her by my side, I can do anything. And I know that together, we will do it all.

EPILOGUE - WILLOW

As I pull the cheesecake from the oven to cool, I can hear the bickering coming from out the back. Every Friday, Tennyson works from my dining table, preferring to spend the weekend here with me than in the city.

"Listen to me, punk, if I throw up, I am going to throw you over the fence back to your mother," I hear Tennyson say as I open the back door and peer out.

"It is a science experiment. We did it today in class. If you do this and I film it, I can hand this in for my homework assignment. You promised you would help me," Josh says in a whine. Something feels off, but I don't say anything. The two of them have a love/hate relationship. But they are best friends, even if neither of them would admit it.

"Fine, give me the Mentos," Tennyson says, grabbing the packet from Josh and putting a few in his mouth.

"Here," Josh says, thrusting a can of Coke to him, and I start to become concerned.

"Ahhh, Tenn..." I say tentatively, starting to step out the door before I get the evil eyes from Josh and retreat just as quickly. I bite my lip so I don't laugh, then grab my cell so I can take the footage. He is going to hate this.

"Okay, so I just hold them in my mouth, then swallow down the Coke?" Tennyson mumbles around the candy in his mouth, and Josh nods all too eagerly. My eyes sweep to the side of the backyard, and I see Bob and Betty in a standoff. A silent feud as they stalk around each other, waiting for the other to pounce. I would like to say that it is a game, but they, too, have a love/hate relationship.

"Okay, go!" Josh says as he starts filming for his pretend science project, no doubt. This is yet another prank he is playing on Tennyson, the two of them in an all-out prank war at the moment. I hit record on my cell as well, as Josh films from the front, and I film from the side.

I watch Tennyson chug the Coke, and I can see it in his eyes the moment he realizes that Josh has set this all up. But he can't yell. He can't even talk. A massive fluffy explosion of Coke and Mentos explodes from his mouth. He stands, spitting out the liquid almost as fast as it went in, causing his shirt to become a black liquid mess. His face is covered in Coke, and he belches before coughing and spluttering and gasping for air.

Josh is in hysterics, laughing so hard he is crying, which makes me stifle a giggle.

"I swear on everything I own that you better run..." Tennyson seethes at Josh, causing him to jump and run like the wind out of my house and back over to his own.

I'm sure he's locking the door and closing all the curtains, keeping Tennyson out.

My giggle escapes me, and Tennyson looks at me sharply. I bite my lip and shrug.

"You think this is funny, hmm?" he says, slowly stalking toward me, Coke dripping from his face and chest. His white shirt is now see-through, and my eyes rest on his perfectly sculpted chest. As he steps closer, I flick my eyes back up to meet his, and heat fills my body as he starts to unbutton and remove his wet shirt, throwing it on the ground.

"No. Not at all. I will have a firm talk with his mother," I state in mock seriousness, holding up my hands in surrender.

"You better run, Cupcake," he warns, and I yelp before I dash back through the door and sprint up the stairs. But I needn't have bothered, as Tennyson is on me before I even get halfway.

"Tennyson!" I squeal as he hoists me up and over his shoulder, running us up the rest of the stairs and into my bedroom.

"You got me," I say, giving up the fight as he plonks me onto the bed.

"What have I always said, Cupcake? I will always get you. You know that," he says, voice low, reaffirming his commitment to me.

Life has completely changed. I am now working with a new client. A female actress who is in some hot water for being drunk and disorderly and a myriad of other things. The prospect to work with the Langford men more regularly is on the cards, before I will move across to Harrison's campaign. His push for the presidency is right around the corner. Tennyson has given me an office in his building in Baltimore, where I spend half my week, and the other half still here at home. He gave me a car and a driver to take me anywhere I need to go. He does the same, working between his office and here with me, hardly ever leaving my side. It has only been six months since the incident, but there are still a lot of frayed nerves, a lot of legal formalities, and sometimes nightmares, but we are getting through it. Together.

"Well, now that you have me, what do you plan to do to me?" I tease, giving him a sweeping look, my eyes running down his half-naked body and back up again. *This man. How did I ever get so lucky?*

Cheesecake on a Friday night is now our new thing. Tennyson is no longer out partying all night, picking up women, and doing the walk of shame the next day. Instead, he stays here, where we talk over cake for most of the night, usually on the back porch, watching Bob and Betty. Except tonight. The Coke will need to be cleaned up at some point. The back porch needs a spray with the hose before I get an ant invasion.

"Well, for the appetizer, I am going to fuck you with my fingers and play with your beautiful pussy until you are a screaming, crying mess on this bed," he says as he stands in front of me, running his finger down my middle. Warmth spreads through me, and I swallow.

"For the entrée, I am going to push my cock inside you so slowly it will be torturous. I am going to make your body shake, your mouth scream, and your toes curl," he growls, and I can make out the hardness of his crotch through his pants. I reach up to undo his belt.

"Then for dessert, I am going to go get the cheesecake and I am going to eat it from your body. I am going to spread it across your perfect tits, down your amazing curves, and to your fucking fantastic pussy that I will fuck with my tongue until you don't even know your own name," he grits out, and I think I lose my breath completely. My hands stall on his buckle.

I look up at him, my eyes wide, my mouth half-open in total awe of this man and how with just his words, he can make me almost melt. Just like the first time we met. That one night in New York. With no names and only each other.

"Just answer me one question..." I whisper as I kneel on my bed in front of him.

He looks at me in question, but nods silently.

"Will there be seconds?" I ask as he moves forward and takes my smile with his lips, reminding me exactly who I belong to.

Want to know what Tennyson and Willow are up to now? Download a bonus epilogue to get a glimpse into their future here.

To read the next instalment of the Langford brothers, download a copy of The Secret Billionaire here.

ALSO BY SAMANTHA SKYE

The Billionaires of Whispers

Tanner

Hudson

Connor

Sawyer

Sutton

Griffin

SCROOGE: A Billionaire Christmas Story

Under The Mistletoe: A Billionaire Christmas Story

The Baltimore Boys

The Charming Billionaire

The Arrogant Billionaire

The Damaged Billionaire

The Secret Billionaire

The Bossy Billionaire

The Billionaire Babe

Men Of New York

My Legacy

My Destiny

My Fight

My Chance

Boston Billionaires

Coming Home

Finding Home

Leaving Home

Building Home

ABOUT THE AUTHOR

Samantha Skye is an international bestselling author. A country kid turned city slicker, she writes spicy and suspenseful contemporary romance novels that leave you hot under the collar and on the edge of your seat.

Samantha lives in Melbourne, Australia and when she's not plotting her next novel, she can be found travelling, drinking margaritas and enjoying a sunset or a stargaze somewhere.

To join in the conversation join Skye's The Limit Facebook group here;

https://www.facebook.com/groups/skyesthelimitbooks

To learn more about Samantha and what comes next in her author journey you can find her on;

Website: samanthaskyeauthor.com